D0557617

BROKEN SCREAMS

CAVENDISH & WALKER
BOOK 12

SALLY RIGBY

TOP DRAWER PRESS

GET ANOTHER BOOK FOR FREE!

To instantly receive the free novella, **The Night Shift**, featuring Whitney when she was a Detective Sergeant, ten years ago, sign up for Sally Rigby's free author newsletter at www.sallyrigby.com

1

Sunday

Adrenaline pumped through Detective Chief Inspector Whitney Walker as she took a bow after her solo with the Rock Choir. She stepped back in line to join the rest of the choir and glanced down at the front row, where her daughter, Tiffany, was clapping furiously, a wide smile on her face. They were going out for a meal after the concert while Ava, Tiffany's young daughter, was being looked after by one of their neighbours.

They didn't get out together much these days – not since the birth of the baby and what with Whitney's job being so full on – so she'd been looking forward to the two of them having some mother-and-daughter bonding time.

Whitney frowned when her phone vibrated in her trouser pocket. She'd put it on silent because of the concert, hoping that she wasn't going to be disturbed, but no such luck. She slid it out of her pocket and glanced down, hoping that no one would catch sight of what she was doing.

Damn. It was a text from DC Doug Baines, one of her

officers, requesting she contact the station immediately. She'd left strict instructions that she wasn't to be disturbed unless it was an absolute emergency, so whatever it was, it had to be urgent and couldn't be ignored.

The audience had only just finished applauding, and the accompanist hadn't yet started the intro for the choir's next song, which meant it was an ideal time for Whitney to slip away. She was close to the end of her row, and as she stepped past the other two singers, she looked across at Betty, the leader of the Rock Choir, who was standing on a podium conducting, and mouthed, 'Sorry.' The woman's expression was unreadable, but hopefully she understood. It wasn't as if she had another solo, so she wasn't dropping them in it. Whitney then looked at Tiffany and shook her head, hoping it was enough for her daughter to understand that something had come up. Tiffany shrugged. She was well used to plans being disrupted.

Once Whitney was outside the hall, she phoned the station.

'It's me,' she said when Doug answered.

'Sorry for bothering you, guv, but there's been a serious physical and sexual assault on a local woman in Willis Park. I thought you'd want to know, rather than it going to DCI Masters' team.'

Masters would be the last person suitable for handling such a case. Not to mention that her team always dealt with serious crimes.

'How badly hurt is she?'

'I haven't been told. All I know is that she's been taken to the hospital.'

'Who found her?'

'Sorry, guv, I don't know that either. The police were called by the person who took her to the hospital. I assumed that you'd want to be the officer to interview the victim, considering the seriousness of the offence.'

'Yes, I do. You made the right decision. I'll be with you in fifteen. Thanks, Doug.'

'No worries. I'll see what else I can find out before you get here,' Doug said.

She ended the call and sent a text to Tiffany, telling her she had to leave for work. Her daughter immediately texted back saying that she'd catch the bus home. Whitney didn't want Tiffany to go home alone, knowing that there was an attacker at large, and told her daughter to ask Betty for a lift because she lived fairly close to them.

Whitney made it to the station in twelve minutes, thanks to every light on the journey being green, and she rushed up to the incident room where her team was situated. There was only Doug and Meena Singh, another detective constable, on duty.

'Okay, tell me what else you know,' she asked Doug, striding up to his desk and leaning against the edge.

'The victim's name is Lorna Knight, and it was her brother who phoned us. She hasn't been questioned yet, nor has he. I spoke to the hospital, but they were unable to tell me the extent of her injuries. Uniform found the place they believe the incident took place and have secured the scene.'

'Thanks, Doug. I'll see if George is available to join me because her input will be invaluable,' she said, referring to Dr Georgina "George" Cavendish, a forensic psychologist from Lenchester University who for several years had been assisting them on their more serious cases, and had become a close friend.

GEORGE TURNED her head at the sound of the hinges creaking on the wooden door of her study as it opened. She'd been miles away, unpacking boxes of books and stacking them in the bookshelves in the home she'd recently bought with her boyfriend Ross. She had carefully separated out texts relating to her research and lecturing at the university from any other fiction and non-fiction books she had. And, of course, all the books were all alphabetised.

Ross stared at her from the doorway, a tentative look on his face. His fists were clenched by his side.

'Is there a problem?' she asked, standing up from her crouched position and turning to face him.

'No, not a problem, but I do have a question for you, and it's probably not the right time to ask, but ...' He bit down on his bottom lip before continuing. 'Is there ever going to be the perfect time?'

'What is it?' she asked, her mind a total blank regarding what it could be.

'W-w-will you marry me?'

She swallowed hard. That was the last question she'd been expecting him to ask.

'Um ...' She wasn't sure how to answer.

'I'm sorry to drop this on you, and thinking about it, asking while you're unpacking isn't great, but while I was hanging the pictures on the wall, thinking how happy we were going to be here ... well ... it just came to me. Despite after the last time I asked, which you'll remember didn't go down as planned.' A wry grin broke out on his face.

How could she forget the last time he'd proposed? It had prompted her to end their relationship. At the time, she'd believed it to be the most logical thing to do, considering her view on romance and marriage. As it had turned out, she'd regretted her decision for a long time and had been relieved when they'd resumed dating several months later. If she'd known that he was planning to propose again, she'd have given it some thought in advance and prepared an answer. But she hadn't.

She still didn't say anything. She was at a loss for words.

'I thought that now we're in such a different place from when we talked about it the last time, and the fact that we've bought this beautiful house together, that I would risk asking you again.' He gave a tiny shrug. 'Whatever you decide, you know I love you. I'll always love you.'

George sighed. He had no difficulty in expressing his emotions. Unlike her. Give her a research paper to write, and the words flowed from her mind faster than she could type them. Ask her to explain her feelings, and it was like speaking a foreign language.

'Why is getting married so important to you?' she finally said.

'You know me, a total romantic at heart, and it just seemed like the next step for us to take. You do love me, don't you?' Uncertainty shone from his eyes.

Did she love him? Did she even know what love was? She was sure she had very strong feelings for him, and she didn't want their relationship to end. And she was happy to be moving in together, so it would seem most likely that she did.

'I believe so.' She nodded.

'I'll accept that, because coming from you, it means so much,' he said, his shoulders relaxing.

He knew her well. Better than anybody else. But was that enough to commit to marriage?

'May I give you my answer after I've had time to give it some thought?'

It was one thing admitting she loved him, but marriage?

She still wasn't sure if she wanted to say yes. But she certainly wasn't going to turn him down if it meant their relationship ending. She had certainly learnt that lesson already.

'Of course, I totally understand. You take as long as you like, and—'

George's phone rang. She picked it up from the top of the bookcase and glanced at the screen. 'It's Whitney.'

'Typical. That woman has some sort of special radar when it comes to us. Every time we're having a meaningful conversation, she calls. What is it between you two?' He sighed, smiled, and raised his hands in mock despair, but he understood. He'd always told her how proud he was of the work she did with the police.

She answered the phone. 'Hello, Whitney. May I call you back later? I'm in the middle of a conversation with Ross.' She didn't want to say about what, although knowing her friend, she would ask when they next spoke.

'Sorry if I've caught you at a bad time, but I thought you'd want to know that we've had a nasty physical and sexual assault on a local woman, and I wondered if you'd like to come with me to the hospital to interview her?'

George stared at Ross. How could she leave him now? Even she realised it wasn't the right thing to do.

'We're busy right now, but I can be with you first thing tomorrow morning. With the students finished for the summer, I've taken two weeks' leave to get the new house in order. We're making better progress than we had hoped, so it's not a problem to join you.' She kept her voice neutral to hide her disappointment at having to decline the invitation.

'Yeah, okay ... Right. That's fine. I'll see you in the morning. Enjoy your evening, or whatever you've got planned.'

Had Whitney been surprised that George hadn't

dropped everything to be with her? Her tone suggested as much.

George replaced her phone on the bookcase.

'I'm assuming a case has come up, and Whitney asked you to assist,' Ross said, walking over to where she was standing and resting an arm around her shoulder.

'Yes and, as you would have heard, I'm going in tomorrow morning to assist. I hope you don't mind. It's an attempted murder and sexual assault.'

'That's dreadful. And of course you should go in. Whitney needs you. But … I noticed that you didn't ask her for any details, which is most unlike you. Is it because of my proposal? And why you turned down Whitney's request?' He turned to face her, his intelligent blue eyes locking with hers.

Was it? It couldn't have been anything else. Normally, she'd have left for the station immediately.

'I suspect you're right,' she agreed. 'I didn't want to leave you in the middle of our discussion because it wouldn't be fair. It wasn't an easy question to ask, and I promise to make a decision soon. I also don't want you to think that I'd be putting Whitney first when it comes to our relationship.'

'George, the one thing you don't have to worry about is how I view your relationship with Whitney. You and Whitney are so close … it's like you're a double act. And I'd never try to come between the two of you. This sounds like a serious case, and she could have probably done with your input straight away. Why don't you call her back and say that you'll go with her?'

George frowned. Had she got it wrong again? Should she have gone with Whitney and not stayed with Ross to continue with their discussion? She found relationships an enigma at times. No, all the time. She'd have to ask Whitney for her advice.

'I'm going to stay here. Whitney didn't mind. She can take another officer to interview the woman with her, and we'll discuss it tomorrow. In the meantime, we need to focus on the remaining unpacking because I can't live or work in this mess.'

They'd bought a beautiful Georgian manor house on the outskirts of a village east of Lenchester. Before moving in, they'd converted one of the outbuildings into a studio for Ross to do his sculpting. It also had a small kitchen, toilet, and office for him to meet clients. It meant that when she worked from home, they could be separate, as he'd be self-contained and away from the main house. It was the perfect situation for them both. They'd be together, but not living in each other's pockets.

Their other outbuilding she was planning to turn into a large garage to house the classic car collection she wanted to start. She'd already been checking online for suitable vehicles to come on the market. But she wasn't going to buy any until her Victorian terraced property in Lenchester had been sold. She did have other money, from an inheritance, but she didn't want to leave herself with nothing to fall back on and was happy to keep that money invested.

'There's no rush. You've taken two weeks off work, and it's not going to be untidy by the end of them.'

'Except if I'm going to be working with Whitney, and that's going to take up a significant portion of my time. Also, I had intended to do some preparation for a research paper I'm going to write next term.'

'Oh, that's a shame.' He averted his eyes. 'I'd been hoping we could get away for a couple of days while you were off work. I was thinking we could take a trip to the Lake District because you love it so much there.'

What wasn't he telling her? Surely he hadn't booked it without consulting her first.

'A visit to the Lake District would be super, but I do need to see what's happening with this case of Whitney's. That might take up my entire annual leave.'

'I understand, and don't worry. I haven't made a booking.' He paused a moment before adding, 'If you'd said yes to my proposal, I thought it would be lovely if we could make it a celebration.'

She frowned. 'But that makes it sound like you've been planning to propose for a while, but you said just now it was a spur-of-the-moment decision while you were hanging the artwork.'

'I've been planning to ask for a while but hadn't decided when.'

'Oh, I see. Does that mean you were really expecting me to give you an answer immediately and didn't want to wait?' When would she get the hang of these things?

'Not at all ... Well ... I'd sort of hoped ... But ...' His voice faded away.

'I promise it's not going to be the same as last time. I just need some time to think it through. And we can still go to the Lake District for a short break. That would be delightful.'

'I'm glad you think so, but I won't make any reservations until you tell me it's okay. Later, we'll go online, and I'll show you some photos of the place I've found. You'll love it.' He smiled. 'Right, I'll get back to it. Do you fancy a glass of wine while you're unpacking?'

'Yes, that would be lovely. Thank you.'

Ross left her study, and she crouched back down facing

the bookcase but couldn't concentrate on sorting out her books. This was a huge deal. And she hadn't even broached the subject of children. She'd never made any attempt to hide the fact that she didn't want any, and he hadn't indicated that he minded, although he'd often said that in an ideal world, he'd like some.

Was that why he wanted to get married? Despite them both only being in their thirties, he had a somewhat old-fashioned attitude towards things like that. Whitney would probably tell her she should talk it through with him, but that was easy for her to say because she had no trouble discussing anything with anyone. George had always admired Whitney for her openness and the fact that she never struggled in social situations.

If only it was that easy for her.

2
_____

Sunday

Whitney replaced her phone on the desk and frowned. Well, that was weird. George hadn't asked anything about the incident. Not a single question. That had to be a first and was so unlike the forensic psychologist. There was definitely something going on, and Whitney would have to find out what it was.

She hoped everything was okay between George and Ross. They'd only just moved into their new house, and it hadn't been an easy decision for her friend to make. The couple were already living together, splitting their time between their respective houses, but then they decided to buy one between them to make their life a bit easier. George hadn't taken the decision lightly, but finally had agreed, much to Whitney's delight.

Whitney would hate to see them separate, especially after the last time, which had been a total disaster, and George had suffered. Still, she didn't have time to dwell on George's private life. She picked up her bag and headed back to the incident room and over to where her officers were sitting.

'Meena, you can come with me to the hospital to talk to the victim. And, Doug, I'd like you to go out and double-check the scene. Confirm that you agree with the position of the attack and make sure it's all cordoned off correctly. Wait until forensics arrive. We don't want members of the public trampling over all the evidence. I'll give you a call once we've seen the victim, in case there's anything you need to be mindful of.'

'Will do, guv,' Doug said, picking up his phone from the desk, sliding his chair away from the desk, and standing up.

'Take a couple of uniformed officers with you. It might be possible for you to make some preliminary house-to-house calls, but it will depend on what time we get to speak to the victim – I don't want you calling on people after ten, because it might cause them unnecessary worry.'

'Got it.' Doug grabbed his jacket from the back of his chair and headed for the door.

After leaving a voicemail message for her boss, Superintendent Helen Clyde, informing her of the attack, Whitney and Meena left for the hospital. On arrival, they stopped at the reception desk.

'DCI Walker and DC Singh. We've come to see Lorna Knight, who was brought in earlier following an attack.'

The woman on the reception glanced at the warrant card Whitney was showing her and then averted her attention to the computer screen on her desk. 'Ah, yes. She's been taken to room one-three, which is in a private area adjacent to the emergency department. Head straight down the corridor and take a sharp left. You'll find it on the right.'

Whitney and Meena hurried to the room, which had a uniformed officer stationed outside.

'Hello, Jade,' Whitney said to the uniformed officer. 'Is the victim able to talk to us yet?'

'She's with the doctor at the moment, guv. Over there is Liam Knight, her brother. He brought her to the hospital and also phoned us. We met him here.' The officer nodded behind them to a row of white plastic chairs next to a water cooler on the opposite side of the corridor. On one of them sat a man. He was leaning forward, his hands wrapped around a white disposable cup. His jaw was tense, and the lines around his eyes tight.

'Okay, thanks, Jade. We'll wait until the doctor has finished.' Whitney walked over to the man. 'Mr Knight?'

He glanced up from staring at his cup and frowned. 'Yes?'

'I'm DCI Whitney Walker from Lenchester CID,' she said softly. 'I'd like to talk to you about what happened tonight.' She pulled over a chair and sat opposite him and then turned and gestured for Meena to join them. 'This is DC Singh.'

'Okay,' he said, drinking the remainder of the water in his cup and placing it on the floor, then sitting upright, his fists clenched in his lap.

'Please could you go through exactly what happened this evening.' Whitney pulled out her notebook and pen from her pocket and handed them to Meena.

He closed his eyes and sucked in a breath, then stared down at his lap. 'I was at home watching the telly with my girlfriend when Lorna phoned ... It was about eight, maybe a couple of minutes after. I was surprised when I saw her name on the screen because I'd been expecting her to phone later if she wanted me to pick her up.' He glanced up at Whitney. 'That had been our arrangement before she left during the afternoon to see her friend.' He paused. 'When I answered, all I could hear was sobbing. Lorna was crying and trying to catch her breath at the same time. "Lorna, what's happened? What's wrong?" I asked, but all I could hear was her saying, "Help me. Help me," over and over again. I—' His voice cracked.

'It's okay,' Whitney said. 'Just take your time.'

'I jumped up from the sofa, grabbed my keys and ran to the car, all the time telling her I was on my way and that it would be okay.'

'Did Lorna tell you exactly where she was?' Whitney asked.

'We have the tracking on for each other's phones for security. It was my idea, and she'd resisted initially. Thank goodness I got her to agree. I found her on Nelson Street, sitting on a wall, all hunched up. There was blood smeared across her face from the cuts, and her shirt was ripped on the arms. I helped her get into my car, and we drove her straight here. I thought it would be quicker than calling for an ambulance, and I called the police on the way.'

'You did the right thing. Did Lorna tell you anything about the attack or her attacker on the way here?'

'No, and I didn't ask. I was just intent on getting her to the hospital as quickly as possible. You better get the person who did this to her. Or ... or ...' He closed his eyes tight and banged his fist on the chair next to him.

'We'll do our very best. I promise. Does Lorna live with you?' Whitney asked.

'Yes,' he said, opening his eyes. 'We're twins and have always been really close. So, after she split up with her boyfriend six months ago, she moved into the spare room of the house I share with my girlfriend. We didn't mind because it helped us with the mortgage payments. But recently, she'd been talking about finding her own place.

She'd needed the time with us to get over ...' He paused, his eyes narrowing.

Whitney went on alert. Could this have something to do with the attack? 'Over?' she prompted.

'Lorna was in a really toxic relationship. But I didn't find out the true extent of what had been going on until she finally left and came to stay with us. I noticed the bruises covering her body and was livid. I wanted to go and sort him out, but Lorna made me promise not to. She was scared he'd hurt me, too. I agreed. Not because I was scared of him – because I'm not – but it was what she wanted. If it was him ... I'm telling you ... I'll ...'

Whitney rested a hand on his arm. 'I understand that you're angry, but we don't know yet who did this to Lorna, so it's wise not to make threats. That said, what is the name of this man?'

'Clark. Fraser Clark,' he spat.

'Did Mr Clark try to contact Lorna after she'd left him?' Whitney asked, taking a quick look in Meena's direction to confirm the officer was taking all of this down.

'Yeah. But she told him she didn't want to see him. He pestered her for a while longer, but then it stopped.' He frowned. 'Until recently, when she had started feeling like she was being watched and followed. We wondered if Fraser had started stalking her. It was the sort of thing he would do, knowing him.'

'Did you report this to the police?' Meena asked.

'How could we? There was nothing specific to tell them. He didn't do anything, and Lorna didn't actually see him in person. It was just an uncomfortable feeling she had that there was someone there. And now look what's happened.' He shook his head.

'Did Lorna think that her attacker was Fraser?' Whitney asked.

'I don't know. All she did in the car was cry and groan. She was in such pain.' He screwed up his eyes and grimaced.

The door to one of the rooms opened, and a woman in green scrubs came out. 'Excuse me,' Whitney said to Liam before jumping up and going over to the doctor. 'I'm DCI Walker, and I'd like to speak to Lorna. Would that be possible?'

She'd learnt over the years not to demand anything from the medics because they could easily say no. When she was reasonable, more often than not, they would be too.

'Yes, but please don't spend too long with her because she's still in a state of shock. We're going to keep her in overnight to make sure there's no concussion, because her head was banged repeatedly on the ground. All being well, tomorrow she should be able to go home, providing she's not going to be alone.'

'I promise not to be in there for too long, but it's important for us to get as much information from Lorna as quickly as we can if we're to have the best possible chance of catching the person who did this to her.'

'I understand. We've swabbed for bodily fluids, and the samples have been sent to the lab. From my examination of Lorna, it would appear that the attacker wore a condom during the attack. Her clothes have been bagged up for forensics, and hopefully, they'll find some evidence on them. It was a nasty attack and could've been so much worse if she hadn't managed to escape. If you need to speak to me again, one of the nurses will find me. It's going to be a long night, judging by the number of people waiting. Whoever said Sunday night was quiet didn't know what they were talking about.' The doctor sighed loudly and left.

After explaining to Liam where they were going, Whitney tapped gently on the door to Lorna's room and pushed it open. She stifled a gasp at the state of the young woman lying on the bed, her cheeks swollen and already purple with bruising. Large marks, which looked like finger-prints, circled her neck. Her short dark hair was plastered to her face.

'Hello?' Lorna said, her voice so hoarse it was barely audible.

'I'm DCI Whitney Walker, and this is DC Meena Singh. How are you feeling?' Whitney grimaced. Was it a stupid thing to ask someone who'd just been attacked? She'd done it automatically to break the ice.

'Lucky to be alive, so I've been told.' Lorna said, the corners of her mouth turning up into a tiny smile.

Whitney nodded, admiring the woman's strength, which was already evident.

'Would you feel up to talking to us about the attack? I know it's going to be hard, but the sooner we get some infor-mation from you, the sooner we can get out there and find the person who did this.'

'Yes.' Lorna moved herself up slightly in the bed and gasped in pain. 'They've given me some painkillers, but they haven't kicked in yet.'

'Don't move. Stay where you are, and I'll ask you a few questions. Although details are important, I don't want you to put too much strain on your voice.' Whitney grabbed a chair from beside the sink, pulled it over, and sat down close to Lorna. 'What can you tell me about what happened this evening?'

'I-I-I ...' She stared back at Whitney, her green eyes glassy with tears.

'It's okay. Just take your time,' Whitney said.

'I can do this,' Lorna muttered to herself, looking down at the bed. 'I can do this.'

'Whenever you're ready,' Whitney said, keeping her voice calm.

'Thank you.' Lorna expelled a long, slow breath. 'I was walking back to my brother's house after being with my friend, Janey. We'd been to the cinema to see the latest *Downton Abbey* film in the afternoon and had got a takeaway and took it back to her house in Waterford Road after it finished. We got back to her house at half-past six. I know that because I remember checking the time. It was such a mild evening and hadn't got dark yet, so after we'd finished eating and chatting, I decided to walk the twenty minutes home instead of phoning Liam to pick me up.' She paused and took some breaths.

'Liam said that your call was earlier than he'd expected?'

'Yes, I was tired and didn't want to stay out late because of work tomorrow. But ... I won't be going anywhere now.' Lorna coughed and grimaced.

'Would you like some water?' Whitney asked, nodding at the glass beside her bed.

'Yes, please.'

Whitney passed her the glass and waited while she took several sips and then replaced it on the side.

'Are you okay to continue?' Whitney asked.

Lorna nodded. 'When I was walking through Willis Park, beside some hedges ... I was grabbed from behind, and ... and ... he dragged me through the hedges and forced me down on the ground, banging my head. Then he was on top; his legs were astride me. I couldn't move. He ... He ... He put his hand over my mouth hard ... banging my head on the ground again. He told me if I screamed, he'd, he'd ... I ... I ...' She shuddered. 'But I couldn't anyway because his hand was over my mouth. I tried to get away, but when I moved, he punched me in the face, and then he put his hands around my neck and started to squeeze. I thought I was going to die. I didn't dare move again, and he ... he ...' She squeezed her eyes shut.

'It's okay. You only have to tell us what you can.'

Lorna sucked in a jerky breath. 'I want to tell you. He *raped* me.'

'How did you manage to get away?'

'He released the pressure on me for a second. I think he was taking off the condom. I managed to lift my leg and knee him hard in the balls. Then somehow, I managed to roll to the side away from him. I scrambled to my feet and ran as fast as I could.'

'Did he come after you?'

'I thought I heard him shout my name in anger, but I can't be sure. I just kept on running until I came to the street and phoned my brother.'

If he did know her name, then already they knew this wasn't a random attack.

'Do you think it was someone you know? Was there *anything* about him that was familiar? His voice. His build. Anything.'

Lorna sucked in a breath, grimacing from the pain. 'When he spoke, it was like he was deliberately keeping his voice low and quiet. He had a northern accent. Maybe Manchester but I'm not sure.'

'You said he threatened you if you screamed. Would you mind telling me the exact words he used?'

Lorna nodded. 'H-he said, "*Scream, and I'll cut your tongue out.*"'

Whitney waited a few moments to allow Lorna time to get her breath back.

'Can you give us a description of him, Lorna?'

'He had a balaclava on, so I couldn't see his face. Black leather gloves. I couldn't even bite his hand because he had it pressed so tightly on my face. Not old, but not a teenager either. Maybe he was in his thirties. He wore jeans. I know that because I felt the material rubbing on my legs. I think he had on a dark T-shirt with long sleeves.' Tears rolled down the victim's cheeks, and Whitney took a tissue from a box beside the bed and passed it over to her.

'You've done very well, Lorna. Can you answer one more question for me?'

'Yes,' she replied, sniffing.

'Liam mentioned your ex-boyfriend, Fraser Clark.'

'You think it was him?' Her eyes widened.

'We've got to look into all possibilities. From the attack, did you get the sense it might've been Fraser?'

'I don't know. There might have been something familiar about him, but I'm not sure. I didn't hear him speak properly. It all happened so quickly. I can't tell you anymore. I'm sorry.' She sniffed and then dabbed at her eyes with the tissue.

'No need to apologise. You've done very well. The doctor said you should be able to go home tomorrow. You'll be safe with your brother. If you do think of anything else, please let me know. I'll leave my card on the side. We will need a proper statement when you're up to it, but you've given us a lot to work with. Thank you.'

3

Monday

Whitney was the first to arrive in the incident room at seven the next morning. She'd let the others on the team know about the assault the night before and had asked them to be there early so they could make a start straight away. She picked up the red marker and wrote *Lorna Knight* at the top of the whiteboard. The fancy electronic one that had come with their brand-new station hung dormant on the wall. It was way too complicated, and Whitney much preferred the old-fashioned, pen-on-board one that she'd bought with her from their old station, where she'd spent most of her career. She still missed the old place and doubted she'd ever get used to working in such a characterless shell. The only redeeming feature as far as she was concerned, was that the new home had a café. Not having to leave the premises every time she wanted a decent cup of coffee had been a godsend. And not just for her. The team knew that unless she had regular caffeine fixes, she wasn't happy.

The door banged, and Brian Chapman walked in.

'Morning, guv,' her sergeant said, heading over to the coat stand and hanging up his jacket.

'Hi, Brian. I'm just getting ready for the briefing.' She wrote *Fraser Clark* on the board and drew a line under it, linking it to the victim.

'We already have a suspect?' Brian said, joining her at the board.

'Possibly. The victim didn't identify him, but he's an ex who's caused her trouble in the past. Which means he's on our radar. Let me know when Frank, Doug, and Ellie have arrived, and I'll come back out to discuss the next steps. I want to make a phone call to forensics to see how they are doing with the samples from the victim.'

'Will do.'

She returned to her office and called the forensics team.

'Jenny speaking.'

'Hi, it's Whitney. I don't suppose you were on duty last night? I'm calling about the attack in Willis Park.' She picked up the pen on her desk and hovered over the piece of scrap paper on her desk, waiting for any information that might be forthcoming.

'No, sorry, it wasn't me or Colin this time.'

She dropped the pen on the desk. 'Damn. I was hoping for some early feedback, and the others aren't anywhere near as efficient as you two.'

'Leave it with me, Whitney, and I'll find out who was there and what was recovered from the scene. It might be a while, though, because there's a meeting first thing, and we've *all* been instructed to attend.'

'Sounds ominous. Do you know what it's about?'

'Staffing, I suspect. We've had two people leave recently, and they haven't been replaced. Budgets. God knows how we're expected to do our jobs.' She gave a loud sigh.

'As long as you or Colin aren't planning to leave, we'll manage. You're not, are you?' she added.

'I'd be lying if I said it hadn't crossed my mind, but, you know, some of us are part of the scenery. Before privatisation.' Jenny gave a hollow laugh.

'You're not wrong, me included. Well, if you can let me know what you have as soon as possible, that would be great. We're lucky not to be investigating a murder, the state the victim was in.'

Whitney replaced the handset at the same time there was a knock at her door, and Brian popped his head around.

'The guys are here, guv.'

'Okay, I'm on the way.'

She followed Brian back into the incident room, headed over to the board, and turned to face them all. The team were all seated at their desks and looking in her direction.

'Bloody nasty business. Why the hell do folks get off doing this sort of thing?' Frank, her older detective constable, said.

'That's what we're going to find out. First of all, Doug, what can you tell us about the scene?' She looked directly at the detective constable.

'I went to check it out, as you asked, but there wasn't much to see. I couldn't tell where the attack actually took place from merely looking, but I left forensics scouring the area within the cordon. I spoke to a couple of dog walkers who were in the park, close to the scene. It turned out that both were regulars there, and they mentioned how where the victim was attacked was a particularly quiet area, mainly because there's no play equipment close by for the kids, and there's no main entry or exit point.'

'An indication that the attack was planned, and it wasn't just a case of Lorna being unlucky to be passing at that time,' Whitney said, writing the word *premeditated* beneath the victim's name.

'Yes, guv, that's what I thought, too. I also called on a house close to the main entrance to the park because I saw the owner putting out his bins. Other than that, I didn't speak to anyone else because it was getting too late, and you'd said not to call on folks if it was after ten.'

'Thanks, that's a good start and gives us a base to work from. Meena and I went to the hospital last night and spoke to Lorna Knight. She was in a bad way and was possibly concussed, but her wounds were relatively superficial, with no broken bones, and she's expected to go home today. If she hadn't managed to escape, it would have been a different story, and—'

'I've just noticed, Meena's not here. Where is she?' Frank asked, interrupting.

'She's off until Thursday,' Whitney answered, waving her hand dismissively.

'Because she worked the weekend? Surely it's all hands on deck at a time like this. It usually is.' Frank furrowed his brow.

Meena's father had been diagnosed with prostate cancer, and she'd arranged to go with her parents to the specialist. They lived on the south coast, and so Meena would be away from work for a couple of days. The officer had offered to cancel, but Whitney said no. It was important to be with family at a time like this. Meena had asked Whitney to keep the reason for her absence confidential, as it wasn't something she wished to share with the team. Whitney understood; the officer kept her personal life private, like several of her team, which was unusual, because most teams that

Whitney had worked with in the past had all been inclined to tell each other everything. Maybe the "compartmentalising" to quote George, was what made her team so effective.

Although Frank shared enough for most of the team put together, he was a good officer. A little lazy and set in his ways, but loyal beyond reproach. He wouldn't be with them for too much longer, though, because retirement was on the horizon.

'Thank you for being my stand-in HR person, Frank, but Meena has my permission to be off duty, and that's all you need to know. Her reasons are nothing to do with you.' Whitney's tone was harsher than she'd intended.

'I didn't mean—'

'Yes, you did. You're sticking your oar in again, Frank. One day you might learn when to butt out,' Doug said, grinning.

'And that applies to you too.' Frank glowered at his colleague.

'Seriously, you two will be the death of me. It's like being back at school. Now, let's get on with it, shall we?'

'He started it,' Frank said.

Whitney narrowed her eyes. 'I'm warning—'

'Sorry, guv.' Frank held up his hands in mock surrender.

Whitney shook her head, forcing back a smile because it would only make the pair of them worse. And if she were being honest, she'd miss their banter. When Frank left, it was going to make a huge difference to the dynamics of the team.

'Back to Lorna Knight,' Whitney said. 'Although she couldn't tell me much, what she did say was that she thought the attacker was quite young but not a teenager, maybe thirties. He had a northern accent which she thought was possibly from Manchester, but she couldn't be sure because he kept his voice low. Of interest is her ex-boyfriend, who has been abusive and threatened her in the past. Lorna's brother mentioned him. His name is Fraser Clark, and Lorna believes he might've been stalking her recently. But it was more of a feeling than anything concrete. It would certainly fit our view that she was targeted. Ellie, I want you to look into him and also do a search on Lorna. Her work. Her friends. Social media. Anything that will give us a picture of her life and how easy it might be for someone to discover what she was doing.'

'I'm on to it, guv,' the DC said.

Ellie was their secret weapon. Her research skills were phenomenal, and there wasn't anything she couldn't discover. Whitney hadn't the foggiest idea how they'd replace her when she left. Although Ellie had said it wouldn't be for a year or two, it all depended on when her boyfriend applied for a nursing job in London.

'Doug, I'd like you to go back and check the area. Do some house-to-house calls. Brian, you can go with him. Frank, you stay here and look at the CCTV around the area. We do know that earlier in the evening, the victim had gone to the cinema with a friend, and then they went back to her house with a takeaway. From there, the victim walked home.'

'Yes, guv,' Frank said.

'Any questions?' She glanced at each of them in turn, but no one had any. 'Okay, we'll meet again at eleven and see where we've got to. I'm expecting Dr Cavendish in later.'

4

_____

Monday

George headed straight to the incident room, rather than Whitney's office, assuming that's where the officer would be. She pushed open the door, scanned the room and saw Whitney standing next to Ellie, and at another desk, she could see Frank staring intently at his computer screen. Apart from that, the room was empty. No doubt they were out making their enquiries. She would've been in earlier, except she'd hardly slept thinking about what Ross had asked, and then ended up dropping off to sleep at six and missed her alarm at seven. Ross had also slept in and so hadn't realised that she hadn't got up.

She walked over to Ellie's desk, and Whitney nodded in acknowledgement.

'Thanks, Ellie, keep going. We'll catch up later when we have the meeting with the rest of the team.' Whitney said before turning to George. 'Thanks for coming in, and I'm glad you're here because we've got a lot on today, including paying a visit to the victim's ex-boyfriend. We've just been discussing him.'

Had Whitney been waiting for her? How could she be late when George hadn't mentioned a time she'd be arriving?

'Sorry, I would have been here sooner if I hadn't over-slept this morning,' she admitted.

Whitney's jaw dropped. 'What? You slept in? I didn't think you were capable of such a thing.'

That made two of them.

'Nor did I, but it appears that was an incorrect assump-tion on my part. You'll need to catch me up on everything because I wasn't able to ask you yesterday when you phoned.'

'We'll do that in the car, but before we see the ex, we'll visit Willis Park, the crime scene.'

After collecting Whitney's bag and jacket, they headed out towards George's car.

'So, let me have the details of what exactly happened,' George said, indicating and pulling out of the station and into the passing traffic.

'First of all, perhaps you'd like to tell me why you sounded so uninterested when I telephoned last night? Did I interrupt something? I know that it does seem to be my speciality, as far as you and Ross are concerned. In fact, I'm surprised he even speaks to me sometimes.' Whitney laughed.

George took a quick look at Whitney, who was staring right back, eyebrows raised. Her friend was going to get it out of her eventually, so why not now? And actually talking about it might help take it off of George's mind.

'Ross proposed to me just before you called.' She took

another glance at Whitney, whose eyes had now widened, sending her eyebrows even higher.

'Oh my God, George! That's fantastic. Did you say yes?' Whitney bounced in the car seat like a child who'd been given free access to the sweet shop. So typical of Whitney to only see the positive side of it.

'I explained that I needed time to think and couldn't give him an answer straight away.'

Whitney expelled a loud sigh. 'Honestly, you make it sound like it was the worst thing in the world for him to ask. How did you feel when he asked? Were you even the teeniest bit excited by the thought?'

George arched an eyebrow. 'Have you ever seen me like that in the past?'

'No, I suppose not.' Whitney sighed. 'I wish you would, though, because it's the best possible feeling.'

'That's not in my biological make-up, as you well know.' And nor was it something that she wanted to experience, because it would only lead to a loss of control, and that wasn't a feeling she desired to have.

'That's as maybe, but let us not forget that you've just bought an amazing place together – which I can't wait to see – so surely you're in the relationship for the long haul. I know he asked you to get married before, but you weren't ready then. It's different now. *You're* different now. Honestly, you don't know how lucky you are having such a fabulous future mapped out for you.'

The wistful tone in Whitney's voice caused George to glance away from the road and look back at her friend. 'Why? Do you wish to get married?'

'Far from it. Anyway, we're not talking about me,' Whitney said, with a dismissive wave of her hand, the movement of which George caught in her peripheral vision.

'I have promised Ross that I would give it some thought, and that's what I'll do. Ross understands me and is prepared to wait.'

Although she couldn't take too long. There had to be certainty in their relationship, whatever she decided.

'What do you think your parents will say?'

'It's nothing to do with them. They know Ross and accept that he's in my life. We hardly ever see them, and they're always polite to him.'

'Wow, I suppose for them that's good. Considering no one is ever going to be good enough for you, unless they're actually royalty. By the way, how's your dad's Parkinson's?'

Her parents' entire life had changed with the diagnosis, and George had been persuading them to move to somewhere more suitable. But they weren't prepared to because they loved their four-storey house in one of the most exclusive areas in central London.

'He's reached a plateau at the moment, and it hasn't got any worse, thank you for asking.'

'But he still can't work?'

'He was a heart surgeon, so obviously not. But he's overseeing the training of the juniors and still seeing patients, but not operating. But how long that lasts will depend on how quickly the disease progresses.'

'I'm glad it's slowed up a bit. That must be a relief for you.'

'Yes, it is. But no need to discuss it now. Tell me about the attack – that's far more important and the reason we're working today.'

Despite not joining Whitney last night, George was anxious to discover what had occurred.

'Not to mention you hate any discussion about your private life. Okay, let's move on,' she added, her tone becoming serious. 'Lorna Knight is our victim. Meena and I interviewed her last night at the hospital. She's lucky to be alive. It was an extremely vicious rape and attempted strangulation, but she fought her way out of it.'

'And you believe the person responsible might be the ex-boyfriend?'

'It's a possibility because he'd been abusive during their relationship, and although she'd warned him off, more recently, she's had the feeling of being watched, but nothing concrete enough to warrant reporting it to the police. She was able to tell us that the attacker had a northern accent, possibly from Manchester, and he wore a dark balaclava, gloves, jeans, and a long-sleeved T-shirt.'

'Obviously trying to disguise himself by being completely covered, considering it was a warm evening,' George muttered, speaking her thoughts out loud. 'When he spoke to her, what did he say?'

'In a low voice, he told her that if she screamed, he'd cut out her tongue.'

'Hmm. Interesting choice of words. Cutting out of someone's tongue to silence them has both religious and historical connotations. Why didn't he just threaten to kill her?' she mused. 'How did the victim react to him?'

'She did as she was told until he was distracted, and then she kicked him and managed to get away.'

'That was a very brave move. But the only choice if her life was being threatened.'

'Exactly. If she hadn't succeeded, this would have been a murder investigation, I'm sure of it.'

'Did you visit the crime scene yesterday?'

'No, that's why we're going now. Doug went while I visited the hospital with Meena. He couldn't see much because forensics were there working, and he had to keep out of the way. They've finished now, so we can have a good poke around. I'm hoping their report should be with us by the time we're back for the team meeting at eleven. Turn left here and park on Nelson Street,' Whitney said.

George did as she was instructed, and once they were out of the car, they headed towards the entrance to the park, a path between two stone pillars.

'Where exactly was the victim found?' she asked.

'She managed to get to Nelson Street and then called her brother to pick her up. But the actual attack took place further into the park in a quieter area behind some hedges. Follow me.'

They headed through the park along the tarmac paths until arriving at a more remote area where the foliage was a little overgrown, and there were some privet hedges. The cordons were still in place, but there was nobody on the scene.

'Do we have to be careful where we tread?' George asked, looking for the plates they usually had to walk on, but seeing none.

'Not now forensics have been. This is more so we can get a picture in our heads of where the attack happened and the direction she ran when she managed to escape.'

They ducked under the tape, and both stood still, scanning the scene.

'There's some flattening of the grass by the hedge over there. Maybe that's where the assault occurred,' George said, pointing to the area.

'Yes, that looks a likely place.' They headed over and observed for a few seconds. 'Do you see how all the blades are flat and pointing towards the hedge? I think that's where he pushed the victim down and her body would have slid a few inches towards the hedge. The ground is particularly hard at the moment. No wonder the doctors were worried about Lorna having concussion from when he banged her head,' Whitney said.

'Let's work out where he would have stood while waiting for her to pass,' George said, striding over to the hedge to see if it gave her a view of the path the victim would have taken.

'Can you see anything?' Whitney asked, coming up behind her.

'Yes. Because of the way the path curves, he would have seen her from ten yards away.'

'That would have given him enough time to get into place,' Whitney said, standing to the side of George and peering through the hedge.

'We should ascertain how the attacker got here, especially if he was disguised, although I suspect he wouldn't have put on the balaclava until he was waiting for her in the hedge.' George did a 360-degree turn to check all the possible ways he might have arrived at the hedge. 'It could have been one of many, especially if he didn't stick to a path and walked over the grass.'

'Yes, I know. But, what else is puzzling me is, how did he know that she was going to walk this particular way and at that particular time, to be in a position to pounce? Lorna herself hadn't planned on walking home – it was a spur-of-the-moment decision,' Whitney said, biting down on her bottom lip.

George considered what her friend had said while scanning the area. 'If he'd been following her and saw her walk into the park, he could have taken a different route to behind the hedge, knowing that she'd be passing that way because she was on her way home. He would have had to run, to give him time to put on his balaclava and gloves.

Which means it was a premeditated and not random attack.'

'Yeah, we've already considered that. Lorna thought she heard him calling her name when she escaped. But she wasn't a hundred per cent certain, but it would confirm it.'

'You mentioned meeting her brother. Could he have been involved?' George asked.

'No, I'm certain that he was nothing to do with it. He was at home with his girlfriend at the time. Lorna and Liam are twins, and she currently lives with them. Lorna phoned him when she got to a safe place after the attack, and he came to pick her up and took her to the hospital. He contacted the police on their way. He alerted us about the ex-boyfriend, and Lorna told us a little more.'

'What do we know about the ex?'

'His name is Fraser Clark and, according to Ellie's preliminary research, he works as a forklift driver for Wickstead, a local fulfilment centre owned by an online retailer. He's been in trouble with the police for fighting, but no charges were brought against him. However, he does have two charges for causing a public nuisance while drunk. He was fined and ordered to keep the peace for six months both times. He boxes at a club, and he originates from Leeds, so we can assume that he's got the strength to attack Lorna.'

'And coming from Leeds, that would give him a northern accent, but it's different from a Mancunian accent. Although you did say the victim wasn't certain about that.'

'No, she wasn't, but plenty of people struggle to distinguish between different accents, so that certainly doesn't eliminate him from our enquiries. He also could have put on a different voice to make sure she couldn't identify that it was him. Clark lives in Edinburgh Street, which isn't too far from here, maybe twenty minutes, but he should be at work, so we'll drive there first.'

They left the park and drove to Wickstead. George parked her car in the visitors' car park, and they headed to the small, single-storey brick-built building beside the large warehouse, with a *Reception* sign above the door. Sitting behind the desk was a balding man in his fifties.

'Hello?' the man said as they walked over to him.

Whitney held out her ID. 'DCI Walker from Lenchester CID, and this is Dr Cavendish. We're here to see Fraser Clark. He works here as a forklift driver.'

'I know who he is. What's he done now?' He rolled his eyes.

An interesting response, especially when speaking to the police.

'Sorry, I'm not at liberty to discuss ongoing investigations. Where can we find him?' Whitney asked.

'Wait here, and I'll put a call out for him.' The man slid a tannoy towards him and pressed the button. 'Fraser Clark to the office. Fraser Clark, to the office. Thank you.' He gestured to the black plastic chairs situated against the far wall. 'He shouldn't be too long if you'd like to take a seat.'

'We'll wait for him outside, thanks. Is there anywhere private we can go with him?' Whitney asked.

'You can use the kitchen. It's small because there's only me and Sharon, our office girl, who uses it. It's through there.' He pointed to an open door opposite the entrance.

'Thanks. We'll do that.'

They went outside, and George turned to Whitney. 'Do you think it's wise waiting here for him in case he sees us and runs off?'

The car park was big and open from all sides. There

were any number of exits off the ground Clark could have taken should he so wished.

'Good point. Even though we're not in uniform, he might be on edge and seeing a couple of strangers here might trigger warning bells. We'll go back inside.' They returned to the reception. 'Change of plan. We'll wait here for him,' Whitney called out when the man behind the desk glanced up at them.

They sat in silence, and finally, after ten minutes, the door opened, and a man wearing a high-visibility top, navy overalls, and heavy black boots walked in. He was around six feet tall, with broad shoulders and wavy dark blond hair. His complexion was rugged, and lips were set in a flat line.

'What's this all about? I was just about to go for a fag break,' he said, striding up to the front desk and staring down angrily at the man behind it, his hands on his hips.

Whitney and George stood, making sure they were blocking the door.

'These officers are here to speak to you.'

Clark swung around and stared at them, eyes wide. 'What?'

'I'm DCI Walker, and this is Dr Cavendish. Come through to the kitchen. We'd like to have a chat with you about one of our enquiries,' Whitney said, stepping forward.

George glanced at the officer. Although she was short, she still came across as intimidating when required. Her slight stature never interfered with her work.

'Am I under arrest?' His eyes darted from Whitney to George.

'Not at present. We believe you might be able to assist us with one of our investigations.' Whitney gestured for him to go through to the kitchen, and after several seconds of scowling at them, he acquiesced.

Once they were in the kitchen, George closed the door. They all sat around the small Formica-topped table in the centre.

'Where were you between the hours of five-thirty and eight yesterday?' Whitney asked.

'Out.' Clark sat back in the wooden chair; his hands clasped behind his neck.

'Please could you be more specific, or we could end up staying in this room for a long time,' Whitney said coolly.

'Tell me what this is about and I might,' Clark countered.

'You used to be in a relationship with a woman called Lorna Knight, is that correct?'

He lowered his hands until they rested on the table and leant forward, his jaw clenched. 'What's the bitch been saying about me now?'

His body language clearly indicated the anger he harboured against the victim.

'I take it, from your response, that there are issues between the two of you?' Whitney said.

'You think? She moaned about me to her brother and said I pushed her around. Well, I soon put him right.'

'How did you do that exactly?' Whitney asked.

'Look, why are you asking me this? I haven't seen the cow in ages. Whatever she's told you is a lie.'

'Where were you last night?'

'I'm saying nothing. Not without my lawyer present. I know what you lot are like. Putting words into my mouth.' He pressed his lips shut and stared belligerently at them.

'That's fine. We can finish this at the station.' Whitney shrugged. 'I suggest you contact your solicitor now while I arrange for you to be escorted there.'

Whitney and George left the room to make the arrangements. Within ten minutes, a car had arrived and taken him away.

'He was certainly quick to ask for his solicitor,' George said while they were driving back to the station.

'Yes, I thought that too, but he clearly wasn't going to give us any information here. Let's hope we get more out of him when we formally interview him.'

5

Monday

'Listen up, everyone. Lorna Knight's ex-boyfriend, Fraser Clark, is in one of the interview rooms waiting for his solicitor,' Whitney said to the team, who were there for the prearranged eleven o'clock briefing.

'How come he's lawyered up already?' Brian asked.

'He asked for one within a couple of minutes of us questioning him. But that doesn't mean we can read anything into it regarding the victim's attack. But it *does* mean that we've got a while before he can be interviewed, so let's make good use of the time and see where we are on the investigation and what, if anything, points to him being responsible. Frank, what have you found so far?'

'I've checked all the CCTV cameras in the area, guv, and I saw the victim with her friend leave the cinema and walk down the side of the building to the car park at six-fifteen. I was able to follow the car until reaching the Bombay Palace restaurant on Kensington Street, where they parked. They were in there for fifteen minutes and came out holding a takeaway. From there, they drove in the direction of the friend's house, but that's where the cameras finished.'

Whitney picked up a marker and wrote the name of the restaurant on the board together with the time Lorna was last seen there.

'Did you pick up the victim later when she was walking back home?'

'No, guv. There are no cameras on the route she took. Not even in the park, which was surprising.'

'Okay, thanks. Ellie, does Clark have a car? He was out last night, but we don't know where yet.'

'Yes, guv.'

'Frank, see if you can spot his car anywhere. Ellie will give you his address and registration details, so start from there. Ellie, what else have you discovered?'

Whitney leant against the desk next to the board and gave the officer her full attention.

'I looked into Lorna Knight's background, and there's nothing out of the ordinary. On her social media, there are lots of posts from when she was dating Clark. Since then, there's no evidence of any serious boyfriends, but she's out regularly with her friends. She works in the office of a local insurance company as an admin assistant. I've checked her finances, and nothing stands out as being questionable.'

'And any more on Clark?'

'Apart from what I've already told you about his run-ins with the police, he's thirty-four, lives alone in a rented flat on Edinburgh Street, and the club he boxes at is in Doncaster Street, which is also close to where he lives and only ten minutes by car to Willis Park. His family live in Lenchester, but he doesn't see them often. He rarely posts on social media, other than a few photos when he was going out with the victim, and since then, either memes, photos of him at the boxing club, and a couple at a stag night. It was clear when his relationship with the victim ended because there was a gap of several weeks before there were any posts at all on his profile. He continued to make comments on some of her posts, although they were different from when they were in a relationship.'

'What sort of comments? Anything threatening?' Whitney asked, alert to potential leads.

'Not threatening as such, guv. More derogatory. One time she posted a photo of herself wearing a new dress that she'd bought and he commented, saying it made her look fat. Lorna ignored and didn't respond.'

'He's a twat,' Frank said.

'Yeah. But that doesn't make him guilty of attacking Lorna Knight. Was there anything in your research into him that showed a violent side?' Whitney asked.

'Only with his boxing, but that's in a controlled environment.'

'Ellie, have there been any other attacks of a similar nature recently? Although this attack appears to have been premeditated, there is still the possibility that he's done something similar in the past,' George said.

'Good point, thanks. Check that,' Whitney said.

'I'll do it now, guv,' Ellie said.

Whitney appreciated George's input because she was always quick to assess the situation and consider other angles, even if she did have other things on her mind, like the proposal. Then again, she did have the knack of being able to compartmentalise. A skill that Whitney wished she could embrace. Her thoughts had kept straying to Martin and their relationship – if you could call it that – all morning, but now wasn't the time to start pondering that.

'Anything from forensics?' Whitney asked, returning to

the matter at hand. 'Jenny promised she'd try and get something to us as soon as possible.'

'Yes, guv,' Brian said. 'They found several dark hairs belonging to the victim, and some wool fibres. Other than that, the site was clean. So not very helpful,'

'The fibres might have come from the balaclava the attacker wore, and now we have confirmation of where the attack took place, which all helps in building up a picture of what happened.' She turned and added further notes to the board.

The phone rang on one of the desks, and Brian picked it up. 'CID.' He was silent for a few seconds. 'Thanks. I'll let the guv know.' He replaced the handset. 'Clark's solicitor is here.'

'Okay. Brian, you and I will interview him. George, can you watch from the observation room? Before we go, Doug, anything from the house-to-house?'

'Not so far, apart from a man who'd been walking his dog in the park, and he thought he saw the victim on her way through. He didn't notice anyone following her. I'm going back there later because there were several houses where there was no answer. Hopefully, someone will have seen something.'

'I hope so, too. Seven-thirty to eight on a Sunday evening is hardly late, especially as it wasn't totally dark.' She let out a frustrated sigh. 'Right, let's go and interview Clark. With any luck, we can pin it on him, and the case will be solved.' She grimaced. 'Damn. I bet I've jinxed it.'

~

GEORGE SAT on one of the stools beside the two-way mirror and stared intently at Fraser Clark, who was seated beside a woman in her forties, sitting upright in her chair, paying no attention to her client. Anger emanated from Clark, from the rigidity of his jaw through to the stiffness of his entire body. George suspected it wasn't just because he was in this situation but because it was one of his personality traits. Even before he knew why he'd been called to the office at his place of work, he was tense and on guard, as if waiting for an antagonistic situation to erupt.

Whitney sat opposite him. She leant across Brian and pressed the record button.

'Interview on Monday, September 12. Those present: Detective Chief Inspector Walker, Detective Sergeant Chapman, and ... please state your names for the recording.'

'Alison Thompson, solicitor.'

'Fraser Clark.'

'Mr Clark, you're not under arrest, but anything you do say may be used in evidence against you in a court of law. Do you understand?'

'Yes. But I've done nothing,' he said, a contemptuous expression on his face.

'When we spoke to you at your place of work earlier, you informed us that you were out yesterday, Sunday, September 11, between the hours of five-thirty and eight, but refused to say where you had been.'

'Why should I tell you if you weren't going to tell me why you wanted to know? You've got nothing on me, so you might as well let me go.'

The solicitor leant in and whispered something in his ear. He nodded.

'You may leave once we've finished the interview. We're making enquiries into a vicious assault on Lorna Knight that took place yesterday at around seven-thirty in the evening. Now perhaps you can tell us where you were?'

'If she told you it was me, then she's lying.' Clark folded his arms and glared at Whitney.

George suspected this aggressive stance was something he used often as a defensive mechanism. 'Whitney, I believe he's hiding something. And he's using intimidation tactics to stop you from pursuing it further,' she said into the mic that linked to the earpiece Whitney was wearing in her ear. The officer gave a small nod to acknowledge that she'd heard.

'We're not accusing you of anything, Mr Clark. However, it would be most suspicious if you don't inform us where you were on Sunday. It's a simple question.' Whitney leant forward slightly.

Good move. It showed he couldn't intimidate her. George would have expected nothing less from the officer.

'Okay. I went to the Lamplighter pub in Perry Street in the afternoon at about three, after I'd been working out at my club. I'm not sure what time I left to go home, but it was probably at just before ten because when I got home, the news was on the telly.'

'And were you with anyone?' Whitney asked.

'No one in particular. I was mainly on my own.'

'So you didn't speak to anyone at all in the pub for all those hours? I find that hard to believe.' Whitney shook her head.

'Of course I did,' Clark said, rolling his eyes. 'I saw lots of people I knew. I go there all the time. So what?'

'Give me a name of someone who can vouch for you being there from three until ten, and once we've checked with them, you'll be free to go.' Whitney leant back in her chair.

'Umm ...'

'He's not telling the truth – his blink rate has shot up. I suspect that he wasn't there for the entire time,' George said.

'Are you sure you stayed at the pub the entire time?' Whitney asked.

There was silence for a few seconds. 'Okay, I did leave the pub for a while at around seven. Maybe a little later, I don't remember exactly.'

'Did you go to Willis Park?' Whitney said.

'No,' Clark said, frowning.

'It's only a ten-minute drive from where you were, if that.'

'I didn't go anywhere near that park, all right?' He folded his arms tightly across his chest.

What was he hiding?

'You can see why we're curious. You were in the vicinity of a vicious attack on your ex-girlfriend at exactly the right time.'

'I've told you I didn't do it. You can't pin it on me. I was with someone. All right?' He thumped the table. 'Now you know.'

'Who is this person?' Whitney asked.

'A girl I met in the pub. We drove to some wasteland close by and ... you know.'

'No. I don't know,' Whitney said coldly.

'I fucked her. Okay? That's what we did, and then after a while, we went back to the Lamplighter.'

'What time did you get back there?'

'I don't know. Maybe half-past eight. I didn't check my watch. So now you know, I can't have done it.'

'Tell me who this girl is, and we'll get in touch with her. If she can verify your story, then you'll be free to leave,' Whitney said.

'I don't know her name.' Beads of sweat formed on his forehead.

He was certainly panicking. Whether it was because he

was telling the truth but couldn't prove it, George wasn't sure. His body was so tense most of the time, it was difficult for her to make a judgement call.

'He's worried. Keep going with this line of questioning,' she said to Whitney.

'You've just told us that you engaged in sexual relations with a woman, and now you're saying that you don't know her name, so it can't be proved. And you expect us to believe you?'

Clark shifted awkwardly in his seat. He glanced at his solicitor, and then back to Whitney and Brian.

'Look. We hooked up in the pub. We'd both had a few and decided to go for a drive. I didn't need to know who she was. When we got back, she left me and sat with her friends. I stayed drinking at the bar until leaving to go home later. And that's it. I didn't go anywhere near Lorna.'

'How convenient. Were you driving while under the influence?'

'Jesus, woman. Give it a rest. So what if I did have a few? I was fine to drive.'

'Is there anyone at the pub who saw you with this woman and can validate your story?' Whitney asked.

'I don't know. You could ask the landlord – he knows me. It's my local.' He sat back in the chair and looked away.

'If that's all my client can tell you, is he free to go?' the solicitor said.

'We'll be keeping Mr Clark here until we have checked out his alibi.'

'What about my job? I won't be paid if I'm not there.' He turned to his solicitor. 'Can they make me stay here?'

'If you'd rather, Mr Clark, we can arrest you and then keep you for up to forty-eight hours. It's your choice. You either wait here while we check out your alibi, or you'll be put under arrest. Either way, you won't be leaving any time soon. Perhaps you can explain that to him, Ms Thompson,' Whitney said.

'That is correct, I'm afraid,' the solicitor said.

Clark grunted and folded his arms tightly across his chest, his whole body tense.

'Interview suspended,' Whitney said, turning off the recording. 'You can wait here, and we'll be back after we've followed up on your story. I'll ask someone to bring you in a cup of tea.'

Whitney and Brian left the interview and met George out in the hall.

'Do you need me to check out the alibi, guv, or are you going to? I've got a couple of things that need sorting out,' Brian said.

'George and I will go, and we'll meet you back here later. What do you think, George, from the interview?'

'It was clear that he was hiding something, but it just could be that he'd left the pub with the woman.'

'Do you think from his demeanour that he could be the attacker?'

'I can't speculate on that. We don't have sufficient information, and he wasn't an easy person to read because his body was in a constant state of tension.'

'Well, we'll soon find out when we go to the pub to see if anyone remembers him being there.'

6

Monday

'So tell me more about this proposal, then,' Whitney said to George on their way to the Lamplighter pub.

If Whitney was to find out any more about her friend's big news, then she'd have to ask, because George was known for keeping things to herself. Not just because she was a private person, but more because the thought of sharing didn't often cross her mind. But once asked, she would usually spill the beans. At least she would to Whitney, not to anyone else. She had begun to think of George as her best friend. Whitney didn't have time to keep in contact with many other people she'd known over the years. Her work and family had always taken priority. She didn't mind; she'd never been one for having lots of different friends. Plenty of acquaintances, but not close friends.

'There is nothing more to tell. Ross asked me to marry him, and although I assured him that I wouldn't be ending a relationship, I did explain my need for time to think. I'm not even sure why he did ask when everything was fine between us.'

'Try because he loves you and wants to spend the rest of his life with you. Surely you can understand that?'

Sometimes it was like speaking to a child with George. She was the most intelligent person Whitney knew, yet when it came to some of the basic things, the woman just didn't get it. When she'd asked George if she'd been diagnosed on the autism spectrum, she'd been assured that she hadn't. George hadn't actually said that she'd been tested, but how else would she know?

'And I want to be with him, too. But that doesn't mean we have to marry. It is, after all, only a piece of paper.'

Whitney gave a frustrated sigh. 'Sometimes I give up with you. Anyway, how did he propose? Was it all romantic over a candlelit dinner?'

'I was in my study unpacking my books at the time.'

Seriously? Why on earth would Ross do it like that? Unless he hadn't wanted to make a big deal about it, bearing in mind what had happened the last time.

'So, no red roses or getting down on one knee, then?' she confirmed, still not quite believing it.

'No. He stood at the door and asked me. Does it matter how?'

'As it's you, then probably not. I'm sure you've never dreamed of being swept off your feet by some romantic gesture.'

'I haven't. Have you?'

'When I was younger. But I got fed up waiting for the right person to come along.'

'What about Martin?'

'I like him a lot. But whether or not that's enough, I can't decide … Look, this isn't about me. Have you and Ross discussed children?'

Tiffany had mentioned that she'd spoken with George about kids, but her friend had never discussed it with her. Whitney wasn't even sure she could imagine George being a mum, although, like everything the woman took on, she would no doubt commit to it totally, if that's what they decided to do.

'I'm trying not to think about the issue of children at the moment. Ross would like us to have them, but I don't. We're at an impasse.'

'You're making it sound like some sort of negotiation. This is your future life with Ross we're talking about it.'

'And you're asking me questions that I can't answer,' George shook her head and let out a long sigh.

Whitney knew anything emotional was hard for her friend, but she also knew that they were a perfect couple, and hopefully, George would see that, too.

'The main thing is you love him, and you're together. I think you should say yes to his proposal. I'd love to go to a wedding.'

'Whitney, I'm not going to get married just to give you somewhere to go,' George said, looking in her direction and rolling her eyes.

'I was only joking. You know what I'm like. I just think it's nice that you and Ross are so happy, and I'd love nothing more than for you both to take the next step and make it more permanent.'

'I'm not prepared to make a rash decision. Would you accept if Martin proposes?'

'It's too complicated. I'd rather we concentrated on your future.'

'That's the third time you've evaded that question today. Do you wish to discuss it with me?'

Did she want to burden George with her problems at a time when she had her own to deal with? Then again, George was probably the perfect person to speak to because she was so rational and saw things clearly.

'Between you and me, I'm not happy with the way things are progressing. I like Martin very much. He's a great grand-father and father, but I just don't feel anything in the rela-tionship. If you get what I mean. There is no spark. I'm not sure if there ever was one, to be honest, maybe just a little fizz. I hope that doesn't sound too mean, because I really do like him, just not in that way.'

'And you've only just realised this?'

'To be honest, the feelings have always been there, but I'd parked them because there have been so many other things to focus on. Finding out what happened to Rob being one of them,' she said, referring to the investigation that her former-Met-officer-turned-PI friend Sebastian Clifford had taken on a few months ago into the attack that had happened to her brother twenty-five years ago and had left him with irreversible brain damage.

'Yes, it must have been a great relief for that to have been resolved. How are Rob and your mother now it's all over?' George asked.

'Rob isn't any different, even though I told him he no longer has to worry about keeping his secret. And as for Mum ... When she was having a good day, I explained to her how Seb had solved the case and that the person respon-sible was going to be punished, but I'm not sure she under-stood. She was more interested in whether Seb and I were an item.'

George frowned. 'You two?'

'Yeah, I know. Funny, isn't it? I explained that we were very good friends, and that whenever I need a private investigator, he'll be the first person I'd call. I mean, really. Can you imagine me with him? I'd have constant neck ache speaking to him, considering he's way over a foot taller than me.'

'It would be tricky. Back to Martin, how do you plan to deal with your problem?'

'I'm trying to find the right time to tell him that it's over between us.'

Saying it out loud confirmed to her that she'd made the correct decision.

'If you do terminate your relationship, how will that leave him regarding seeing Tiffany and Ava?'

'That's the issue I'm struggling with. I don't want him to stop seeing them. Or me, even. I want us to remain friends, and I'm hoping that he'll agree to that.'

'He's a sensible man. I'm sure he won't want to lose all contact with his only daughter and granddaughter.'

'I hope you're right. I really do. Right, we're here. Let's forget about our personal issues and instead focus on what we can find out about Fraser Clark's whereabouts last night.'

The pub was quiet, with only a couple seated at an oblong table beside the window, and an old man seated with a pint in front of him at the bar. As they approached, a six-foot tall, wiry man with dark brown hair who looked to be in his late forties stepped forward from his position beside the till.

'How may I help you, ladies?' he said, smiling, his teeth stained with nicotine.

Whitney held out her warrant. 'I'm DCI Walker from Lenchester CID. I'd like to speak to the manager, please.'

'I'm Bob Cross, the landlord.'

'Is there somewhere we can talk?'

'We'll go into the snug. It's quiet, but I can still keep an eye on what's going on from there. I'll have to pop back if a customer comes in.' He came out from behind the bar and led them through the pub into a smaller room, which had an unlit open fire with stacks of logs either side of it.

'We are here to ask you about a customer. Fraser Clark. Do you know who he is?' Whitney asked once they were all seated.

'Yeah, I know him, all right. He's one of our regulars, and he's a right pain in the arse. Comes in at least two or three times every week.'

'Was he drinking here yesterday?'

'Yes. He arrived mid-afternoon, I believe, and stayed quite a few hours, although I'm not sure exactly what time he left. Is that important?'

'Yes, we need an exact time for when he left. You referred to him as a "pain in the arse" – what did you mean by that?'

'In the past, I've had patrons and also members of staff complain about his behaviour towards them. He comes on to the ladies and can be quite insistent. He's not too bad when he's sober, but when he's had a few to drink, he can be obnoxious.'

'And have you spoken to him about this behaviour?' Whitney asked.

'Oh, yes. I've warned him several times to cut it out. He'll be okay for a while after I've had a word, but then the behaviour starts again.'

'Why don't you bar him?' Whitney asked.

'If I barred every person who played up, then I'd go broke in a few months. Fraser's a good customer, providing he's handled correctly. I make sure that my staff are safe, and if any patrons complain about his behaviour, I ensure that they're not left alone with him. Look, I've probably made him out to be worse than he is. He doesn't try it on all the time, and it's mainly when he's been drinking that issues arise. And, let's face it, some women like the attention.'

'What?' Whitney stared daggers at him. 'Are you implying that what he does is okay?'

'No, no, of course I'm not. What I meant was that he's a good-looking man and some women like him, that's all.'

Whitney sucked in a breath. They weren't going to get anywhere if she lost her cool.

'We really need to find out what time Fraser Clark left the pub yesterday. Who else was on duty with you?'

'Hannah. She had an issue with Clark at one time, which I sorted out, and he's left her alone since then.'

'What are her working hours?'

'She's here three or four nights a week, depending on when I need her. She's a student at the university. She's been working here for a couple of years now. She's very reliable, and I'll miss her when she finishes studying. But she's got at least another year to go.'

'What about the university holidays? Does she still stay in Lenchester?' George asked.

'Yes. She comes from round here and lives with her boyfriend.'

'If you could let me have her details, we'll contact her to find if she knows what time he left,' Whitney said.

'I've got them in the office.'

They followed him back to the bar, and he left them. When he returned, he handed Whitney a piece of paper with the name and address written on it.

'Here's my card. If you do think of anything, please let me know,' Whitney said, handing it to him.

They left the pub and went back to the car.

'I assume we're going to Hannah's house,' George said.

'Yes. Let's see if she can give us any information about Clark.'

7

Monday

George drove them to Flitwick Road, which was two streets away from the pub to the terraced house where Hannah Pyke, the Lamplighter's student bartender, lived. Whitney knocked on the door and, after a minute, heard footsteps coming down the stairs. The door was opened by a man in his early twenties. His hair was sticking up, and he looked like he'd only just got up.

'Yeah?' he said, staring at them both.

'Is Hannah Pyke here?' Whitney held out her warrant card.

'What's it about?'

'We need to speak to Hannah in person. Is she in?'

'She's upstairs. I'll call her.' He left them standing on the doorstep and went to the bottom of the stairs. 'Han, the police are here to see you.'

There was a loud thump on the ceiling, and then footsteps as a young woman dressed in pink-and-white-striped pyjamas hurtled down the stairs, a look of panic etched across her face.

'What is it?' she said as she got to the bottom. 'Has something happened to my family?'

'No, it's to do with your work at the Lamplighter pub. We'd like to speak to you regarding your shift last night,' Whitney said, stepping inside.

'Oh. My. God. I thought someone had died.' She leant against the banister, her hand resting on her chest.

Whitney could've kicked herself. She should have said straight away that it wasn't an emergency and there was nothing to worry about.

'My apologies. Is there somewhere we can sit down and talk?' Whitney asked.

'Sure. We'll go in the kitchen – I could do with a glass of water.' Hannah turned to her boyfriend. 'Babe, could you go upstairs and put my tablet on charge? I was just about to do it when you called me down.'

'Sure.'

He took the stairs, two at a time, and they followed Hannah down the narrow hallway into the galley kitchen, which had a small table close to the back door.

Whitney pulled out one of the chairs furthest away from her to give George enough space to squeeze in next to her, and after filling a glass with water from the tap, Hannah sat on the remaining chair.

'Have you lived here long?' Whitney asked.

'Since Tim and I moved in together at the end of our first year at uni.'

'What do you study?' George asked.

'Media and communications. I've just finished my second year and found out on Friday that I'd passed. Thank goodness. Next year I'm determined to work harder.' She laughed. 'I said that this time last year. I blame the nightly happy hour in the student union bar.' She picked up her glass and drank almost half of it. 'Sorry, what do you want to know about yesterday?'

'Do you remember Fraser Clark being at the pub?'

Hannah turned her nose up. 'Yeah.'

'Do you still have issues with him? The landlord told us that it had been dealt with.'

'It had, but that doesn't mean I like him. Fraser had a thing for me, maybe twelve months ago – I can't remember exactly when it started. He'd stand at the bar, staring at me. It really gave me the creeps. I almost left the job because of it. Bob persuaded me to stay and had a word with him.'

'I sorted him out, too,' the boyfriend said.

Whitney turned her head. She hadn't noticed him standing by the entrance to the kitchen, leaning against the door.

'What happened?' Whitney asked.

'Fraser waited for me after work a couple of times and asked if I wanted to go out for a drink to a club in the city centre. I kept telling him no. But one time, he followed me home and started getting insistent when I was about to go inside. Luckily, Tim arrived home from being out with his friends at just the right time and warned him off.'

'Clark doesn't seem the type to be warned off easily,' Whitney said.

'I was with several of my mates, and two of them play rugby. They're massive, and no one messes with them,' Tim said.

'Did Fraser leave you alone after that?' Whitney asked.

'Mostly. Occasionally, he makes a creepy comment about how I look, but other than that, he's okay. A little while after the warning from Tim, he got fixated on Penny, another girl who works behind the bar.' Hannah picked up her glass and took another long drink.

'Do you remember Fraser's girlfriend, Lorna, coming to the pub with him?'

'I didn't even know he had a girlfriend. Although a couple of times last year, he was at the pub with the same girl. But I didn't speak to her. She sat at a table while he came to the bar to be served.'

'Why do you remember that so clearly?'

'Mainly because he usually came into the pub on his own, so it stood out.'

'What about friends? Does he come into the pub with them?'

'No, he usually drinks on his own. I've seen him chatting with some of our regular customers, but I've never seen him out with the lads.'

'Do you know that he's a boxer?'

Hannah laughed. 'Everyone knows. He's always bragging about how good he is and which world champion he could beat, given the chance. He's such a show-off.'

'He's all mouth,' Tim said. 'If he was that good, he wouldn't have backed off so easily when faced with me and my mates.'

But that didn't mean he wasn't prepared to attack someone like Lorna, who was so much weaker than him.

'Back to last night. Do you know what time Fraser arrived at the pub?' Whitney asked.

'He was there when I started my shift at five, sitting on a stool beside the bar. I remember my heart sinking when I saw him.'

'Do you remember the time he left?'

'No, I'm sorry, I don't. I was rushing around all over the

place, serving customers, collecting glasses, and washing up. Rinse and repeat,' she said with a grin.

'Do you recall seeing him with a woman?'

Hannah was silent for a while. 'Yes, now you mention it, I think so. He was standing towards the back of the pub talking to one. I can't remember what she looked like, though, apart from I didn't recognise her as being a regular. I'm sorry. Sunday can be crazy, especially as it was only me and Bob working last night because Penny called in sick.'

'Did you notice them leave the pub together?'

She chewed on her bottom lip. 'No. I'm sorry, I don't recall seeing them after that one time.'

'Thanks for your help. If you do remember anything further, please let me know.'

They left the house and went back to the car.

'It seems to me that Clark targets single, young women who he sees as vulnerable. Once warned off, he'll move onto a different target,' George said.

'So, where does that leave him regarding the attack on Lorna?'

'He's still a person of interest,' George said.

'My sentiments exactly. We know he stalks women. We know he has a temper. We know he doesn't have an alibi for the whole evening. And we also know that Lorna believed she was being followed in the weeks leading up to the assault. We'll interview him again. Perhaps this time we'll get more out of him.'

8

Monday

'Guv, I've got some important info for you,' Ellie called out excitedly as George and Whitney returned to the incident room after interviewing Hannah Pyke.

Whitney had hardly spoken on the return journey, which was most unlike her. George had half expected her colleague to be discussing wedding dresses, venues, and possible honeymoons. Unless it was the Martin conundrum that had occupied her thoughts? It was somewhat disconcerting to see her friend struggling in this way, even though George was happy not to be discussing her own issues further.

'Listen up, everyone. Ellie has something,' Whitney said, although the other team members were already looking up from their desks and staring in the young officer's direction.

'I've been researching into unsolved sexual assaults over the last few years to see if the attacker had offended in the past, as Dr Cavendish suggested, and I found three assaults where the exact words spoken to Lorna Knight were spoken to these other victims. "Scream, and I'll cut your tongue out." Also, which is further confirmation that it's probably the same man, these other victims all claimed that their attacker had a northern accent, but that it was hard to pinpoint where exactly he was from because of his whisper-like voice.'

'Excellent work, Ellie. But how come these three weren't linked together, and we've only just discovered similarities between them?' Whitney tilted her head quizzically.

'It couldn't be helped, guv. No one would have thought to look. There were two in Lenchester, but those were twelve months apart, and the other one happened in Harleston.'

'Hmm. I suppose so, although the two Lenchester ones could have been linked if proper research had been undertaken. Which teams worked on them?'

'Both were investigated by DCI Masters' team, guv.'

Why didn't that surprise her?

'I see,' Whitney said, narrowing her eyes. 'Tell me more about these three cases?'

'The first one happened eighteen months ago, and the victim, Jessie Wood, is twenty-four and lives in Lenchester. The next one is Tina Bennett, and she also lives in Lenchester. Her attack occurred twelve months ago. Then Cheryl Hughes, aged fifty, who lives in Harleston, and that took place six months ago.'

'So, the victims weren't chosen because of being in a certain age band,' Doug said.

'No, and the Tina Bennett is thirty-five.'

'And there were six months between each attack, including the one yesterday on Lorna Knight,' Whitney said.

'Except, I suspect there may have been more attacks that weren't reported, when considering the statistics relating to sexual assaults and how many victims refuse to contact the police,' George said.

'That's true. Many sexual assaults are kept quiet. But then, how can we account for this six-month gap between each of them? Surely it can't be a coincidence,' Whitney said, glancing at George, a twinkle in her eye.

Whitney knew full well George's view on coincidences, and she would often tease her about it.

'I certainly don't believe it to be. However, until we have a motive, we can't speculate. Were they six months apart to the very day, Ellie?' George asked.

'No. They were within a couple of weeks either side of the six months.'

'In that case, it puts a different perspective on it. The length of time between the attacks that we are aware of is something to consider, but I wouldn't get too wedded to that notion,' George said.

'No, we shouldn't get *wedded* to it,' Whitney muttered, loud enough for only George to hear.

George glared in her direction, then relaxed into a smile. Her friend was only having a bit of fun with her.

'I have photos of the three other victims, guv. I've printed them off. Shall I put them on the board for you?' Ellie said.

'You know, you can use the smart board and send them straight there,' Brian said.

'And you know my view on that. Which I know it makes me sound like a dinosaur, but I don't care. So, yes, please, Ellie.'

Ellie placed the photos on the board, and George and Whitney stared at them.

Straight away, George observed certain similarities between each image, sufficient to convince her that they were dealing with the same attacker. 'Look at the bruising over the mouth on each of them. They're all identical,' she said.

'Yeah, the exact same sized hand and fingermarks.' Whitney turned to face the team. 'See the fingermarks on the faces of each victim? They're all the same, including those on Lorna.' She pointed to Lorna's photo. 'I'd say we're definitely looking at the same assailant.'

'Fraser Clark?' Frank asked.

'He's our chief suspect in respect of Lorna, but now we have the other victims, we'll need to dig deeper. Ellie, see what else you can find. Frank, check CCTV from six months ago and see if Clark's car was anywhere near Harleston. We'll interview Clark again. He might speak without his solicitor present if he thinks he'll get out sooner than if he waits for her to return. Ellie, please print me off all these victims' details. I want dates, times, locations, and photos. If he is our man, then I want to make sure that I have all the ammunition available to get a confession.'

∼

WHITNEY AND BRIAN headed back to the interview room. George wasn't with them because she'd received a message from Ross that the builder they'd employed to do some work on the house was going to be there earlier than expected, and typically, George didn't want any decisions made without her being there. But she promised to be back in the morning.

Clark was seated with his arms folded across his chest and his lips set in a flat line. Whitney placed the folder she was holding on the desk in front of her and nodded for Brian to start the recording equipment.

'I want to leave now. You've got no right to keep me here

when I've done nothing,' Clark said in a voice much less aggressive than in their previous interview.

'Your solicitor has already explained our legal entitlement. We are here to continue with our interview. Do you wish to wait for your solicitor to return, or are you willing to speak to us now?'

Clark sighed. 'What choice do I have? It could be hours before she comes back, and I want to get home. I've already missed most of today from work, and knowing them, they'll dock my pay. Just ask your questions and let me get out of here.'

'Mr Clark, do you recognise this woman?' Whitney took out the photo of Tina Bennett from the file on the table and slid it over for him to see.

He glanced down, his eyes widening. 'Hang on a minute. I thought we were talking about Lorna. That's not her. Surely, you're not saying that I beat this woman up?'

'Please answer my question. Do you know this woman?'

'Nope. I've never seen her before in my life.'

'Where were you on the twentieth of September last year?'

'How the fuck am I meant to know what I was doing on a certain day over a year ago? That's stupid. Ask Lorna, she might know, because we were still together then. She used to keep a diary, but I don't.'

'Do you know Grafton Street in Lenchester and any people who live there?' Whitney asked.

'Yeah, it's close to where I grew up. My mum still lives the next street over, and I know some of her mates. Most of my old school friends have left the area.'

'In that case, is it possible you could've been in the vicinity of Grafton Street twelve months ago?'

Whitney stared at his face, looking for any signs of deceit, but so far, there was nothing.

'I've told you, I don't know. Maybe I was. I visit my mum every week. Unless I've got other things on. But if you think I did that to this woman, then you're wrong.' He stabbed his finger at the photo.

'We've been to the pub to check your alibi and, unfortunately for you, no one can vouch for how long you spent there. We have established that you were there, but not the time you left. We've also learnt that you have a reputation for pestering women.'

He eyes flashed. 'Who the fuck said that? I'll kill 'em—' He stopped himself. 'I don't mean I'd really do it. That's just a saying. Look, if I see a woman I like, I'll approach her. What's wrong with that? It's better than going on one of them dating app things.'

'Do you have an issue when women tell you no? Because we've been informed that you were very insistent in pursuing one of the bar staff. So much so that the pub landlord had to warn you off and threaten you with being barred.'

'If that's what he said, then he's lying. If you ask me, he wanted her for himself. She didn't mind me coming on to her. We were having fun.'

'I am going to have to disagree with you there. Now, let's go back to last night when Lorna was assaulted. You still don't have an alibi.' Whitney steepled her fingers and rested them on the table. She stared, unblinking, at Clark, who shifted awkwardly in his seat.

'Look, I've just remembered someone who saw me leave because I said goodbye to him. I also had a chat with him while I was in there. He saw me go outside with that girl because he winked at me. And then gave the thumbs up when we came back.'

'And you've suddenly remembered this? How convenient,' Brian said.

'I'd been drinking, okay? Some things are a bit fuzzy. Ask him. He'll tell you. The thing is, I'm not sure of his proper name or how you can contact him. Bob, the landlord, might know. The man's called Digger, and he's always in there. You better ask him because I'm not going down for something I didn't do.' He thumped the table, his temper suddenly returning.

'You can stop that for a start, or you'll find yourself here for much longer. Wait here quietly, and we'll check,' Whitney snapped, sliding back her chair and standing.

Clark stared at her open-mouthed, but silent. Clearly, her words had some impact.

They left the interview and headed back to the incident room.

'Do you want me to call the landlord, guv?' Brian asked.

'No. I'll do it. He knows me.' She returned to her office, found the number, and called.

'Lamplighter pub, Bob speaking.'

'Hello, Bob. It's DCI Walker. We came to speak to you earlier about Fraser Clark, one of your customers. I have further questions for you.'

'Sure. Fire away. The bar's empty, so I'm all yours.'

'You have a regular customer called Digger, is that correct?'

'Yeah. He's been coming here for years. What's he to do with your investigation into Fraser?'

'Mr Clark has suggested that he'll be able to vouch for the time he left the pub yesterday. Do you happen to know Digger's real name and have any other details for him?'

'I've only ever known by his nickname. But I do know that he works for Macintosh Construction, if that's any use.'

'It is. Thanks for your help.'

Whitney ended the call and went through to the incident room to speak to Brian.

'Digger works at Macintosh Construction. Give them a call and see if they have a mobile number for him, or if they can put you through to him. Let's see if he can confirm Clark's alibi.'

'Will do, guv.'

The door opened, and she glanced over to see Doug headed towards her.

'Got anything?' she asked.

'We've now spoken to everyone in the area, guv, and although we have two witnesses who actually saw Lorna enter the park, neither of them noticed anyone following her.'

'Damn. It's never easy,' she muttered.

'But if the attacker knew where she lived and could see the road she was heading down, he'd have known that she would be cutting through the park. That meant he could take another way in and be in place to ambush her.'

'From the direction Lorna Knight was heading, what, in your opinion, would be the route he'd have taken?'

'To get into the spot he did and be ready to pounce on her, the most likely place would be down the walkway off Blenheim Street because it cuts off a whole section of the park that Lorna would have walked through before reaching the spot.'

'So, why didn't she take the shortcut?'

'At that time of night, even though it wasn't totally dark, I imagine she'd have wanted to keep to the main streets. The shortcut isn't well lit because of the overhanging trees.'

'But the place she was attacked was?'

'Yes. Until she was grabbed into the bushes, she could have been seen by people in the vicinity. Except there weren't any who saw her beyond the park entrance.'

'Okay. I want you to speak to uniform and arrange a house-to-house in the area surrounding Blenheim Street. Ask Frank to check CCTV from there, will you?'

She noticed Brian heading in her direction and walked over to meet him halfway.

'I spoke to Digger, guv, whose real name is Kevin March, and he couldn't confirm Clark's story. He said he remembered the man being in the pub, but only after I'd described him. He didn't know his name.'

'Right. Let's go and tell Clark that he's remaining in custody.'

'He won't like that.'

'That's not my problem. He stays there until we know for certain that he's not our assailant. Which won't happen until we've investigated these other assaults.'

9

Tuesday

The next morning, Whitney and George sat in a café close to Wentworth Way where Jessie Wood, the first victim Ellie found, was working. When Whitney had called and spoken to the woman, she was reluctant to meet with them, saying that she couldn't talk about it, but after Whitney had explained about Lorna and the fact that they'd found two other similar attacks, she had agreed to meet with them, providing it wasn't at the police station. She said she couldn't face going there again. Whitney had then arranged for them to meet at the café.

Whitney recognised the woman when she walked in and raised her hand. Jessie acknowledged she'd seen her with a nod and, after ordering at the counter, came over with her drink. She was small, around five foot two or three, and had straight mid-brown hair that hung to her shoulders, which was held back off her face with a black hairband. She looked a lot younger than twenty-four.

'Thanks for agreeing to speak to us. I really appreciate it,' Whitney said, gesturing for her to sit down when she reached the table.

'It wasn't an easy decision to make. I know it happened eighteen months ago, but it's still my first thought every morning when I wake up, and the last one at night before going to sleep. All those memories, dredged up from where I just want to bury them.'

Whitney's instinct was to reach out and give the young woman a hug. She reminded her so much of how Tiffany was after she'd been subjected to a vicious attack. The haunted look in her eyes, the constant checking around her. Tiffany had recovered enough to lead a normal life, thanks to help from George and other professionals. Jessie didn't appear so lucky.

'Do you live at home with your parents?'

'Yes. I'd been planning to move into a flat with my friends before it happened, but I changed my mind. My mum wanted me to go to counselling, thinking that would help, but I said no because it would just mean going over everything again and again each time I had an appointment, and I couldn't face it.'

'Counselling isn't like that. You wouldn't be pushed into talking about what happened if you didn't want to. But what they can do is help you to find ways of coping. I can recommend a good counsellor you could go to and see if it's something you would like to consider,' George said.

'I'm sorry, I didn't introduce you to Dr Georgina Cavendish,' Whitney said gently. 'She's a forensic psychologist who helps us on our cases. And she is exactly the right person who would be able to point you to someone suitable to help.'

'Thank you for your advice. I'll have a think about it.'

The closed expression on Jessie's face implied that she wasn't going to do anything of the sort, whatever George suggested. If only Whitney could do more to help.

'I know this is going to be really hard, but please, could you go through what happened on the evening of the attack?' Whitney took out her notebook and pen. 'Do you mind if I take notes?'

'Umm … no, if you want to, that's fine.' She sucked in a breath. 'It was my birthday, and I'd gone out with friends to the Bear pub in the city centre to celebrate. At the end of the evening, we all left the pub together. It was probably around eleven to eleven-thirty. It wasn't late because we all had work the next day. I was going to phone for a taxi, but then the bus came along, so I jumped on instead. The stop is literally at the top of the road where I live, so I didn't think there'd be an issue. I got off the bus and was walking down the road when, suddenly, I was grabbed from behind and pulled into an alleyway. That's when he, you know …' She was silent, her eyes glassy.

'I understand from the report that he held his hand over your mouth and spoke to you.'

'Yes, he said, "Scream, and I'll cut your tongue out."'

'Did you recognise his voice?'

'No. He had a northern accent that could've been Geordie, but it was hard to tell because his voice was low. I tried to fight him off, but he was bigger than me, and he punched me in the face. All I could think of was that I didn't want to die, so I forced myself to stay still.'

Whitney hated having to ask the woman to relive the attack again in such detail.

'Did he also put his hand around your neck and attempt to choke you?'

'No. His hand stayed over my mouth for much of the time.'

'Do you recognise this man?' Whitney asked, holding out a photo on her phone of Fraser Clark.

Jessie stiffened and stared at the phone.

Was this it? Had they got Fraser Clark?

Jessie remained motionless for a while, but then her body sagged, and she shook her head. 'No, I don't. Is it him? Is he the man who raped me?'

'He's a person of interest, but he hasn't been charged. It's early stages in our investigation. We wanted to speak to other women, like yourself, who we believe might have been attacked by the same man, to look for any clues as to his identity.'

'I didn't see his face because he wore a balaclava, but that aside, I think my attacker might have been bigger than the man in this photo. More solidly built. But I don't know for sure. I was too scared to pay attention. I kept my eyes closed most of the time, just willing the whole thing to be over.'

'Could you tell how old he was?'

'No, but he was definitely fit. The way he dragged me and pushed himself on top of me, it seemed easy for him, even when I was struggling to get away. He hardly seemed to exert himself at all.'

Fraser Clark was fit from all the boxing he did, and it wouldn't have taken him much effort to immobilise her.

'And sure his exact words were "Scream, and I'll cut your tongue out"?'

'Definitely. I hear them every day in my mind.' She pulled the sleeves of her top over her hands. 'How many people do you think he has attacked?'

'We're currently looking at four attacks, including yours.

The reason we've linked the cases is because of how he spoke, and the words he used.'

'You have to catch him before he hurts anyone else. I wouldn't wish this on anyone. It's always there. At the back of my mind. I go over it time and time again, wondering if I played it right. Whether I should have tried harder to get away. But all I could think of at the time was that I didn't want to die, so I did what he asked. The attack didn't last long. It was over in a few minutes, and then he ran off. Maybe I should've tried harder to get away. It's not like we were far from the street.' She lifted her cup and took a sip, her hand trembling.

'Jessie, since you reported what happened to the police, have you remembered anything else that might help us catch the man who hurt you?' Whitney asked.

'No. I told them everything.'

'Did he seem confident in what he was doing? Did he hesitate at all?' George asked.

'Well ... he did sort of fumble a bit with my clothes. B-b-but ... I don't know.' A tear rolled down her cheeks, and she wiped it away with a tissue, which she'd pulled out from her jacket pocket. 'I'm not sure. I can't say. Why does it matter?'

'I was wondering if this was his first assault, and he was unsure about what he was doing.'

'Do you think he actually knew who you were?' Whitney asked.

'I don't know. He didn't act as if he did, but ...' She hesitated. 'Leading up to the attack, sometimes I had the feeling that I was being followed, but there was never anyone there. I've always been a bit jumpy when I'm out on my own, and so I thought it was just that.'

'Did you tell the police that at the time?' Whitney asked.

'No, because I couldn't prove anything. But I'll tell you something, I'm never going to celebrate my birthday again. And that's a promise.'

'You will in the future, I'm sure,' Whitney said gently.

'Well, it's only every four years on the actual day, which is something to be grateful for, I suppose.'

'So your birthday is on the twenty-ninth of February? A leap-year baby.'

'Yes, that's right, and it did sort of make it easier this year. Not that I went out celebrating with my friends. All I did was go for a meal with my family,' Jessie said.

Whitney leant over and rested her hand on Jessie's arm. 'Thank you very much for taking the time to talk to us about this. We understand how hard it was for you to relive the assault, but hopefully, with your help, we can prevent this monster from hurting again. We'll let you know how the investigation goes, and once he's been caught, that might give you some peace of mind.'

The words sounded pathetic and futile to Whitney's ears, but what else could she say? It wasn't like she could ever take away what had happened to Jessie.

'If you mean I'll be able to stop constantly looking over my shoulder, I doubt it. But if he could be caught, that's something.'

'Please do contact me if you change your mind on the counselling, because you might find it helps,' George said.

They left the café and headed back to the car.

'That poor girl. The trauma she's gone through— is *still* going through. We've got to succeed in catching him. But one question I have: if it's the same man, then why didn't he try to strangle her, like he did with Lorna?' Whitney said.

'If this was one of his earlier attacks, then I'd say it's

because, with each one, he's needing to be more aggressive to fulfil his needs. Initially, the rape was enough, together with the hand over the mouth to act as a warning. But as he progressed, then he needed to increase the level of violence. We need to catch this man before he progresses from sexual and physical assault to murder.'

10

Tuesday

'And who's this new member of the team? The new recruits get younger every year,' Whitney said, smiling, when she returned to the incident room and saw a little girl sitting at Frank's desk, where the officer was showing her photos of cars on the screen. Just beyond, Whitney then caught sight of a familiar face, standing next to Ellie, chatting.

'Matt!' she called out, heading over to them. 'What are you doing here?'

'Hello, guv,' he said. 'Just thought we'd pop in to see the old folks.'

'Good to see you again, Matt,' George said, joining them.

'You, too, Dr Cavendish.'

'So, you must be Dani,' Whitney said to the pretty little girl with cute dark curls who had turned her head to look at them.

'Yes. I'm Dani Price. Daddy brought me here.'

'It's lovely to meet you, Dani. How's the new job going, Matt?' Whitney asked, turning back to face him.

After the restructure and merger, Matt had decided to move to a smaller force thirty miles away so he could look after the baby, and his wife, Leigh, could pursue her career as a nurse.

'Quiet, guv. Not like here. But it's fine, and I seldom have to do any overtime. Mind you, looking after this one makes police work seem like a doddle,' he said, nodding at his daughter.

'I know exactly what you mean. Did you know that Tiffany's had a baby?'

'Yes, Ellie told me. So, now you're a granny.'

'No need to remind me. It makes me feel very old. How's Leigh getting on?'

'They're giving her more and more responsibility, and she's in line for another promotion. We definitely made the right decision because her career is really taking off, and the extra money is great. It means we can pay for childcare for Dani.'

'So why are you back in town? I highly doubt you drove all this way to say hi to your old boss,' she asked, not wanting to push him away, but conscious of the fact that they had work to do.

'I have an appointment with a solicitor in the city and was a few minutes early, so thought I'd come and see you all. Ellie's just been telling me about the case you're working on. Grim stuff.' He ruffled his daughter's hair. 'Dani, it's time for us to go.'

'But I don't want to, Daddy. Frank is showing me lots of cars. We're looking for a blue one.'

'I can't believe how well she talks. She's not even two,' Whitney said.

'She started at nine months and hasn't stopped since. She's really bright. Takes after her mum.'

'I'm sure there's plenty of you in her, too. It's been lovely to see you. Come and have a drink with us all sometime, so we can have a proper catch-up.'

'Okay, I will. I miss the old team,' Matt said, a wistful tone in his voice.

Was he regretting leaving and deciding to stay as a sergeant instead of taking his inspector exams like Whitney had wanted him to?

'We miss you, too,' she said, and meant it. Nothing against Brian, her new sergeant, but Matt was special, and they went back a long way.

'Thanks, guv. Come on, Dani, we can't be late for our appointment.'

He managed to prise the child away from Frank's desk, and once they'd left, Whitney called the team to attention.

'We've just been to see Jessie Wood, one of our earlier victims. She's still very traumatised by what happened, despite it being eighteen months ago. Which is understandable. There were similarities in her account of the attack and the one that Lorna gave us, so we're going to work on the assumption that we're dealing with a serial rapist.'

'Was she able to give you any more details regarding what this bastard looked like?' Frank asked.

'No, but she also believed the accent was northern, but maybe Geordie and not from Manchester. She did say he spoke with a low voice, so it was hard to tell, which is exactly what Lorna told us. Jessie's attack took place on the evening of her birthday – what a day for that to happen. A constant reminder. The only good thing, if it can be called that, is the reminder, in theory, will only be every four years because she was born on the twenty-ninth of February.'

'Hang on a minute, guv,' Ellie called out. 'Lorna Knight was also born on the twenty-ninth of February. I remember seeing posts on social media from when she celebrated her birthday last year with her friends.'

Whitney exchanged a glance with George. Did they have a link already?

'Check the other victims you've found, Ellie. If it turns out that the rapist has been choosing women with leap-year birthdays, that would be proof positive that these attacks were targeted and not random.'

'But where would that leave Fraser Clark? Wasn't he going out with Lorna then?' Frank asked.

'Yes, he was. He's still in the frame, and I'm very interested in knowing why she celebrated with her friends and not him?'

'Maybe they'd had a falling-out, and he took out his frustration on other women with the same birthday?' Frank said.

'How would he have known that Jessie had that birthday?' Doug said.

'It could have been by chance. He didn't go out with Lorna, for some reason, but he went out somewhere else instead and happened to come across Jessie out with her friends. It could have been a spontaneous thing,' Frank said.

'What do you think, George?' Whitney asked, turning to face her friend, who was staring at the board.

'It's a possibility, but I'm reserving judgement until we know for certain whether the birth date is a determining factor.'

'Guv, they're all the twenty-ninth,' Ellie called out.

Whitney turned to the board, and in big letters at the top wrote, *Born: 29 February.*

'Right. Ellie, I want you to do a search on all sexual

assaults over the last five years and find any victims who were born on that date. Is it possible to find out how many have that birthday? There can't be many.'

Whitney turned to George, who was staring at the screen on her phone.

'According to the national statistics, just under eleven thousand babies have been born on the twenty-ninth of February since 1995. That averages out at almost eighteen hundred a year. It's a rare birthday, but not impossible to locate people with it, thanks to the databases that are around these days,' George said.

'Do the stats specify how many live in each area and, in particular, how many are women?' Whitney asked.

'No, I don't know that information here.'

'Ellie, what's the chance of finding out how many women live in Lenchester and surrounding areas with a twenty-ninth of February birthday?'

'It might take some digging, but it's not impossible.' Ellie pulled her keyboard closer and started tapping on the keys.

'What do you think is special about the date?' Frank asked.

'That's what we need to discover, because it's quite likely that it's linked to our motive. George and I are going to visit the third victim, Cheryl Hughes, who lives in Harleston. Her bruising appears significantly more severe than Jessie Wood's.' Whitney turned to the photos on the board and pointed to them. 'In fact, they do get steadily worse with each attack from Jessie Wood until Lorna Knight. George, what's your view?'

George took a step back and stared ahead at the board. 'It's my opinion that Jessie Wood was either the first, or one of the first. There are no marks on her neck, and the main bruising occurred from the hand being placed over her mouth. If we take Tina Bennett, the next one, which was six months later, she has several bruises on her cheeks, implying that he'd hit her. There do seem to be some abrasions on her neck, but no discernible finger-marks. Cheryl Hughes had a cut below one of her eyes, bruising around her mouth and then some lacerations on her neck. With each attack, the assailant has stepped it up a gear, culminating with Lorna, the latest victim.'

Whitney looked away from the board, back at her team. 'If we run with the theory that it's linked to Lorna's birthday and her not seeing Clark that night, then we need to speak to her to find out more. We'll visit her after we've been to see Cheryl Hughes.'

'I think that's a good idea,' George said. 'If only to confirm my theory.'

'Although Clark is currently our chief suspect, we need to be mindful that it might not be him. Ellie, check the database for all known sex offenders within a fifty-mile radius of Lenchester so we can follow up on their whereabouts at the time of the assaults. Brian, you can give her a hand. Doug, any joy on yesterday's house-to-house in Blenheim Street.' Whitney asked.

'No, guv. It's like people go around with their eyes closed. There are still some houses where no one was in. I'll speak to uniform and make sure someone goes to visit.'

'Good. Well done, everyone. We're getting somewhere.'

11

Tuesday

Cheryl Hughes lived in a 1970s semi-detached house on an estate on the outskirts of Harleston, but the woman who opened the door appeared older than fifty.

Whitney held out her warrant card. 'Are you Cheryl Hughes?'

'Yes, I've been expecting you.'

Cheryl opened the door and ushered Whitney and George straight into an open-plan lounge, which had stairs going up along the right wall. At the rear of the large room was a small dining table and a door that Whitney assumed led to the kitchen. Whitney and George sat on the black leather sofa, and Cheryl on one of the matching easy chairs.

'Thank you for agreeing to see us,' Whitney said.

'Why, after all this time, do you want to speak about the attack? I thought the police had forgotten all about it.' She bit down on her bottom lip. 'Lucky them. Because I never will.'

Whitney wanted to tell her that it would get better over time. But how could she? Because it might not. Even when the culprit had been taken off the streets, the woman would most likely spend the rest of her life looking over her shoulder, never truly trusting men again.

'A sexual assault occurred on Sunday night, and we believe that the attacker might be the same man who attacked you six months ago. There have been several others, which we believe this man is also responsible for. I know this is going to be hard, but please, could you go through what happened that evening?' Whitney hated having to put the woman through it all again, but she had no choice.

'I told everything to the police at the time. They were very kind and supportive and kept in contact for a while. But they didn't catch him, and then I stopped hearing from them. I took that to mean that they'd closed the investigation.'

Whitney shook her head. Even if they had stopped investigating, the woman deserved to be told as such.

'I'm sorry that you weren't officially told the position. We're reopening your case, but because we're from Lenchester and your assault was dealt with by Harleston CID, we need to go through it all again with you. It's because we don't have automatic access to their files, and it may take a while to get them. By speaking to you directly, we can move quicker and hopefully catch the man who assaulted you. From our investigation so far, it seems that with each assault, he's becoming more and more violent. Fortunately, the woman who was attacked on Sunday managed to get away because he had tried to strangle her. Then we'd have been dealing with a murder.'

Should Whitney have given away those details about the case? *Yes. If it helps.*

Cheryl's hand shot up to cover her neck. 'Oh my God. That's even worse than what happened to me. But ... his hand was around my neck, and he squeezed, but not hard enough that I thought he was trying to strangle me.'

'Now you understand why it's so important for us to know everything we can about this man so we can put together a picture. Would you mind going through everything that happened that night?'

Cheryl closed her eyes for a few seconds and sucked in a breath. She looked directly at Whitney. 'I was coming back from church, and it was about five o'clock on a Sunday evening. It was dark, but the streets were well lit. I was walking along Moreton Street when suddenly, I was grabbed from behind and pulled by my arm into a dark alleyway, which is a shortcut to some waste ground ...' Her voice was low, and she spoke in a monotone, like she was reading from a script.

'What happened next?' Whitney asked after Cheryl had been silent for many seconds.

'Sorry. I thought I'd be okay speaking about it. B-but ...'

'Take your time. It's okay,' Whitney reassured her.

'Thank you.' Cheryl sat upright in the chair, her hands resting in her lap. 'I tried to escape. But he was strong. His hand was over my mouth. It was pressed so hard I could hardly breathe. He told me if I screamed, he'd cut out my tongue.' She stared ahead; her eyes had a distant faraway look. 'He dragged me a few yards to the waste ground, and then he pushed me hard onto the ground. He straddled me with his legs so I couldn't move. And then ... then ... he raped me ...' Her voice cracked, and she bowed her head.

'I'm really sorry to have to put you through this,'

Whitney said, hating how they were raking up all this pain again.

'It's okay, I understand. What else do you need to know?'

Whitney admired Cheryl for the bravery she was showing them.

'Did you get a look at him?'

'No. He was wearing a hoodie and, under that, a balaclava. It was dark – I couldn't even see the colour of his eyes.'

'And when he spoke, did you recognise his voice?'

'He sort of whispered. All I can tell you was he spoke with some sort of northern accent. But I can't tell you where from – I'm not great with accents anyway – but his voice was all raspy, so it was hard to tell.'

'What happened afterwards?'

'He ran off, and I lay there on the ground, too scared to move in case he came back. After a little while, I reached for my bag, took out my phone, and called my husband. I forced myself to walk to the main road and wait for him. When he got there, we went straight to the police station and then they took me to hospital to do all the checks. The irony of it is I have a personal-defence spray in my bag, but he was too quick, and I couldn't get hold of it. I had no idea that he was even behind me.'

'Thank you for going through it with us. Do you recognise this man?' Whitney asked, showing her a photo of Fraser Clark on her phone.

Cheryl stared at it, her eyes wide. 'No. No, I don't. Do you think it was him? Was he the one who did this to me?'

'He's a person of interest in the latest attack, and at the moment, we are looking into all possibilities. Did you have the feeling that your attacker knew you?'

'I don't know. He didn't say my name, but then he didn't say anything other than threatening me. But if it was someone I know ... then ... that means—' She clamped her hand over her mouth.

'It's a question we ask all victims. Please don't start assuming that it's going to be someone close to you. It's just one of our many lines of enquiry.'

Cheryl's emotions were clearly still very raw, so Whitney decided against asking if Cheryl thought she was being followed prior to the attack. She didn't want to make the woman's suffering any worse.

'When it happened, it was a complete shock. I'm fifty – who'd be following me, at my age? You always imagine it happening to younger women, but ...' She stopped speaking and stared into space. 'The attack has totally changed my life. I used to work part-time, but I've given up that job now. I tried counselling initially, but it didn't stop the nightmares. Sometimes, I think about going again, but I feel safe in my own home, and I only go out if I'm with my husband.'

'I'm sorry to hear that,' Whitney said gently. 'Your birthday is on the twenty-ninth of, isn't it?'

'Yes. Is that important?'

Whitney hesitated. If she mentioned to the woman about the birthday connection, Cheryl would know she'd that she'd been targeted by someone who knew her movements and where she lived. That wasn't a good idea.

'It's just unusual.'

'Yes, there aren't many of us around.'

'Thank you very much for your help. We'll keep you informed of our progress, and if we do charge anyone, we'll let you know straight away. We may also be in touch to discuss the attack some more, if you're up to it.'

'I have to be. Because until the bastard's caught, there's no chance of me being able to resume a normal life.'

12

Tuesday

'Hello, Liam,' Whitney said when he opened the door to the semi-detached property on the Wessex Estate. Dark circles had formed under his eyes, and worry lines were etched across his forehead.

'Are you here to see Lorna?' he said.

'Yes. This is Dr Cavendish.' Whitney stepped to the side so he could see George. 'We won't be too long, but there are a few more details I'd like to discuss with her, if she's up to it. How's she doing?'

Whitney had been reluctant to speak to Lorna again so soon. But it was important, so they could fill in the missing pieces.

'She's been very quiet and has mainly sat reading in the living room. After I picked her up from hospital yesterday afternoon, I thought she should stay in bed, but she didn't want to. She said she didn't want to be alone because it made her feel isolated. She was up most of last night. We all were. I just wish I knew what to say to her. I feel so helpless.'

'It's never just the victim who finds it hard – it can't be easy to see her in such pain,' Whitney said gently. 'But give her time. Be there if she wants to talk, but don't push her if she doesn't.'

'Why did it have to happen when she was beginning to get her life straight? Lorna's a good person. She'd never hurt a fly. I just don't get it. Do you have any clues about who did this? Was it Clark?' He ran his fingers through his dark hair, making it stick up at right angles.

'Mr Clark remains a person of interest, but it's early days in the investigation. We do believe that Lorna's attack is part of a series of sexual assaults on women going back over the past eighteen months or so. We've only just made a connection between them.'

'After all this time? Why?' His brows furrowed.

'They were far apart in distance and time, and not all handled by the same force.' The excuse sounded pathetic, even if it was the truth.

'Does that put Clark in the clear? He was with Lorna eighteen months ago, so surely she would've realised if he was raping other women.'

'It's what we're investigating. But now we have linked the attacks, it will make it easier for us to catch him. Have you taken today off work to be with Lorna?' Whitney asked.

'The whole week. Penny, my girlfriend, would have liked to be here with us too, but she is in the middle of an important stocktake at work, and they wouldn't let her have the time off at such short notice. Come on through, and you can speak to Lorna.'

Liam took them into the lounge, which had large windows at either end, filling the room with light. The furniture was modern, with chrome-and-glass coffee and dining tables. The L-shaped sofa was an oatmeal colour with large, blue-striped cushions scattered on it. Lorna was seated on a matching easy chair, staring ahead, not looking at the book she was holding in her hand. Whitney winced at the sight of the bruising on her face and neck, which was now a very dark purple with slight tinges of yellow.

'Lorna?' Liam said softly.

She glanced over at them. 'Hello,' she said, her voice still hoarse.

'How are you feeling?' Whitney asked, walking over to Lorna and sitting on the edge of the sofa next to her.

'Numb.' Lorna placed the book she was holding on the small table beside her.

'I hope you don't mind, but we'd like to have a quick word with you. This is Dr Georgina Cavendish. She's a forensic psychologist, and she advises on our more serious cases.' Whitney gestured to George, who sat next to her.

'I'm very sorry to hear what happened,' George said.

'Thank you.'

Whitney exchanged a glance with George. Lorna's one-word answers were a clear indication that the shock and trauma of the last thirty-six hours were sinking in.

'I'd like to ask you a little more about Fraser Clark, if that's all right with you?' Whitney said.

'Was it him?'

'It's too early to be certain, but currently he's a person of interest. What we've also discovered is that several other attacks have taken place over the last eighteen months that were very similar in nature to yours. In particular, the words that the attacker spoke and the way he placed his leather-gloved hand over your mouth.'

'Oh.' Lorna sat forward, hugging her knees.

'I'd like to take you back to your birthday celebration eighteen months ago. Although you were dating Fraser at the time, according to your social media pages, you didn't go out with him that evening, but went out with your friends. It was on your actual birthday of the twenty-ninth of February.'

'Yes, I remember. We'd been rowing a lot, and I refused to go out with him on my actual birthday and instead made other plans. I couldn't go out with Liam because Penny was taking him away for a surprise mini-break, so I asked all my friends.'

Talking about something other than the attack was clearly the way forward because Lorna was already far more lucid.

'How did Fraser take it?' Whitney asked.

'He said he didn't care because he didn't want to go out with me that night anyway. But when I was getting ready to go, he started acting jealous and said he wanted to come out with us. I said no because no other men were going. My friends didn't like him and wanted it to be just us. But I didn't tell Fraser that ... He'd have gone off on one if I had.' Lorna fiddled with the gold ring on her little finger, turning it backwards and forwards.

'What you mean by "acting jealous"?' Whitney asked.

'He threatened that if I spoke to any men in the pub, or if I went to a club after that, there'd be trouble ... He then said he was going out, too.'

'Do you know where he went?'

She shook her head. 'But knowing him, it was to the local pub. That was all he ever wanted to do.'

'Has Fraser ever been to the Bear pub in the city?' Whitney asked, referring to the place where Jessie had gone to celebrate her birthday.

'I don't know,' Lorna said, shrugging.

'The first of the attacks that I'd mentioned to you was

actually on that night of your birthday. The victim was also celebrating their birthday.'

Lorna froze and stared directly at Whitney, her eyes wide. 'And you think Fraser did it?'

'We're looking into all possibilities. Was he home when you got back that night?'

'Yes, he was fast asleep in bed.'

'And was he different in any way when you spoke to him the following day?'

Lorna chewed on her bottom lip. 'Yes. He made me a coffee first thing, and we chatted before going to work. I thought he was going to start questioning me and demanding to know who I'd been talking to, but he didn't. Weird, now I come to think about it.'

'How long after this did you finish the relationship with him?' George asked.

'A year. It got too much. Every time he went out drinking, he'd come home and ...' Her voice cracked. 'I can't do this.' Lorna grabbed her book from off the table and hurried out of the room. Whitney could hear her footsteps as she ran up the stairs.

'I'm sorry about that,' Liam said.

'No need to apologise. I'm surprised at how much Lorna was able to tell us. We'll go now. If she does think of anything which might help, here's my card.'

'Thank you. Please, for all of our sakes. Catch the man who did this to my sister.'

13

Tuesday

Whitney sat at her kitchen table, her empty coffee mug pushed to one side, reading the file relating to the second victim, thirty-five-year-old Tina Bennett. When Brian had tried to contact Tina at work to arrange an interview, he'd been informed that she was on holiday, somewhere overseas, and wouldn't be back for a further ten days. To make sure that was correct, they'd tried her home, but there was no answer.

From what Whitney could ascertain from the file, the attack was similar in nature to all the others. Tina's happened twelve months ago and, from the photos, appeared less violent than what had happened to both Lorna and Cheryl. There was not a lot else Whitney could glean from the records apart from that it had happened on her way home from a leaving party for a colleague. Tina had taken a taxi and was dropped off outside her block of flats in the south Lenchester area. She was grabbed while walking along the path towards the entrance door, dragged around the back to the grassed area and raped. The only words spoken by the assailant were, "Scream, and I'll cut your tongue out." The police questioned the residents in the flats, but no one saw or heard anything.'

Whitney sat back in the chair and sighed. Whoever they were dealing with was clearly clever and planned everything, because nothing was left to chance. There was no evidence, even from what appeared to have been his first attack. Victims were targeted, their movements known, and were assaulted in areas where they wouldn't be seen.

Was it the work of Fraser Clark? It was appearing less likely. He didn't come across as capable of such meticulous behaviour, but when the search warrant came through for his house, that might provide further evidence.

Her phone rang, and she picked it up from the table. 'Walker.'

'Guv, a woman's body has been discovered in a park in Claxton. Reports are that the death is suspicious,' an officer said.

Crap. The team were stretched enough as it was.

'Okay. Text me the details, and I'll go straight to the scene.'

She ended the call and phoned George. 'A body of a woman has been found in Claxton. Would you like to come out with me?'

'Is it linked to the assault cases?' George asked.

'I sincerely hope not, but we'll soon find out. Meet me there.' Whitney texted the address to George and then hurried to the bottom of the stairs. 'Tiffany, I'm going out and don't know when I'll be back. Sorry, love, you'll have to eat alone,' she called out.

'I'm just putting Ava down. Don't worry. I'll see you whenever.'

When Whitney arrived at the park, George was already there, standing beside her car, talking with Dr Claire Dexter, the forensic pathologist.

Whitney went over to them. 'Claire, I'm so pleased to see it's you on duty. What do we know?'

'I've only just arrived myself, so can you let me take a look first?' Claire said, looking at Whitney from over the top of her glasses and shaking her head in typical Claire fashion.

'Did we interrupt something important?' Whitney said, glancing at the pathologist's attire; a blue lurex jacket over a tweed skirt with a pair of gold lace-up trainers.

'I was at home with Ralph, and we were in the middle of a game of chess – which I was about to win, might I add. So, yes, you did interrupt something.'

That outfit for chess? Whitney forced back a giggle.

'Sorry about that. Let's head towards the scene.'

'Remember to keep your distance,' Claire barked.

Uniform had already put cordons around the area and foot boards for them to walk on. After signing themselves in with the uniformed officer on duty, they walked across to the crime scene in single file, with Claire leading the way. The weather had been so warm recently, the ground was hard.

Whitney and George came to a standstill a few yards from the scene and waited while Claire pulled on her gloves and took out her camera from the bag on her shoulder. She placed the bag on the ground away from the body and took some photos. She then bent down and assessed the scene.

From where Whitney stood, she could see the victim was wearing a pink spotted summer dress with spaghetti straps, which had been hitched up to her thighs. A pair of knickers and handbag were on the ground next to her.

Bruising on the woman's face and neck was clearly visible. Did that mean George was right and they were dealing with the same assailant?

Nausea washed over her. 'I'll never get used to this. Never,' she muttered.

George rested a hand on her shoulder. 'You wouldn't be such a good detective if you did.'

'Maybe.' She turned her attention to the pathologist. 'What can you tell us, Claire?'

'I put time of death at somewhere between midday and six, but I'll know more once I've got the body back at the morgue. That's it. I'm not prepared to make further suppositions.'

'Was she strangled?' Whitney asked.

'Did you not listen to anything I just said?' Claire scowled in her direction.

'Look, I'm just trying to see if this is linked in any way to the current sexual assault cases we are investigating. Have you photographed the handbag? I'd like to see if it has any identification in there.'

'Yes, you can have it.' Claire picked up the small shoulder bag and gave it to Whitney.

She opened it, and inside the small black leather purse was a driving licence. Her heart sank. 'Paula Moore. Aged thirty-eight. Another February twenty-ninth birthday. Damn. It's definitely him.'

'That's an unusual date of birth,' Claire said.

'Our attacker is targeting women born on that day. He's now progressed from sexual assault to murder. This is exactly what we feared would happen. But for it to happen so quickly after the last attempt on Sunday is worrying. Does that mean we're fighting against the clock before another woman is murdered?'

'Let me get on, and I'll do what I can for you as soon as possible,' Claire said.

Whitney was surprised at the sudden change in Claire's manner. Clearly, some murders she found more abhorrent than others, and this must be one of them.

'Thanks, Claire. We'll see you first thing tomorrow morning, if that's okay?'

'It will have to be,' Claire said back to the usual self. That didn't take long.

Whitney and George stepped away from the scene.

'It's what I suspected might happen, but why so soon? Unless ...' George paused for a moment. 'Unless it's because Lorna Knight managed to escape his clutches. If his intention had been murder, then he would have believed that the job was only half-done. That could be why he needed to find someone else.'

'Yes, but this is someone who had the same birthday. So surely he must have already known the victim because this is only two days later.'

'That's correct. The attacker doesn't appear to leave anything to chance. Paula Moore might already have been in his sights, and he brought her attack forward.'

'We have to inform the family and ask for a formal identification. But before we do that, let's talk to whoever found the body. I didn't actually notice anyone there. Did you?'

'No. Unless they were in one of the police cars.'

'Hmm. Maybe. Let's find out.'

They returned to the officer who was on duty.

'Where's the person who found the body?' she asked the constable.

'It was two young boys, guv. Ten-year-old twins. Billy and Archie Wright. They were out on their bikes when they came across it. Their dad took them home after we arrived. He was the one to phone emergency services.'

'You let them go without even making a statement?'

'Sorry, guv. They were in no state to say anything. I thought it would be okay because they only live around the corner at Brinkton Street.'

'Okay, it sounds like that was the best course of action. We'll call round there. We'll need to arrange for them to come into the station to make full statements, but I'd like a chat with them now, if we can.'

Whitney and George walked to the house and knocked on the door.

A man in his late thirties wearing jeans and a T-shirt answered.

'Are you Mr Wright?' Whitney asked, holding out her ID.

'Yes. If you've come to see the boys, I'm not sure whether they're up to speaking about it yet. They're only young, and what they've just seen. Well ... It would affect anyone, let alone a child.'

'I totally understand, but it would be very helpful for the investigation if I could speak to them. We have to catch the person who did this before he tries it again.'

'Yes, I understand. We'll do what we can to help.'

'Thank you. First, I'd like a word with you. Could you tell me what time the boys went out?'

'Yes. They had their tea at five-thirty and then asked if they could go out on their bikes for an hour or so because it was still light. It's usually fine around here, and being twins, they look out for each other. All they do is cycle to the park and then ride around there. They've both got phones, so we can always keep in touch with them. They'd been gone about an hour and a half, so it would have been about six forty-five when Billy phoned and said they'd found this body. He was panicking and clearly upset, so I told him that they should stay together and wait for me. I drove round to find them.'

'Why didn't you walk?' Whitney asked.

'I don't know. I suppose it was so that I could bring them back and put their bikes in the back of the car. To be honest, I didn't actually think it through. I just acted on instinct.'

'What happened when you got there?' Whitney asked.

'They showed me the body, and I phoned the police straight away. I put the boys in the car and their bikes in the boot, and we waited until the officers arrived. The boys were in no state to speak at the time, so I left them sitting in the car and explained everything to the officers. One of them said it would be okay for me to bring the boys back home.'

'Did the twins tell you whether they'd seen anyone in the area?'

'I asked them that, and they said there was no one around. Are you sure questioning them can't wait until tomorrow when they've calmed down a little?'

Whitney sucked in a breath. They'd already learnt enough – in particular, that there was no one lurking around in the vicinity – and she didn't want to put the children through further distress.

'Yes. We can do that. Will you bring them to the station first thing?'

'Thank you. I'll have them there by nine.'

Whitney and George left and returned to their cars.

'You made the right decision not speaking to the twins now. It's going to be hard enough for them to get over the shock as it is,' George said. 'Are we going to see the deceased's family now?'

'Yes. We'll drop my car off at the station first and go in

yours. Having to break the news to someone that their loved one is dead really is the worst part of this job, especially in these circumstances.'

'It's never easy. You also know what finding the body means?' George said.

'That Fraser Clark isn't our man. He's in custody and couldn't possibly have done it. I'll phone the station and have him released.'

14

Tuesday

George observed the tight lines around Whitney's eyes and the way her face was set hard as they drove to the address cited on the driving licence belonging to Paula Moore. Although Whitney had said that this was the worst part of her job, in fact, she was probably the best person to deliver such news to a family. George had witnessed her doing so in the past, and she always spoke with compassion yet was still able to extract the information she needed to enable them to carry out their investigation.

Paula Moore lived in a modern detached house in a suburb south of the city, and when they arrived, George parked in the drive behind a silver Audi.

'Is this the address for Paula Moore?' Whitney asked the man who answered the door.

The man, who looked to be in his forties and was casually dressed in dark jeans and a white T-shirt, frowned.

'Yes.'

Although the victim's driving licence had this as her

address, some people forget to change it when they move, so Whitney needed to check that first.

'My name is DCI Whitney Walker, and this is Dr Cavendish. May I ask who you are?' She held out her warrant card, and he glanced down.

'I'm Paula's husband, Graham. What's happened? Is Paula okay?'

'Please may we come inside, Mr Moore?'

He ushered them into a square hallway with a window seat looking out onto the street. 'What is it?'

'It might be better if we could sit down,' Whitney said.

'Just tell me what it is. Obviously something bad has happened. Please ... just tell me.' His eyes darted from Whitney to George.

George heard Whitney suck in a breath and observed her body tense.

'I'm very sorry to inform you that the body of a woman has been found and, from the driving licence, we believe her to be your wife, Paula.'

The man froze. 'Paula? Dead? How?'

'We're treating her death as suspicious, and that's all we can say at the moment because we're waiting for the pathologist's report. We would like to ask you a few questions, if you're up to it?'

George scrutinised the man's face, looking for any tells that he might have been involved in his wife's demise. Although they suspected it to be the work of the rapist, that didn't mean they should be blinkered and not consider all possibilities. But so far, his reactions appeared genuine.

'She was murdered?' His eyes stared at Whitney and George, but he wasn't really looking at them.

'Is there somewhere we can sit down, Mr Moore?' Whitney asked, resting a comforting hand on his arm.

'Um ... yes. Yes. Come into the kitchen.'

They followed him through to a large room, which had an island in the middle and two sofas to one side.

'Shall I put the kettle on?' George asked.

Whitney flashed a grateful look in her direction. 'That's a good idea.'

George went over to the kitchen section and watched while Whitney led Mr Moore over to one of the sofas, where she sat opposite him.

George hunted in the cupboard and found some instant coffee, teabags, and sugar. She'd make him a sweet tea, which was good for shock, and it would give her a chance to continue observing his reactions to the questioning.

'Do you know what Paula's movements were for today?' Whitney asked.

'Yes, she was working in the office this morning, and this afternoon she had an appointment with a prospective client. They'd arranged to meet in a local café.'

'What sort of work did she do?' Whitney asked.

'We're a marketing consultancy and work from home. Normally, our work is all done via Zoom or on the phone, because our clients are all over the world, but this particular person lives locally, and when he phoned yesterday, he asked to meet Paula in person. She always does the client-liaison stuff, and I put together packages and do any graphics or advertising. I'm more behind the scenes. It made a change for her to get out of the house, and she was looking forward to it.'

Drinks made, George put the mugs on a tray and brought them over to where Whitney and Mr Moore were sitting. She offered the cups around, which were received gratefully before Whitney asked her next question.

'Do you know the name of the person Paula was meant to be meeting and their contact details?'

'All the details should be in Paula's calendar on her computer. Do you think it was them who did this?'

'We don't know at this stage. Please could we check her computer?'

They left the kitchen through the back door and headed into the garden, where there was a large wooden building accessed via a path which cut the lawn in half.

'This is where we work. It helps keep a good work-life balance by keeping us separate from home,' Mr Moore said.

He opened the door, and inside were two large desks, a four-drawer filing cabinet, a large whiteboard, and some other storage units. On one desk was a computer screen, and he went over and clicked the mouse. 'According to this, she was meeting a Mr Lewis at the Tea Room café in Claxton. Only about twenty minutes from here. She left home at three.'

That would narrow down the time of death.

'Weren't you concerned when she didn't come home?' Whitney asked.

'No, because she said she might go and see her friend Glynis afterwards, and I know that when they're together, they can talk for hours. To be honest, I'd been too engrossed in my work to notice the time. It was only by chance that I heard the doorbell when you rang because I'd come in to go to the toilet.'

'Do you have contact details for Mr Lewis and also Paula's friend, please, so we can get in touch with them?' Whitney asked.

'Yes. I'll write them both down for you.' He grabbed a piece of scrap paper beside Paula's computer and wrote down the details.

'Mr Moore, what were you doing between the hours of three and six today?' Whitney asked.

'I was here, working.'

'And is there anyone who can vouch for you?'

'Surely you don't think I had anything to do with what happened to my wife. That would be ... I mean ...' He ran both hands through his hair. 'Look, I had a couple of phone conversations with clients, but other than that, there is no one to prove that I was here. Unless ... you can check my computer because that will have the date stamp of the work I've been doing today.' He exhaled a loud breath, headed over to the other desk, and opened the laptop. 'Look, here it is.'

Whitney walked over to him, peered over his shoulder and confirmed that the files were dated for the time of death. 'Thank you. I asked so we can eliminate you from our enquiries. Is it just the two of you living here?'

'We have a daughter who's away on a school trip to France until Friday— Oh my God, I've got to tell her. What should I do?'

It was as if suddenly, the enormity of what had happened had hit him. A delayed response to this sort of news wasn't untypical.

'I'm going to arrange for a family liaison officer to be with you, and they will help and advise you. However, we do need someone to formally identify Paula. Will you be able to do that?'

'Does it have to be done now? Can I do it tomorrow? I have to phone Paula's parents and my parents, and the school. There's so much to do.'

He'd compartmentalised and gone into automatic pilot, thinking of all the things he needed to do. A defence mechanism to stop him from having to work through everything.

He'd most likely break down at a later date. George had witnessed that on a number of occasions.

'Tomorrow will be fine. Here's my card. Phone when you're ready, and we can sort something out for you.'

'Thank you.'

'Before we go, we noted that Paula's birthday was the twenty-ninth of February,' Whitney said.

'Yes, she hated it because she said three out of four years, when she had a birthday, it wasn't real. Why do you ask?'

'It could be important, but we're not sure yet. Is there someone we can ask to stay with you? A neighbour or friend?' Whitney asked.

'No, thank you. I'm fine.' His fists were tightly clenched by his side. His sweet tea remained undrunk on the side.

How long before he gave in to the grief?

'I will arrange for the family liaison officer to be with you. It won't take long. We're very sorry for your loss. Please give me a ring anytime if there's anything you'd like to discuss.'

'Thank you.' Mr Moore sat there staring into space.

'We'll see ourselves out.'

They left the house, and Whitney then made a call arranging for the FLO to go there straight away.

'Why did you mention Paula's birthday?' George asked, curious as to what the officer's reasoning was.

'I wanted to see his reaction, but it didn't seem to faze him at all.'

'Agreed. I focused on him while you were asking questions, and there was nothing out of the ordinary.'

'If it was him who'd been carrying out the attacks, I imagine there would have been some sign that we'd made a connection between the birthdays.'

'Yes, he wouldn't have been able to hide that. I'm used to spotting even the most minute of tells.'

'Let's hope that whoever the attacker is, he won't have realised we've connected the dates of birth, because that's the only clue we have so far.'

15

Wednesday

Whitney arrived at the office to discover everyone, including George, already there – and she wasn't even late. She would've been even earlier if it hadn't been for the fact that she'd drifted back to sleep, dreaming about Martin and all the different scenarios surrounding their relationship. Sometimes, she was convinced that ending things between them was the right thing to do. Then, at other times, she wasn't sure.

But now wasn't the time to dwell on it. She scanned the room, watching everyone hard at work. She was so proud of her team. They stepped up without being asked when there was work to be done. She looked over at Meena at her desk and caught her eye. 'Everything okay?' she mouthed.

'Yes, thanks, guv,' she mouthed back, giving a tiny shrug. Whitney hoped that the specialist had managed to catch Meena's dad's cancer early enough. If she had the chance, she'd speak to the officer later, when they were alone.

Whitney caught sight of Frank frowning. He'd seen their

exchange and, knowing him, was desperate to know what it all meant. But if he pestered Meena to find out, the officer was well able to put him in his place.

'Attention, everyone. Let's get started. This is now a murder investigation, and our prime suspect has been released, having a cast-iron alibi for this latest attack.'

'Unless he had someone working with him,' Frank said.

'From what's happened in the previous assaults, I doubt that very much, but that doesn't mean we won't consider it. Ellie, you researched local sexual offenders. What did you turn up?'

'There were ten within the area you designated, and I gave the list to Brian.'

She turned to face her sergeant.

'I've contacted seven, and they have alibis, which I've checked for at least one of the offences. The other three are proving harder to track, but I'll keep on it,' Brian said.

'Okay, thanks. Ellie, have you also been looking into similar attacks countrywide?'

'Yes, guv, but so far, I've found no more. I'll continue searching, in case I've missed any, but I don't think I have.'

'Thank you. I'd also like you to look into a client named Shanon Lewis, who Paula Moore met with at the Tea Room café yesterday. That's Shanon with a single *N*, according to Paula's diary. Not that I've ever seen it spelt that way. Unless it was a mistake.' She wrote the name up on the board.

'It's a Gaelic spelling of the name,' George said, 'although it's more commonly spelt with a double *N*.'

'Oh. Thanks. So now we know. I want checks into both Paula and Graham Moore. They have a marketing consultancy, and this man was a potential client who had phoned on Monday morning and arranged to meet. Ellie, I'll let you have the phone number and contact details her husband gave us. I tried the number last night and got no reply. See what you can find out. Meena and Brian, look into the couple, their finances, client list, friends, social media, etc. Frank, I'd like you to check the CCTV close to the café where Paula went to meet this man. Doug, after the meeting, I'd like you to go to the café to confirm they were there, and the time they arrived and left. Also, get descriptions of him and anything else you can that might be relevant. He could be our man.'

'Yes, guv.'

She turned and stared at Paula Moore's name on the board. 'Now what is it about February twenty-ninth? And how does our attacker find out their birthdays?'

'The twenty-ninth? That's my birthday,' Meena said, her eyes wide. 'I didn't notice it written up on the board. Sorry, guv.'

'No problem. What can you tell us about having your birthday then?'

'It's a right pain,' Meena said.

'Mr Moore said Paula didn't like it either. Why?'

'Because every time people find out, they go on and on about it. "Oh, you're only ten, ha, ha, ha." Or whatever age I am. It's driven me mad my whole life. And then there's the case of when to celebrate my birthday. February twenty-eight or the first of March? The trouble with March is every four years, suddenly I have a February birthday. I know this sounds weird, but it sort of makes you feel like part of your identity is missing.'

'I understand that. When do *you* celebrate your birthday?' George asked.

'I do it on the twenty-eighth, because then I feel like February is my birthday month. Even though in reality it makes it a day earlier.' Meena shrugged.

'The question is, how does our attacker know the birth date of his victims?' Whitney said.

'Could it be someone who works in a hospital? They would have birth records,' Frank suggested.

'Then that would depend on each person having visited the hospital to have their records there, but check the hospitals, anyway, Frank. Remember, one of the victims lives in Harleston, so it's unlikely that they're in the Lenchester system,' Whitney said.

'What about someone who works for the DVLA? Driving licences have dates of birth on them,' Brian suggested.

'That's a good place to start. Brian, perhaps you can look at all of our victims to see if they drive and have a driving licence. Or passports. Ellie, are there any other general databases that would enable our attacker to access dates of birth?'

'Yes, guv. There are plenty online, if you know where to look.'

'Why do you think this attack was so soon after the other one?' Doug asked.

'I'll leave George to explain that.'

George, who'd been sitting at one of the vacant desks in the incident room, walked over to where Whitney was standing.

'Of the attacks we have been made aware of, there was a six-month gap between them, although I suspect there might've been others on women who haven't come forward. However, that aside, it's my belief that because Lorna Knight got away from him, the attacker felt the need to commit another assault straight away, to finish off what he started. He needed closure. From the way each attack has worsened in severity, and after what happened to Paula Moore, it would be safe to assume that Lorna was lucky to get away because he had intended to murder her. The reason he was able to attack again so soon was because he already had his next victim in his sights and all he had to do was bring his plans forward.'

'Do you think that Shanon Lewis is the murderer?' Frank asked.

'The fact that he made the appointment with Paula Moore after Lorna Knight's attack certainly ties into that theory,' George said.

'George, could you give us a general profile of our attacker? I know we've discussed it a little, but it would help the team to hear something more concrete,' Whitney said.

'Certainly. This is a basic profile of the man we're looking for. Once we have more information from the pathologist and the manner in which the victim was killed, whether it was frenzied or not, we might be able to add more to it.'

'We already know that he's increasing in violence, though,' Whitney said.

'Yes, that's true. I would suggest that we're looking for a man, who's exceptionally well organised and also patient. He not only had to identify his victims, but also he took the time to watch them and learn their routines and, from there, work out a plan for him to carry out his attacks. Also, the fact that he already had Paula Moore lined up as a backup indicates him being well prepared.'

'But Lorna's attack was after a night out with a friend. How would he know about that?' Brian asked.

'He could've used social media to discover that Lorna was going out and then follow her,' Doug said.

'Yes, that's correct. He also might have made sure to be prepared to attack at any time, having with him a balaclava and condoms and the appropriate clothing. If this was the case, then he'd be able to take advantage of any situation that presented itself.'

'Does him wearing a condom indicate anything?' Whitney asked.

'Good question. There is, of course, the obvious that he doesn't wish to leave any of his DNA. But also, and this would tie into his threats to cut out his victims' tongues, he didn't want to impregnate any of them.'

Whitney chewed on the inside of her cheek. She didn't get it.

'Sorry if I'm sounding dense, but how do they link together?'

'It wouldn't surprise me to learn that our assailant had a religious upbringing. The belief that children shouldn't be born out of wedlock and also, cutting out of a tongue is symbolic of silencing a person for speaking out against religious doctrine.'

'It sounds a right load of bollocks, if you ask me,' Frank said.

'Frank,' Whitney snapped, glaring at him.

'Sorry, Doc. I didn't mean your analysis. Just that this killer is bonkers.'

Whitney laughed, and the others joined in. 'Now you see what I have to put up with on a regular basis. At least you're only with us some of the time,' she said to George. 'Is there anything else you can add to his profile?'

'He's proficient with IT, enabling him to target people with the correct birth date. Also, he would need a job that gave him scope to pursue his victims.'

'Or he could be unemployed,' Meena said.

'Yes. I would put him between the age of twenty-five and forty-five, judging by the descriptions we have and the strength that would be required to commit the attacks.'

'Shall we contact all women born on the twenty-ninth of February in, say, a fifty-mile radius of Lenchester to warn them?' Brian asked.

That was a question Whitney had been grappling with for a while.

'If we do, then it might come out that we know his potential targets. For the moment, we'll keep that to ourselves. But I will speak to the super later about having a press conference regarding the murder and other assaults. I'll ask her to inform women to be careful. We do have some time to play with because he's unlikely to attack again for a while,' Whitney said.

'Unless he's switched it up a bit,' Brian said.

'We know that he's methodical and well organised. Assuming that he works alone, which we believe he does, it seems likely that he would only be following and preparing two attacks at any one time. He would need to regroup,' Whitney said,

'Okay, guv. That makes sense,' Brian said.

'Good. Right, we have plenty to be getting on with. George and I are going to see Claire, and we'll be back later.'

～

WHEN THEY REACHED THE MORGUE, Claire was standing beside one of the large rectangular stainless-steel tables on which the body of Paula Moore was laid out. The ruby-coloured V-shaped incision on Paula's chest in stark contrast to her body's white skin.

'Good morning, Claire. Is it okay for us to approach?' Whitney said.

Claire turned her head and glanced at them over the top of her glasses.

'Yes. I have just got the body out of storage for when you arrived. I undertook the post-mortem last night.'

Pathology fascinated George, and had she pursued the medical career that she'd first embarked on, then she may well have ended up as a pathologist. Of course, it was a moot point because her aversion to blood had put paid to any medical career. Forensic psychology had more than made up for it, though, and she didn't regret the direction her career had taken. Fortunately, the hours of hypnotherapy she'd undergone many years ago meant that she could tolerate being in the presence of blood. Providing it wasn't spurting like a geyser, though. She was unable to cope with that.

'Thanks. I was hoping that you'd be ready for us. Is everything okay?' Whitney asked.

What had Whitney spotted that George hadn't? Claire didn't appear to be any different from usual. Her officious manner seldom changed.

'Of course it is. Come over here – I don't have all day to spend with you.'

They took a few steps forward until they were standing beside the table. George stared at the body, which from the neck upwards was covered in bruises of varying shades, some almost black.

'Time of death was between four and five in the afternoon, and the cause was manual strangulation. There are petechial haemorrhages caused by ruptured capillaries. I'll show you.' Claire lifted the eyelid on the victim's left eye. Whitney and George both leant forward and stared at the eye. 'Do you see the small red dots on the white of the eye? That's what I'm talking about.'

'Did the victim struggle?' Whitney asked.

'Most definitely. Look at the contusions on the neck. The

prominent bruising shows the fingers and thumb, but there's some faint bruising to the sides of these where there was a struggle. Do you see the bruising on the victim's hip?' Claire pointed to a circular bruise that was about three centimetres in diameter. 'There is an identical one on the other hip.'

'What caused it?' Whitney asked.

'The attacker straddled her, and she was restrained by the insides of his knees,' George suggested.

'Exactly, yes. I found small tears on the inside of the vaginal wall and bruising on the inside of the upper thighs, indicating that the victim was raped. The attacker wore a condom, so it's unlikely that there will be any DNA present, but samples have gone for testing. It's not unheard of for condoms to split, although there isn't any indication that this occurred in this instance.'

'Did the rape take place pre- or post-mortem?' George asked.

'There was extravasation of blood around the tissue at the entry site, which indicates it happened ante-mortem.'

'Did you find any foreign substances on the victim?' Whitney asked.

'There was dirt under her fingernails, which I suspect was from the place the attack took place. If the victim had her hands flat and then clenched her fists during the attack, it would have come from there. I've sent samples away for testing, along with some dirt samples I took at the site to see if they are a match. I also found some leather fragments around the victim's mouth and also on her teeth.'

'We know that during previous attacks, he wore leather gloves,' Whitney said.

'Why wasn't I involved in these?'

'They weren't murders, but sexual assaults. We believe

the murderer is the same man who's been sexually assaulting women for at least the last eighteen months, possibly longer. He's progressed from sexual assault to physical assault, and now to murder. His last victim was only two days before this one.'

'Oh, I see. If it is the same person, then the glove is most likely where the fragments came from in that case. There were traces of blood in the fragments, but I suspect they belong to the victim because it would have been extremely difficult to bite through the glove and cause the attacker to bleed, especially under the circumstances. But she could have easily bitten the inside of her mouth or lips at the time. I'll find out for certain when it comes back from toxicology. How is your investigation going? Do you have any leads yet?'

George frowned. It was unusual for Claire to take an interest in the mechanics of an investigation. She was an exceptional pathologist, one of the best in the country, and her input was instrumental in Whitney's team being so successful. But in the past, Claire had been careful to keep their two operations separate. Why was this different?

She glanced at Whitney, who had a puzzled expression on her face. No doubt she was having similar thoughts to George regarding Claire's interest.

'It's not like you to enquire into our work,' Whitney said.

'I've been asked to present a workshop at a pathologists' conference in two months and hadn't decided which case to use. This would make a perfect example of how the police investigation uses my findings. Unless you haven't solved the crime by then, but with your track record, I'm assuming that you will have.'

'Am I to take that as a compliment?' Whitney asked, smirking.

'You can take it however you wish,' Claire said, waving her hand dismissively.

'Well, to fill you in on what we have so far, we did have a suspect, but he was in custody at the time of the murder and had to be released. What we have discovered, though, is that the women he targets all have their birthday on the twenty-ninth of February,' Whitney said.

'Have you yet ascertained why this birth date is so important to him?' Claire asked.

'No. But it's going to be the key to solving the case,' Whitney said.

'That's obvious,' Claire said, rolling her eyes. 'You can go now. As soon as I hear back from the tox screen, I'll let you know.'

16

Wednesday

Whitney knocked on the door of Superintendent Clyde's office. The super was her immediate boss and, apart from Don Mason, the inspector in charge when she'd first joined the force as a police constable, she'd been the best boss Whitney had ever had. It had helped that the super was a woman, so there wasn't any chest puffing and all those other things that Whitney had encountered from the majority of her male superior officers, who seemed to think it was their duty to act dominant at all times.

'Come in,' the super called out.

'I've come to see you regarding the suspicious death from last night,' Whitney said as she walked into the office.

'I was expecting to hear from you after reading what had happened in the dailies. What else can you tell me?' The super indicated for her to sit on one of the chairs situated in front of the desk and gave Whitney her full attention.

'Thank you, ma'am. We believe that this death is

linked to several unsolved sexual assaults that have occurred over the last eighteen months. The mode, together with the words spoken by the attacker, was similar in all cases. The most recent attack, aside from yesterday's murder, was the one that occurred on Sunday evening.'

'Why do you believe it was the murderer that carried out these other attacks? Obviously, you can't know what was spoken to the victim.'

'All the victims, including last night's murder victim, were born on the twenty-ninth of February. This is the first time he's carried out two attacks in such a close time frame, and we believe that he'd intended to murder the victim from Sunday night, but because she managed to escape, the murderer struck again yesterday. To finish the job, so to speak.'

'I see. Where are you with the investigation so far?'

'We've identified three other victims from police records in both Lenchester and Harleston, but I'd like for us to hold a press conference to see if anyone else comes forward. Dr Cavendish believes there may be more.'

'Women born on the twenty-ninth of February only gives the assailant a small pool, if he's keeping his attacks within this region of the country. Have you thought about contacting all of them to warn them to be vigilant and not go out on their own?'

'It was a discussion we've had but decided against it at the moment, ma'am. We don't want the killer to get wind of the fact that we've already homed in on who his potential victims are. He'll realise that we've linked the attacks together because of his MO. I think it will be enough to talk about the murder and earlier assaults more generally. Considering that, in the past, there has been around six months between attacks, I believe it does give us a little leeway.'

'Apart from this latest one. I don't want to have another victim on our hands because the targets weren't warned.'

Did the super think that she wanted more deaths? That was crazy.

'No, ma'am. But I still believe it's prudent not to warn anyone born on that date just yet. We don't want to lose what little advantage we might have.'

'It's your call, Whitney. But please be mindful of the possible consequences.'

'Yes, ma'am. I think it's enough to announce to the public that we have a sexual predator on the loose and that women should take care.'

'Do we have any other evidence?'

'Two of the victims believe they were being followed in the days leading up to their assault, although they didn't actually see anyone. With regard to the attack on Sunday, the victim believed he called out her name when she ran off. Although the attacker spoke in a low voice when with the women, almost all of them believed he had a northern accent. No one so far has been able to identify him at all because he was completely covered in balaclava, gloves, long sleeves, and trousers.'

'I'll arrange a press conference for this afternoon. I'd like you with me for this one. And please email me everything you have, including a profile if you have one.'

'According to Dr Cavendish, we should focus on looking for a male aged between twenty-five and forty-five, who is well organised and methodical.'

'Not much to go on, but it's something. Okay, I'll go with your suggestion, and we won't mention the birthday connection yet.'

'Thanks, ma'am. By holding that back, it will also weed out any information that isn't relevant to this particular attacker. We may well have women assaulted by someone else approach us, which we will also need to investigate.'

'Yes, I agree, that seems the sensible way to proceed. My assistant will email the details once it's set up, and I'll see you later.'

Whitney headed back to the incident room and called the team to attention.

'The press conference is going to be sometime this afternoon. I'm waiting to hear when. We need to make sure there's someone on the phones at all times through until midnight. If we do have calls from women who have been assaulted, it's going to be hard for them to make the call, and we don't want them to have to phone again if there's only an answer machine.'

'I can take the first shift, guv, but I'm out with the wife this evening,' Frank said.

'Why is it you never want to stay late?' Doug said, rolling his eyes.

'Why is it you can never learn to mind your own business?' Frank replied, glaring at his colleague.

'Like you do, you mean,' Doug said.

Whitney ignored the spat between the officers and then turned to George. 'I'm hoping we'll get a good response to the press conference and will be interviewing people tomorrow. Are you free then?'

'Yes, I can come in. If you no longer need me, I'm going home to continue with the unpacking.'

George left, and Whitney moved to her usual position by the side of the board. 'Okay, I want you to sort out the phone rota between you. But now, let's share what we have so far. I'll go first. According to Dr Dexter, our victim was raped first and then strangled. She was subjected to a great deal of trauma. We can't allow this man to attack again. Has anyone got anything to report back?'

'I picked up Paula Moore's car on CCTV as she drove into the car park next to the café and then when she left, forty minutes later.'

'Did you see her leave the actual café?'

'No, guv. For some reason the café entrance can't be viewed. I wonder if that was why it was chosen.'

'It could have been. Did you see another car leave soon after Paula?'

'No, guv. I watched the footage for half an hour after, and there wasn't anyone.'

'Okay, so the man she met must have been on foot and knew where the CCTV cameras were situated. Where did Paula go after leaving the café?'

'I lost the car after she drove into a more residential area. If I had to guess, I'd say that she was heading in the direction of her friend's house,' Frank said.

'Who contacted the friend?'

'I did, guv,' Meena said. 'Glynis, her friend, told me that Paula had called to see her after pitching for some work. Paula said that if they got the job, it would involve some rejigging of their current workload to fit it in. Glynis also said that the victim received a call while she was there and was pleased with the outcome. All Paula said to Glynis was that it looked like they'd secured the contract she'd just gone for. Glynis asked the victim more about it, but she was reluctant to say anything further. Glynis thought that was strange but didn't follow up on it.'

'Where's Paula's phone?' Whitney asked.

'With forensics, guv,' Meena said.

'Ellie. Get onto Mac and hurry him up. Tell him it's urgent that we identify who called our victim.'

Ellie had a special relationship with Mac, who was in charge of digital forensics. If anyone could get their work escalated, it was her.

'Yes, guv.'

～

WHITNEY GLANCED at her watch and increased her pace. The press conference started in five minutes, and she'd arranged to meet the super there. She headed down the corridor towards the conference room, and Melissa was the only one waiting. That was unusual for the super because she was invariably early.

'No super?' she said as she approached the PR officer.

'Yes, she's just gone in with Chief Superintendent Douglas.'

Whitney's heart sank. What the hell was Dickhead doing there? It wasn't something for him to get involved in.

'And they didn't think to wait for me?'

'The chief super insisted they went straight in and told me to wait outside for you. Which is weird, seeing as I'm the one to open the conference. I'm not sure the purpose of going in.'

Douglas didn't need a purpose, if you discounted trying to derail Whitney's career at every possible opportunity.

'Do you know why he's decided to attend?'

'Sorry, Whitney, your guess is as good as mine.'

Whitney opened the door, followed by Melissa, and was greeted by the sound of chattering voices. The room was full, with reporters at the front and only two cameras at the back. Nowadays, most of the conference was filmed on a phone and emailed back into the media outlet's office.

'You're cutting it a bit fine, aren't you, Walker?' Douglas said to her as she headed over to the podium, where he was standing with the super.

'Sorry, I was caught up on the phone. Do we need three of us here?' She'd welcome the chance to leave, if at all possible, especially now that he was there.

'I'm being watched as part of my appraisal. The chief super won't be taking part,' the super said, giving a tight smile.

Only Douglas could want to do that in such an open forum. Did he want to intimidate the super? Fat chance of him succeeding with her, though.

'Surely you can be filmed and your performance judged from that?' Whitney said, stating what she believed to be the obvious.

'How I decide to conduct my appraisal is nothing to do with you, Walker,' Douglas said.

'Sir,' Whitney muttered, glaring at him but refraining from pursuing it further. Their relationship was never going to improve however far up the career ladder he was promoted. There was too much history between them, and he knew it. It went back to the time when he'd made an unwanted move on her when she was a constable and him a sergeant and she'd turned him down, in no uncertain terms. He'd never made advances again, but when he'd been promoted and moved away, she'd breathed a sigh of relief. Unfortunately, his latest promotion had brought him back to Lenchester. At least she had the super to act as a buffer between the two of them. And she had done on a number of occasions.

'Right, we'll start,' the super said, turning to Melissa, who was standing next to them.

'Yes, ma'am.'

The PR officer stepped up onto the podium and called everyone to attention. She then handed over to the super.

'Thank you for coming in. I'm here to inform you that yesterday the body of a woman was found at a park in the Claxton area, and the death is being treated as suspicious. The victim was strangled and brutally sexually assaulted. We are interested in locating a man we believe to be aged between twenty-five and forty-five with a northern accent. We are of the opinion that this man has also carried out sexual assaults on women in the past, at which time he warned them not to scream, or their tongue would be cut out. We're asking if anyone knows anything about this or has been subject to an attack of a similar nature to please contact us here at the station. Everything will be kept confidential.'

Whitney and the super hadn't discussed mentioning the actual words that were spoken by the attacker, but then again, if they didn't release that piece of information, there wasn't a lot else to go on, especially if they wanted other victims to come forward.

'What's the name of the victim?' One of the reporters in the front row asked.

'At the moment, we're not divulging the woman's identity until we've had a formal identification. All we can tell you is she was aged thirty-eight and lived in the Lenchester area.'

'Do you have any suspects?' The same reporter asked.

'Our investigation is ongoing, and we do have several lines of enquiry.'

Questioning went on for a while longer, and Whitney

was unsure why she was needed as the super fielded them all and she wasn't called upon to assist.

'Thank you for coming. As soon as we have further information, we will let you know,' the super said.

They left the conference room and stopped outside.

'Fingers crossed somebody gets in touch with some evidence,' Whitney said.

'I agree, because it's most likely that his next attack will also be murder. He's hardly going to go back to sexual assault only. Not after progressing this far,' the super said.

'You may go now, Walker. I wish to speak to Superintendent Clyde,' Douglas said, giving a flick of his hand to dismiss Whitney.

She was more than happy to get away from them. She not only had a murder to solve, but she was going to end her relationship with Martin when she saw him later. She could wait until after the case was solved, but if she did, then it would be playing on her mind all of the time, and she should be focusing on finding the killer. This was the right thing to do. Even if it meant that nothing was ever going to be the same again.

17

I glare at my computer screen and thump the desk with my
fist.

Damn.

The police have linked the murder back to all the other
attacks. *I wasn't ready for that for that to happen yet. It wasn't
how I'd planned it.*

How the hell did they do it so quickly?

There's no way I left any evidence.

*The attacks were well spaced apart and not all in the same
vicinity. I was meticulous.*

Was it Lorna?

*Did I give something away when she kneed me in the groin?
It fucking hurt, I'll tell you that much. But I pulled myself
together quickly enough and scarpered before she could alert
anyone. And I'll bet my last penny that nobody saw me leave the
scene. The place was deserted, as it usually is. That was the
whole point in me doing it there.*

*I should go back and finish her off, but I doubt I'll be able to
get anywhere near her now.*

I spend hours upon hours researching and strategising. Plan-

ning who's going to be next. When and where. And now that pain in the arse woman has messed it all up.

Okay, so I had someone to take her place, but it's like the domino effect. Now I have to move my plans forward for the next one. And I'm not ready yet.

18

Wednesday

'But, Mum, why?' Tiffany said.

Whitney had thought her daughter might take the news badly that she was going to break things off with Martin that evening, but hoped that once she'd explained that it wouldn't change anything between her and her father, it might ease the situation. Judging by the shocked expression on Tiffany's face, it was going to take a while for her to accept it.

'It's not something I've decided on a whim, and it's been a difficult decision. But I've been feeling for a long time that our relationship isn't going anywhere. And more to the point, I don't want it to. Martin's a great guy, and I really like him, but there's nothing between us other than friendship. There's no fizz. None of that heart-skipping-a-beat kind of stuff. And, before you say anything, yes, I know that those feelings are only temporary and don't last, but to be honest, they weren't ever there in the first place. I've made my decision. We're far better off being just friends, and I'll explain that to him. I'm sure he'll understand.'

She'd tried to sound confident, but to be honest, she wasn't totally sure of how he'd react. But one thing she was certain of; he wasn't going to walk away and leave them. It wasn't in his nature.

'You make it sound simple, but what if Martin doesn't want to be *just friends*? What will you do then?' Tiffany asked.

'It will be fine,' Whitney said with a smile, not only to console Tiffany but also herself.

'What about me and Ava? It's going to make a huge difference to us, you know.'

'No, it won't. Martin is always welcome here at the house, and you'll always be able to visit him and take Ava whenever you like. He's your dad and Ava's grandad. Nothing's going to change that, whatever happens between me and him. I promise.'

'Mum, stop treating me like a child—'

'I'm not, it's just ...' Whitney's voice fell away. Tiffany was right, but it was only because she wanted to protect her. 'I'm sorry. I know it might be difficult but I was trying to cushion the blow.'

'I get it, Mum. I do. But I wished you'd given me some warning. Because whatever you say about it not going to change things, you're wrong. Of course it will. He might meet someone else, and then he won't want to see me and Ava so often. Or he might stop coming to visit us here because it's so awkward. Or you might meet someone, or—'

'Tiffany, stop. However Martin feels about me, and whatever happens between us, he's never going to turn his back on you. Never. You're forgetting that he'd always believed he couldn't father children, so when he first met you and discovered that you were his daughter, it changed his whole life. And that was before we got together, too, remember. Trust me on this.'

'I hope you're right,' Tiffany said, folding her arms across her chest and staring at her.

Whitney had denied Martin's entire existence for over twenty years until she'd met him at a school reunion and discovered that she'd been totally wrong in thinking that he'd ignored her after their drunken night together. It turned out that Whitney had totally blanked him afterwards, but that wasn't in her memory bank. But what he'd told her had made sense. She'd been so mortified at the time that she'd probably made sure to keep out of his way.

It wasn't until after his wife had died that Martin had discovered about Tiffany being his daughter, and it had changed his life completely. She was going to feel guilty about ending the romance between them, but she was confident they'd still remain friends because of Tiffany and Ava. She had to make it clear that she didn't want a physical relationship with him. It sounded easy, but she was dreading it, which was ridiculous considering the job she had and the difficult decisions she had to make, not to mention having to inform people on a far too frequent basis of the deaths of their loved ones. On paper, this should be a piece of cake.

The doorbell went, and Whitney picked up her bag from off the sofa.

'Well, I'm about to find out. I'll see you later.'

'Just you, or Martin as well?'

'I've no idea.'

Whitney went to the door and opened it. Martin smiled and leant in to give her a kiss on the cheek.

'You're ready. I thought I'd have time to see Tiffany and Ava,' he said.

Whitney didn't want him to go inside in case he sensed something was wrong with Tiffany. 'Later, after our meal. Tiffany's trying to settle Ava, and you know you'll only wake her up because she gets so excited when she sees you.' Guilt at lying to him coursed through her veins. She stepped out of the house and closed the door behind her before he tried to insist he pop in just for a few minutes.

Martin drove them to their favourite pub, which was in a village just outside of Lenchester. They sat outside at their favourite table, on the patio. The weather was unseasonably warm, and the garden was beautiful, but Whitney couldn't enjoy it. She chatted about nothing in particular to him, but the words stuck in her mouth. She kept telling herself to lighten up, but it didn't work. Martin didn't seem to notice, though.

Despite ordering her favourite meal from the menu, home-made burger with fries, it might as well have been cardboard, the amount she actually managed to eat.

'Is there something wrong? You've not been yourself the whole evening,' Martin said after they'd looked at the dessert menu and decided to just have coffee.

And she thought she'd been hiding it so well. What the heck did she know?

It was now or never.

She hitched in a breath. 'You're right. There has been something on my mind. I'll tell you, but please don't take it the wrong way.' She winced at the sound of her ridiculous words. There was only one way to take the news. Unless, by some chance, he'd been thinking the same. But how likely was that?

'What is it?' He reached over and covered her hand with his.

Tears filled her eyes, and she blinked them away. Now wasn't the time to get all emotional.

'I've been thinking a great deal about us and our relationship. You know I like you very much. You're a great father to Tiffany and now granddad to Ava ...'

'I sense a *but* coming,' Martin interjected, removing his hand from hers and sitting upright in his chair.

He could read her like a book. Was that a good thing? In this case, probably yes, because he'd already be guessing what she was about to say.

'But ... you and I, together as a couple ... It's just not really working. We're great as friends, but I just don't see it as anything more.' Her body, which had been so tense for most of the evening, relaxed. She'd done it. She picked up her glass of wine and took a large swallow.

Martin stared at her and then gave a hollow laugh. Whitney was stunned. She had gone through various scenarios of how Martin would react to the news, but laughter hadn't even figured.

'Sorry, I don't think it's funny,' Martin said, picking up on her confusion. 'It's just that your news came at a rather inopportune moment. I was about to tell you that I'd booked us a holiday overseas. To the Maldives.'

She looked away, unable to face the pained expression on his face. This was even worse than actually telling him. She'd told him once that the Maldives was on her bucket list. And he'd remembered.

'I'm sorry,' she muttered. 'Can you get your money back?'

'I haven't actually made the booking. I should have said I'd looked into provisional dates because I know you can't up sticks and go, especially now the case you're working on. I was going to clear it with you before making any firm booking. But it doesn't matter, now.' He shrugged, trying to look nonchalant, but the hurt shone from his eyes.

'I'm sorry, Martin. But I don't want this to change anything. You're welcome to come round to see Tiffany and Ava any time you like. I want us to stay friends.'

'That's going to be very hard for me, Whitney. I'll be honest, I really thought that we had something special that was going to be forever.'

Her heart ached. Was she wrong in doing this? Should she give it another try to not give up so easily? Is what they had worth fighting for?

'But there's no fire in our relationship. It's just ... well, you know how it is. We get on great, but I don't have butterflies in my tummy every time I see you. We're comfortable together, and I like you. But there's no real excitement.'

'Whitney, that's what relationships are all about once you get over that initial stage. Friendship is important. I suppose you and I got there quicker than a lot of couples because we have history and have a family. Tiffany and Ava. Please don't give up on us just yet,' he implored.

Was he right? Did she have an idealised view of love that didn't exist? Perhaps she was acting rashly, without any consideration of the future. It wouldn't be the first time. Why couldn't she be more like George and see things rationally?

'I don't want to lead you on. It's not fair. Not after all we've been through.'

'I understand. All I'm saying is, let's give us some more time.'

'Okay,' she finally said.

Why had she given in so easily? Maybe because it was the right thing to do. Or was it because underneath it all, she did want to continue being with him?

'Let me make a suggestion,' Martin said. 'After this case is over, why don't you take some leave, and we'll go away somewhere warm and relaxing? It can be the Maldives, or somewhere else. Wherever you like. It will give us a chance to be together on our own without any interruptions from work or family. Then we'll know for certain if we can make a go of this relationship.'

Whitney nodded. 'Okay, it's a deal.'

And now she could give the case the full attention it required.

19

Thursday

'Guv,' Frank called out while George and Whitney were standing next to the board discussing the case. 'A call has come in from a woman who reckons she has information regarding the murderer. I thought she could be trying it on, but she mentioned seeing something on Sunday which wasn't mentioned in the press conference, so she could be genuine.'

Whitney's eyes flashed with excitement as they always did when there was some prospective evidence.

'That's great. Get her in, pronto.' Whitney rubbed her hands together.

'Already done. She should be here around twenty minutes. Her name is Josie Merton.'

'Thanks. George and I will speak to her.' She raised an eyebrow in George's direction. 'Okay?'

'Yes, I'm here for the day,' George said, trying to ignore the nagging thoughts at the back of her mind that kept reminding her of the unpacking that she'd left Ross to do. It would be fine, providing he didn't try to unpack anything of hers, because she liked to decide where to place her belongings. Apart from kitchen utensils. They shared the cooking. In fact, he was more proficient than she was, so she was happy to acquiesce.

Also, she suspected he'd spend most of his time setting up his studio, so wouldn't do much in the house. He already had two commissions needing his immediate attention. His modern hyperrealistic style of sculpting meant he was always in demand, and it was exacerbated by him being so high profile in the sculpting world. These days, he was turning away more work than he was taking on. She was delighted because him being busy meant he didn't mind when she was engrossed in her research and other university work or working with Whitney on a case. Unlike her previous boyfriend, who, despite also being an academic, was always nagging her to stop working so hard. It had been a nightmare with him constantly challenging her work ethic, and it was that experience which fuelled her reticence regarding moving forward with her relationship with Ross.

George pushed away her thoughts and focused on following Whitney back to the board, where they resumed their conversation.

'Guv,' Frank called at just after eleven. 'Josie Merton's here. Interview room five.'

'Thanks. Come on,' she said to George.

They headed downstairs and waiting in the room was a woman in her late sixties, and next to her a man in a wheelchair, who looked a little younger.

'Josie?' Whitney asked.

'Yes, and I've brought my neighbour, Wilson Neash, with

me because it's something we've both noticed. I hope that's okay.'

'Of course,' Whitney said, smiling, as George and she sat down. 'What would you like to tell us?' Whitney asked, pulling out her notebook from her pocket.

'I saw on the telly last night about the woman being murdered and wasn't sure whether to say anything. You know, it might be nothing. But it played on my mind, and so this morning I asked Wilson what he thought, and he'd seen it on the telly, too. So that's why we decided to come to see you. Didn't we?' She turned to look at Wilson.

'Yes. We thought it best you should know,' the man said, nodding.

'You've made the right decision. What is it that you've both seen?' Whitney asked.

'We're not saying we definitely know who the murderer is because, of course, we don't. But there is someone who lives near us who we've both noticed acts in a suspicious manner.'

She stared at Whitney and then at George, biting down on her bottom lip, as if debating what to say next.

'And who is this person?' Whitney asked after a few seconds of silence.

'He's across the road from us and lives on his own. He's always in and out of the house at strange times. And it's not for work because he has a day job.'

'When you say "strange times", what do you mean?' Whitney asked, beginning to write.

'I've seen him from my window when I can't sleep. He's always on his own, and the other evening – Sunday, I think it was – at about ten or maybe a little earlier, I watched him park his car a little up the road because there were no spaces in front of his house. That was because two doors down from me, they had all their family around for a party—'

'So he had to park a distance from his house?' Whitney interrupted.

'Yes, sorry. I wanted to give you a full picture. Anyway, I watched him walk down the street to his house, and he kept looking over his shoulder like he was worried someone was coming after him. I might be wrong. It's just that after watching the news, it made me think of him. He comes from up north, too. That was the main reason I decided to contact you. It all seemed too much of a coincidence.'

'And did you see this, too, Mr Neash?' Whitney asked.

'No. I have seen him go out at other times. But ...' His voice fell away, and a worried expression crossed his face.

'What is it?' Whitney asked.

'Please don't say it was Josie and me who told you. I don't want him coming round and threatening us. We wouldn't stand a chance. He's a big man.'

'Mr Neash, I can assure you that everything you tell us is in confidence, so there's no need to worry. We're well used to not divulging our sources. What's this man's name, and where exactly does he live?'

'Kyle Gray, and he lives at number 128 Hilton Road. But he's not there now. I saw him leave for work a few hours ago,' Josie said.

'Where do you both live?' Whitney asked.

'I'm at 129, and Wilson's at 125,' Josie said.

'Are either of you friends with him?' Whitney asked.

'Not really. We say hello if we pass each other in the street,' Josie said.

'That's the same for me. Not that I go out much on my own. I have to rely on someone to take me,' Wilson said.

'One time, he stopped and had a chat – that's how I

know about his accent. I only know his name because a letter was delivered to my house by mistake when there was someone new doing the postal round, and it was written on the envelope. I took it over and pushed it through his letter box,' Josie said.

'Did you happen to see what he was doing on Tuesday afternoon?' Whitney asked.

'Ummm ... Yes,' Josie said. 'He went to work at the usual time, I believe. And after that, I didn't see him until the evening when he came home at around seven. Look, I don't want you to think that I spend all my time looking out of the window. It's just that sometimes I see him, that's all.'

'Same for me,' Wilson said.

'Have you lived in the street long?' Whitney asked.

'I've been there for fifteen years,' Josie said.

'And I've only been there for a couple of years. I rent my house. Josie owns hers,' Wilson said.

'How long has Mr Gray lived in the area?'

'I'm not sure exactly, but definitely longer than Wilson. He rents his house, too,' Josie said. 'When I first moved here with my husband – he's dead now – most houses were owned, but now loads are rented. It's a sign of the times, isn't it?' she said, sighing.

'Yes, I suppose it is,' Whitney agreed. 'Thank you for your help. We'll definitely look into what you've told us.'

'We're glad to be of help. I hope it doesn't turn out to be him. We live in a nice neighbourhood and ... well ... you know.'

'I understand. The main thing is that we check so we can eliminate him from our enquiries. We'll show you both out. Thanks for coming in to see us.'

'Shall we go over there now?' George asked once the couple had left the building.

'No. We'll head back to the incident room first and I'll
get the team to look into him. Their evidence was sketchy at
best, and not much to go on. But – and don't say anything –
I've got a good feeling about this. We've caught people from
a lot less.'

20

Thursday

'Eyes forward, everyone. We've got a lead,' Whitney said the moment they entered the incident room, anxious to get moving on the latest info they'd received.

'That's great, guv,' Frank said, flashing a smile in her direction.

She headed over to the board, with George following, and waited until they were all looking in her direction.

'George and I have just been speaking to Josie Merton and her neighbour Wilson Neash, who phoned in following the press conference. Although Josie didn't actually say it in so many words, it appears that she spends a lot of time staring out of the window at what her neighbours are up to. Neash to a lesser extent, I think.'

'Typical nosy parkers, you mean,' Frank said, rolling his eyes and turning to the side where Doug was sitting. His colleague nodded his agreement.

'Don't mock. We need so-called "nosy parkers" to assist

in our enquiries. It's often where we get our breaks,' Whitney said. 'Anyway, they are suspicious of Kyle Gray, the man who lives on the opposite side of the road. According to Josie, Gray comes and goes at all hours, and last Sunday night, after parking his car a little way from his house because there were no spaces, Gray walked down the street in an agitated manner.'

'If it was after Lorna Knight had escaped, maybe he was worried that the police were coming for him?' Brian said.

'Exactly. I want this man looked into before we bring him in for questioning. We've already wasted valuable hours on Clark. We've got to catch the killer before he strikes again. Ellie, you can research into Gray's background. According to Josie, he comes from somewhere up north. Check the usual stuff. Work, family, friends. Meena, please look at his social media presence. Frank, find his car registration and check CCTV footage close to where both attacks took place and see if his car was in the vicinity at the right times. Doug and Brian, you can give him a hand.'

'Yes, guv,' the officers said in unison.

'Have we any more to go on regarding the meeting Paula Moore had at the café?'

'Not a lot, guv,' Doug said with a sigh. 'I went to the café, but the owner didn't remember them being there. He did say they're always very busy at that time of day, so it's hardly surprising. I also spoke to a couple of staff members, and neither of them could help either. The café does have a security camera above the counter, but it's for show and didn't record anything. If the killer was aware of all this, that could be why he chose that place for them to meet.'

'A logical conclusion, based on what we already know.' George said. 'The assailant is an intelligent man, and he wouldn't have chosen to meet Paula Moore at a place where he could have been identified. Did you ask the café owner whether any of his regulars were there at the time?'

'I did, but he said he didn't know. Shall I go back and question some of the customers?' Doug asked, picking up his phone from the desk and sliding his chair back.

'Not yet, because there's no guarantee that the customers there now would have been in the café at the same time Paula was on Tuesday,' Whitney said. 'Stay here and assist researching into Gray. Have we heard back about Paula's phone, Ellie?'

The officer glanced up from her screen where she'd been clicking furiously on the keys. 'I spoke to Mac in forensics, and the call came from a burner. Paula had phoned the number, but there's no way to trace it now.'

'Okay, you lot carry on. George and I are going to grab a coffee and will be back in ten minutes.'

~

WHEN THEY RETURNED, Whitney closed the door to the incident room harder than she'd intended, making a loud bang, which caused Doug, who was standing behind Frank, staring over his shoulder, to start. Both officers glanced across at her and George.

'Great timing, guv. This is really interesting,' Frank said. 'I picked up Gray's car in the vicinity of where Lorna was attacked on Sunday night. I tried to track it as far as the park, but the trouble is, there aren't any cameras there. But he was certainly in the area. That we do know for sure.'

'Excellent,' Whitney said.

'Tell guv the rest,' Doug said, excitement in his voice.

'I will, if you let me get a word in edgeways ... Gray's car was also seen around the time of Paula's murder, too. Look.'

He pointed at the screen showing a silver Toyota Corolla stationary at the traffic lights in Junction Road.

'Excellent work. Ellie, what do you have on Gray?'

'He's forty-five and works for Cheston Media in Lenchester as a senior sales executive, and he's been with the company for five years. He spends much of his time on the road, meeting with clients. I was able to access his work diary on their network.'

'What? You hacked into their system?' Whitney said.

Ellie might be the best researcher they had, but she still had to keep within police guidelines.

'No, guv. It's made public to enable people to book their appointments with him online.'

Whitney let out a sigh of relief. She should have known better than to think Ellie would step outside of the law.

'You should become a professional hacker,' Frank said. 'You'd make an absolute killing.'

'And you'll be looking for another job if you start making those suggestions.' Whitney grinned so he knew she was joking.

Except, she sort of wasn't. She didn't want Ellie to think about leaving them any sooner than she'd already planned to in a year or so.

'I'd never do anything illegal like that,' Ellie said, the palm of her hand over her chest.

'That's why I said it,' Frank said. 'But you have to admit that his job is perfect for being able to stalk these women without his colleagues thinking he was acting suspiciously.'

'I agree,' Whitney said. 'What else do you have on him, Ellie?'

'He lives within his means, and his credit card is paid off regularly. He doesn't have a police record, although they were called out to his home three years ago because of an argument with a woman that had got out of hand. The neighbours phoned it in. By the time the police arrived, it had calmed down and no charges were pressed.'

'Hmm. Interesting. So he may have violent tendencies. That's worth bearing in mind. Anything on social media, Meena?' Whitney said, turning to her other detective constable.

'No red flags there, guv. So far, I've found that Gray has a profile on one social media platform, but he rarely posts. He often likes his friends' posts, so he clearly goes on the platform. I'm still checking other platforms to see if he uses one of those more regularly.'

Whitney nodded her head. Everything was pointing in the direction of Kyle Gray, and the sooner he was brought in for questioning, the better. Josie and Neash might be "nosy parkers" to quote Frank, but without their input, they'd have never come across Gray.

'Brian, give uniform a call and ask them to bring Kyle Gray in for questioning. You'll probably need to get in touch with his company to find out where he is exactly, especially if he's mainly out on the road.'

'Or I could check the online diary that Ellie found?' Brian suggested.

'We don't know how accurate that is. Call the company first.'

~

GEORGE POSITIONED herself in the observation area while Brian and Whitney went into the interview room to question Kyle Gray. The man had closely cropped grey hair and a receding hairline, making him appear older than his mid-forties. He was smartly dressed in a well-cut, and most likely expensive, dark navy suit with a pale blue open-neck shirt. He was sitting up straight with his lips set in a firm line.

'Why am I here?' he demanded the moment Whitney and Brian sat down opposite him.

'Good morning, Mr Gray. I'm DCI Walker, and this is DS Chapman. You've been brought in for questioning because we'd like to speak to you about your whereabouts on Tuesday, the thirteenth of September this year, between the hours of three and six in the afternoon. Before you answer, we'll turn on the recording equipment.' Whitney nodded at Brian, who leant forward, pressed the button and then made the introductions.

'I was working,' Gray said once Whitney had given him the go-ahead to answer.

'What is your job?'

'I sell advertising for a local media outlet. I'm out a lot of the time, visiting local businesses. My area spans a fifty-mile radius area from the centre of Lenchester.'

Very interesting, because that meant he could legitimately be in Harleston, where Cheryl Hughes was assaulted.

'And during this time, can anyone vouch for you?'

'Not for the whole of the time. I had an appointment at two and then one at four-thirty. I didn't bother to go back to the office because the appointments were fairly close to one another, so I just got myself a coffee and sat in the car by the river.'

'Most convenient,' Brian said.

'What's that meant to mean?' Gray asked, his brows drawing together.

'We're investigating the murder of a woman whose body was found at a park in Claxton which, according to CCTV, is in the vicinity of where you were for the entire time.'

Kyle Gray's eyes widened. 'B-b-but surely you can't think it's me?'

He appeared genuine, but the speed with which he moved from outrage to shock was faster than George would have normally expected for genuine shock, considering his brain needed time to process the information. She'd continue watching for other telltale signs that he was acting.

'We're just making enquiries at this stage. I notice from your accent that you're not from round here.' Whitney asked.

'No, I'm not. My accent is a bit of a mixture because we moved a lot when I was a kid. I was born in Leeds, but also lived in Manchester and Birmingham.'

'I see. As part of our investigation, we're looking into a series of sexual assaults on women over the past couple of years. Do you know a woman named Lorna Knight?' Whitney leant forward in her chair, resting her arms on the table.

'No.'

'Where were you on Sunday evening between seven and eight?'

'At home.' He touched his neck.

'He's lying and feeling stressed,' George said into Whitney's earpiece. 'Touching his neck in that manner is a pacifying action designed to soothe himself in difficult situations.'

'Try again. Your car was seen in the vicinity of Nelson Street.'

Gray continued to massage his neck and stared at the table for a while. 'Okay. I'd gone out to meet someone in a pub. But she didn't turn up.'

'That's the truth,' George said.

'Who is this person?'

'All I know is her first name is Sonia. We met online, and this was going to be our first date. I'm guessing that she might've arrived, seen me and then changed her mind. It's not uncommon for women to do that.'

Was he regularly stood up on dates? Was this a motivator for him to resort to rape and murder?

'Pursue this further,' George said.

'How did you feel when you were left high and dry by Sonia? Did it make you angry?' Whitney asked.

Gray ran his hand over the top of his head. 'It didn't bother me.'

'Really? I'd have thought you'd have been very upset. Or angry. You made the effort to get ready and go out to meet someone, and then they stand you up. How dare she?'

'Look, I don't know what you're getting at, but you've got it all wrong. Of course, I was a little upset. Who wouldn't be? But that was it. It was no big deal. Once I knew she wasn't going to turn up, I had a couple of drinks and was home by ten.'

'So you have no alibi for the time between seven and eight that anyone can verify?'

His fists clenched in his lap. 'Not unless they remember me in the pub, but it's not one I've been to before, so they probably won't. You'll have to take my word for it. Is that it? Can I go now? Or should I be phoning a solicitor? I know my rights.' He stared defiantly at Whitney and Brian.

'Three years ago, the police were called to your house because of a domestic disturbance?' Whitney said, not answering his question.

'It was just a misunderstanding between me and my girlfriend at the time. It was nothing important.' He shifted awkwardly in his chair and blinked several times in succession.

'I think it is, Whitney. Keep going,' George said.

'And where is this girlfriend now?'

'We finished a few months after that incident. She died of cancer not long after.'

Whitney visibly stiffened. If the girlfriend was dead, they couldn't follow up on the incident and find out whether or not he was abusive towards her.

'Do you live on your own?'

'Yes, and I'm perfectly happy. I've tried the marriage-and-babies lark, and it wasn't for me. I'm divorced but still paying my way, hence why I live where I do. It's the only thing I can afford. It's a rental. Is there anything else? Because I've got appointments today, and you've taken me out of my workplace – no doubt causing gossip while they wonder why you wanted to question me and why it was so important that I had to be escorted out of there. It was pure luck that I was actually in the office and not out on the road.'

'That's all for now. Thank you for your assistance. We may wish to speak to you again soon. DS Chapman will escort you out of here.'

Once Brian had taken Gray away, George met Whitney in the corridor.

'Apart from the one time he was lying but then said it was because he was out on the date, I got nothing from him,' George said.

'We don't have anything concrete to hold him on at the moment, but that doesn't mean he's in the clear. There's definitely something about him and we'll find out what it is. He won't get away with hiding anything from us.'

21

I close my eyes, reliving the moment when Paula Moore's last breath extinguished. I was able to pinpoint exactly the time it happened. Her legs stopped shaking and her body went perfectly still. It was peaceful, in the end.

Not peaceful for me.

My heart was beating so hard, and the euphoria was so strong that I almost screamed. But, of course, I didn't. I was too much in control for that.

But ... despite all that, it wasn't right. Because it hadn't been Paula Moore's turn. I hate it when my plans get disrupted.

It was all down to that bitch, Lorna Knight. How the hell I let her get away, I do not know. Luckily, I had a contingency plan. Not so lucky for Paula, though.

On a more positive note – and no one can say I'm not a glass half-full guy – I've learnt by my mistake, and I'll never be caught wanting again.

No one will escape from me. And that's a promise.

I laugh, reliving again actually meeting with Paula Moore, face to face, on Tuesday. She was the first of my 'girls' to have that honour. Even if I was in disguise.

It certainly added some spice to the proceedings. Pretending to be interested in what she said. But of course, I wasn't. If anyone had looked at us, they would have seen two people sitting together, but clearly not as friends. The folder she'd placed on the table indicated that it was a business meeting.

And the way she picked up her pastry and took a dainty nibble, hardly enough to even have tasted it. It was all so ... so ... false and designed to impress. I can still picture the crumbs that had attached themselves to the side of her mouth and how she wiped them away with the edge of her paper napkin.

She'd talked non-stop. But I didn't listen. All I saw was her mouth opening and closing. Blah, blah, blah. She gave the occasional, white-toothed smile in my direction, along with a flutter of her eyelashes while trying to persuade me to sign up as a client. And she even paid for the coffee and cake.

If only she'd known that from the very moment she'd walked into the café to meet me, her days were numbered. Which is a ridiculous thing to say because she'd never have been drawn into my trap if she'd realised.

I finish my cup of tea and head upstairs to my office.

I have some planning to do and decisions to make.

Who's going to be next?

22

Thursday

'No, ma'am, we've let him go for now, but we'll be investigating into him further.' There was a knock on Whitney's door, and she beckoned for Meena to come in and sit on one of the chairs in front of her desk. 'Will do, ma'am.' She replaced the phone back onto the handset. 'The super wanted to know where we were with Kyle Gray. Do we have anything more on him yet? I haven't had time to go back into the incident room since letting him go.'

'Not that I know of, guv. But I haven't been paying close attention to what the others are doing. While I was looking into Gray's activity on the different social media platforms, I had a thought that I wanted to share with you. Remember, you were wondering the places where the attacker can get dates of birth from?'

Whitney frowned. 'Yes, but we found plenty of places already.'

'I know, but what I'd totally forgotten about was groups

on social media. I'm a member of a private group that was set up for people born on February twenty-ninth. You have to apply to join, and it's been going for at least ten years, if not longer. I've been a member since it began. I'm not very active on there, to be honest, which is probably why it's only just come to mind. I'm really sorry I didn't mention it sooner.'

'No need to apologise – you've got enough on your plate at the moment. How did it go at the hospital?' Whitney had intended to ask the officer yesterday, but the time had got away with her, and by the time she'd remembered, Meena had left for the day.

'It wasn't easy, guv. Dad seems to have gone to pieces, but Mum was there comforting him. The doctors are hoping that it's been caught early enough and have explained about the different treatment options. They're going to decide which one is most suitable. We're waiting to hear more.' Tears filled the officer's eyes, and she brushed them away with her hand.

'I'm sure he's in good hands. If you need any more time off, just let me know, and we'll sort something out.' Whitney could ill afford to lose an officer at such a crucial time, but they'd manage.

'Thanks, guv. We'll see how it goes. I don't want to be a nuisance, especially during a murder investigation.' Meena gave a watery smile.

It can't have been easy for the officer, being so far away from her family, particularly if her dad wasn't coping well. It reminded Whitney of how difficult it was when her father had died. It had left her mum in sole charge of Whitney's older brother, Rob, who'd had a brain injury as a teen and was unable to look after himself. Now, with both of them in separate residential care homes, because her mum's dementia meant she could no longer look after Rob, it was easier on a day-to-day basis, but Whitney was constantly plagued with guilt that she was unable to look after the pair of them. She shook her head to rid her mind of the thoughts. There were more pressing things to deal with.

'Back to your suggestion that the details might have come from a group. Let's go back into the incident room and I'll ask Ellie to look into it.'

Meena bit down on her bottom lip. 'She's on to it already. I've mentioned it to her when you were interviewing the suspect. I hope you don't mind me asking her.'

If the team were already on to it, then it hadn't really been necessary for Meena to come and tell her. Unless she'd wanted to offload with someone about her dad.

'Of course I don't. We're all working the case together. Come on, let's see if she's got anything.'

They went into the incident room together and headed over to Ellie's desk.

'Perfect timing, guv. I've got something for you,' the officer said, her eyes flashing with excitement.

'Attention, everyone,' Whitney called out. 'Ellie's been doing her magic and is about to astound us.'

The keyboard clicks stopped, and all the team members stared in their direction.

Ellie cleared her throat. 'Meena had mentioned a particular social media group for people born on the twenty-ninth of February, and it turns out that all the victims belonged to it. I took each victim in turn and identified who had actually personally friended them, and there's only one person who features in every friendship group. Evan Cox.'

'Am *I* friends with him?' Meena asked.

'Don't you know?' Frank asked, frowning.

'I belong to so many groups that I can't keep up. People

are always friending me, and I never turn anyone down. I've got hundreds of friends. Haven't you?'

'No. And that's exactly why I'm not on any of these stupid social media platforms,' Frank said. 'People brag about how many friends they have, but they're not real friends. It's just a number.'

Whitney agreed with Frank, but now wasn't the time to get into a debate regarding the pros and cons of social media groups.

'It doesn't matter. I want focus. We need to find Evan Cox and bring him in for questioning,' Whitney said.

'That's the problem, guv,' Ellie said. 'I think the name's an alias because I can't find a record of him anywhere.'

'You're kidding. It's like one step forward, two steps back.' Whitney gave an exasperated sigh.

'That doesn't mean I *won't* find him. It will just take a little longer. I'm looking into the IP address Cox uses to see if I can track him that way.' Ellie looked at Meena. 'He hasn't friended you.'

Whitney breathed a sigh of relief. If Meena had been on the killer's radar, she might have been a potential victim.

'That's great.' Whitney headed over to the board and wrote *Evan Cox* across the top.

The door opened, and George entered the room.

'Sorry to be longer than I thought. I had to go into work because there were some issues with a member of staff's research, and they wanted me to represent the research committee.'

'Even though you were on annual leave?' she asked, shaking her head.

That didn't seem fair to Whitney. George worked all the hours God sent, so surely she deserved to be left alone when she was on holiday. The irony of her own attitude to the sanctity of annual leave didn't escape her, but working with the police was different.

'It wasn't an issue. I'd informed the departmental admin office that I was available if any emergency cropped up and—'

'Guv,' Ellie called out, interrupting. 'I've tracked the IP address of Evan Cox.'

'You're never going to believe this,' Frank said, who was standing behind the officer, staring over her shoulder.

'She might if you let Ellie actually tell her,' Doug said, glancing over from his desk and rolling his eyes.

'Shut up, or—'

'Carry on, Ellie. Ignore them,' Whitney intervened.

'The IP address is registered to Kyle Gray.'

Whitney's heartbeat quickened, and she rubbed her hands together. Finally, they'd got something concrete to work with.

'That's fantastic work. Well done,' Whitney said.

'Drinks all round, I'd say,' Frank said, punching the air.

'Hold your horses, Frank. We might be closer to solving the case now than earlier, but there's a lot of work to do to ensure that we have sufficient evidence against Gray, or his barrister will walk all over us. We don't want him getting off on a technicality. Right, Brian, arrange to have him brought back in straight away.'

'Providing he hasn't done a runner after your interview with him,' Frank said.

'That would be admitting his guilt. If anything, he'd go back to work and continue acting as he always has. Remember, he doesn't know that we've established the birthday link, which gives us a distinct advantage.'

'Yeah, you're right, guv,' Frank said. 'But I still think we'll be celebrating very soon.'

23

Thursday

'Why have you brought me back here?' Kyle Gray demanded as Whitney and Brian stepped into the interview room. 'I'd literally just got home when there was a knock at the door, and your officers took me away. In full view of the entire street. How do you think that looks?'

George stared intently at the man. His anger was genuine, and he appeared mystified as to why he was being interviewed again. That didn't mean he was innocent. Not by any stretch of the imagination. He came from a successful sales background, and that meant he would be used to convincing people that he was genuine.

'We have further questions for you,' Whitney said coolly as she placed the Manila folder she was holding on the table in front of her and sat opposite the man.

'And, of course, you couldn't just phone and ask me to come back here. Instead, you had to go in all guns blazing. I'm already going to miss an appointment that I had to

rearrange from earlier after this morning's charade to in' –
he turned his arm and glanced at the silver watch on his
wrist – 'an hour's time.'

'Don't bank on making it,' Brian said icily.

Whitney's back stiffened. She wouldn't be happy with
her sergeant's comments. Antagonising Gray so early on
wouldn't help them.

'Whitney, making him angry won't help. I know it was
Brian and not you, but you need to let him know that it's
important to keep things on an even keel,' George said into
her mic.

Whitney nodded in acknowledgement and scribbled on
a piece of paper, which she then slid over to Brian.

'I'm warning you. If I lose my job because of this, then
I'm going to sue your arses off. And I don't make idle
threats.' He folded his arms across his chest and stared at
Whitney.

'Mr Gray, instead of getting angry and wasting valuable
time, why don't you allow us to do our job and ask the questions? The sooner we can do that, the sooner this will be
over,' Whitney said in a placating tone. 'The reason you're
here is because further evidence has come to light, which
we'd like to discuss with you.'

Whitney's manner was perfect. An irritated Gray
wouldn't help in this instance because he would clam up. If
Whitney could get him onside, he might be more open and
let his guard down. In George's opinion, a more relaxed
and congenial Gray was more likely to give something
away.

'How many times do I have to tell you that I don't know
anything?' Gray let out a sigh. 'But if it makes you feel better,
ask your questions. As long as you're quick about it because
I want to get out of here.'

He sat back in his seat, his hands now resting in his lap. Obviously calmer.

Whitney leant over and pressed the recording equipment. 'Interview on Thursday, September 15. Those present: DCI Walker, DS Chapman, and … Please state your name.'

'Kyle Gray. As you well know.'

'Mr Gray, before we begin, I need to inform you that you do not have to say anything. But it may harm your defence if you do not mention when questioned something which you later rely on in court. Do you understand?'

Gray brows furrowed.

Was he beginning to put two and two together?

'Yes. But what do you mean "my defence"? There's nothing—'

'You are entitled to have a solicitor with you during questioning if you'd like one,' Whitney said, interrupting.

'Well … I mean … No. It's not necessary … Just get on and ask your questions. I've done nothing, and if I wait for a solicitor to arrive, I could end up being here for hours, and I've got more important things to do with my time, as you well know.'

'Thank you. Mr Gray, do you know anyone who has a birthday on the twenty-ninth of February?' Whitney asked.

Gray's eyes widened, and he glanced at Brian and then back to Whitney.

'That question certainly had an impact on him. Keep pursuing this line,' George said, observing the panic on the man's face, which he still hadn't got under control.

'Um … Not that I recall.' He rubbed the back of his head.

'Try again, Mr Gray. Do you know anyone with a birthday on February twenty-ninth?' Whitney repeated, leaning forward slightly in her chair.

'Not now. But the girlfriend I mentioned in my previous

interview did. But I don't see what she's got to do with anything. I thought you were investigating the murder of a woman the other night.'

'Let us be the judge of what's relevant and what isn't. What was your ex-girlfriend's name?' Whitney asked.

Gray sat forward in his chair and glared at Whitney. 'Why do you want to know? I've already told you that she's dead. This is ridiculous. You're using this line of questioning to waste my time. Or to make me say something that will incriminate me. And anyway, it's pointless asking about her, because it's not like you can interview her. Unless you have a hotline to up there.' He pointed towards the ceiling.

'Why is it proving so hard for you to answer a very straightforward question?' Brian asked, banging his palm on the table.

Whitney rested her hand on Brian's arm, and he sat back in his seat.

'Mr Gray?' Whitney asked.

'Her name was Deirdre Jones. Happy now?' He glared at Brian. 'We were together for a while, but I didn't find out about the cancer until after she'd left me.'

George kept her eyes focused on Gray. His lips were set in a flat line. Was he going to admit something?

'You may have tapped into a motive for the attacks, Whitney. If this woman died and he was affected by it, or he was bitter because something untoward happened in respect of her dying, then it could have had some psychological impact on him. I'm not saying for certain, because he needs to be questioned further and the truth elicited, but it is something to consider and probe,' George said.

'I'd like to know more. When exactly did Deirdre die? It must have been devastating for you at the time,' Whitney said.

'Not really, no. It wasn't. I've already told you we'd broken up by the time she got sick. So it wasn't even a big deal.' He shrugged.

'That's rather heartless,' Whitney said.

'I didn't mean it like that. All I'm saying is we weren't together at the time of her illness. Of course it was sad when she died, especially for her family and friends. And it's not like I went around cheering. But I was distant from it.'

'Why did you and Deirdre split up?' Whitney asked.

'Why does any couple break up? We did. It's ... what do you call it ... irreconcilable differences.'

'Was it anything to do with the incident when the police were called out to your place that we spoke about earlier?' Whitney asked.

'It might have been part of it. I don't remember. You still haven't explained why it's so important. Or why you wanted to know when her birthday was.' Gray's voice was increasing in volume, and his fists were clenched and resting on the table.

'Was Deirdre a member of a social media group for people born on February twenty-ninth?' Whitney asked.

'I've no idea. When we were together, I don't recall her going on any social media sites. But I don't know about after we split.'

'Are you aware of a group for people with that birthday?'

'No. Why would I be? It's not my birthday. Look, if this is all you want to ask me, then I've told you everything I know, so may I leave now? I might just make my appointment.' He glanced at his watch.

'We'll leave that line of questioning for now,' Whitney said. 'I'd like to go back to Tuesday night. You mentioned you were stood up by a woman you'd met on a dating site. Do you know her date of birth?'

Gray frowned. 'I have no idea because it didn't come up during our very few online interactions. We made all the arrangements via email and didn't get too personal. All I know is her first name and that she's aged thirty-one.'

'Mr Gray, please could you tell us your movements on the following dates. February 29 and September 20 last year, and between four and six in the afternoon on Sunday, April 17 this year. Also, last Sunday between six and eight, and Tuesday between three and six.'

He stared at Whitney, open-mouthed, but whether it was due to uncertainty, or disbelief that he'd been caught, it wasn't possible for George to tell at this juncture.

'You already know about Tuesday. Sunday, I was at home alone. As for the other dates, they are a long time ago, so I'd need to consult my calendar, which is in my phone. May I get it out to look?'

'Be my guest,' Whitney said, sitting back in her chair and gesturing with her hand for him to do so.

Gray pulled out a phone from his jacket pocket and stared at the screen for a while, frowning. 'Damn. I can only tell you about this year because, for some reason, last year's calendar isn't showing. This week you've already asked me about and I've given you my answer. I'm not telling you about April until you explain exactly why you want to know about all these different dates.'

'Tell him, Whitney. I want to gauge his response,' George said, focusing on Gray's face.

'We're investigating one murder, one attempted murder, and several sexual assaults, and you've come up in our enquiries.'

His jaw dropped a little, and his right eye twitched. There was definitely something he wasn't telling them.

'Keep going along this line,' George said. 'He's hiding something.'

'It's not me. I didn't do anything to those women.'

'Then I take it you won't mind me taking a DNA sample?' Whitney said.

'Um ... no. Go ahead. Then you'll know it wasn't me.'

The attacker had left no evidence, and if it was Gray, he'd have known that, so he'd assume that it would be fine to give a sample. Whitney took out a kit from her bag, which she'd hung on the back of the chair, pulled on some gloves and walked around to where Gray was seated. She placed the swab inside his cheek and took a sample, which she placed into a tube.

'Thank you,' she said once finished and returned to her seat.

'May I go now?' Gray asked.

'No. We have further questions. You say you don't know of a social media group for people who have leap-year birthdays, yet we have found posts on there from a man using the alias of Evan Cox, and we traced his IP address back to your house. We know you live alone, so it can only be linked to you. How do you account for this?'

Uncertainty flashed in his eyes. 'You're making this up. It's not me. It can't be. I don't even know how to make an alias on the internet.' He threw his hands up in despair.

'You could have googled it. It's not that hard,' Whitney said.

George smiled to herself. Whitney would have no idea how easy it was or not because her IT skills were so limited.

'I think I need a solicitor,' Gray said quietly, sinking into his chair and appearing less sure of himself than at any other time during the interview.

'That is your right. I will arrange for you to call one, and in the meantime, you'll remain at the station. I am currently waiting on a search warrant for your house. Once it's here, we will execute it immediately.'

Gray paled. 'You can't do that. You can't search my home when I'm not with you.'

'That's where you're wrong,' Whitney said.

'But ...'

George went on alert. Whatever it was he was hiding from them, she suspected they'd find it when they searched his house.

24

Thursday

'I suppose you want to know how it went last night,' Whitney said to George while they were on the way to Kyle Gray's house in Cotton Fields.

George hadn't actually given Whitney's predicament with Martin much thought since she'd first learnt about it. She'd been too busy deliberating over her own dilemma with Ross and whether or not to accept his proposal. On the one hand, it wouldn't make much difference to the life they already had. And if it would make him happy, then why should she deny him? But on the other, she wasn't fond of change and much preferred the certainty of knowing the state of every aspect of her life. She'd already kept him waiting for four days, and she knew she couldn't delay her decision for much longer. She'd sit down with him later and discuss it. That would be the appropriate thing to do.

'I was waiting for you to mention it to me,' she said, knowing that Whitney wouldn't question her response because it wasn't out of character. 'Did you manage to resolve the situation with Martin?'

'Not exactly. It was a bit of a pickle, really. There was me wanting to end it and plucking up the courage to tell him. And when I did, he turns around and tells me he's been planning to take me on holiday to the Maldives. The Maldives! Can you imagine it? You do realise that it's been on my bucket list since forever. I felt so awful that I ended up agreeing to go on holiday with him after the case is over, so we can have some time together and decide our future.'

'So you're not going to end it with him just yet?'

'I want to remain friends, and he does, too. As for anything more *romantic*, I'm prepared to wait and see for a while longer ... and before you ask, it's not just so he can take me on holiday.'

George tossed a glance in Whitney's direction. 'The thought hadn't even crossed my mind.'

'Oh well, it must have crossed mine, then.' Whitney laughed. 'Anyway, enough about me, we're almost here.'

George pulled up outside Gray's house in Hilton Road, and they waited until Brian, Doug, and Meena arrived too.

'Do you have a key?' Doug asked once they were all standing outside.

'Yes, so there's no need to break the door down. He wasn't happy about it, but he knew it was the lesser of the two evils. This is a rental, so any damage he'd most likely be liable for.'

'That should be the least of his worries, guv,' Brian said.

Whitney opened the door, and they all piled into the small, terraced house. She led them into the reception room on the left. It was a small square room and was sparsely furnished with a three-piece suite, TV and a light oak sideboard. There were no paintings on the wall or any ornaments.

'Right. I want every inch of this house inspected. If there's any evidence here, we're going to find it. George and I will take upstairs. Meena, you can search the kitchen, Brian, you do this room, and Doug, take the garden. Shout out if you find anything.'

George followed Whitney up the threadbare carpeted stairs, which were situated on the right-hand side of the house, and into the first of the two bedrooms. It was a square room, with coving around the edges of the ceiling, and Anaglypta wallpaper painted an ivory colour. Again, there was very little furniture, just white fitted wardrobes running alongside one of the walls, a chest of drawers under the window and a small set of drawers beside the bed on which stood an empty beer bottle. There were clothes hung neatly over a chair, and the bed was unmade.

'This is certainly his room, and he could do with letting in some fresh air,' George said, screwing up her nose and shaking her head.

'Here, take these gloves,' Whitney said, handing George a disposable pair. 'I'll take the drawers, and you go through the wardrobe.' George pulled open the double doors on the left-hand side and stared. There were shelves on the left and a rail on the right. Hanging up were jackets, trousers, and shirts, many of them unworn with their tags still on. The shelves were the same. She counted twenty T-shirts and a similar number of jumpers.

'This is weird,' Whitney called out. 'I've just opened the top drawer, and there are multiple packs of unopened boxer shorts and socks.'

'I've got the same here with his clothes.' George crouched down to the floor and picked up a pair of clearly brand-new trainers. 'The wardrobe is full of items still with their labels on.'

'I don't get it,' Whitney said. 'If these are all unworn, where are the clothes he wears on a daily basis? Or does he wear something once and then throw it away?' She laughed. 'And who wouldn't want to be rich enough to do that?'

George opened the second set of doors to the wardrobe. 'I've found the clothes he wears every day.' Several clearly worn jackets and trousers were hanging up, and she flicked through them and felt in the pockets. They were empty. 'Nothing of any interest, though. What about you?'

'I've found his regular underwear in the second drawer. But what do you make of all this new stuff?' Whitney asked, frowning as she turned to face George.

'He could be a habitual shopper. Or perhaps someone is buying him gifts. It's impossible to know without further questioning.'

'I think he might be a shoplifter.' Whitney walked over to the wardrobe on the left and flicked through the new items. 'Have you seen the designer names on some of this lot? There must be thousands and thousands of pounds' worth of stuff here. I couldn't even afford a tenth of this. And it's not like he's in some high-powered job where he earns megabucks, so how does he afford it?'

'What are we to do with all of these? Take them as evidence?' George asked, thinking that it would take an enormous number of evidence bags to do so.

'No, we have no reason to at this stage. But I'll take a few photos of the clothes, so we can investigate further. We'll definitely question him about it at some point. But we have to be mindful that it's most likely tangential to the murder investigation and mustn't get in the way. I wonder if he's got other unused goods elsewhere in the house?'

'Shall we look in case—'

'Guv.' Doug's voice came echoing up the stairs. 'You'll want to see this. We've got something. Come to the kitchen.'

'We're on our way,' Whitney called, exchanging a glance with George and running out of the room and down the stairs.

They headed to the rear of the house and hurried into the kitchen.

'Look what I found in the back of the garden shed,' Doug said, grinning from ear to ear while holding up an evidence bag. 'A black balaclava and a pair of leather gloves, complete with a set of teeth marks on two of the fingers. Let's see him try to get out of that.'

Whitney nodded in agreement. 'Forensics will give a positive identification, and if they do, that will be enough to charge him. Did you come across any unused goods, possibly still with the price tag on them? Or any new items in boxes that clearly haven't been opened.'

'Yes, guv. On the top shelves in the pantry are sets of saucepans and cutlery, and also loads of crockery. I thought it was odd, because he has loads of stuff in the drawers that he can use,' Meena said.

'It was the same upstairs. We found so many clothes the guy could open a shop.'

'Sounds like it needs investigating,' said Doug. 'But is it anything to do with the murder and other attacks?'

'It doesn't appear likely, which is why we won't make asking him a priority. The murders come first. We'll reinterview Gray on our return. By the way, have we found his laptop yet?'

'No, guv,' both Doug and Meena replied.

'Okay, we'll ask him where it is when we speak to him.

But first, George and I will finish checking upstairs, and you two continue down here.'

'You take a look in the second bedroom, and I'll finish up in the first and will then do the bathroom,' Whitney said to George when they returned to the top of the stairs.

The second bedroom was smaller than the first, and all it contained was a single bed and an old-fashioned free-standing wardrobe, which was empty. She peered under the bed and there was nothing there either. She left the room and returned to Whitney, who was facing the chest of drawers.

'George,' Whitney shouted when she was only a couple of feet away.

'I'm here,' George said.

Whitney started. 'What the ...? I thought you were next door.'

'The room is empty of all personal possessions.'

'Look what I've found.' She smiled at George, excitement shining from her eyes.

George stepped closer to see. The officer was holding a small notebook book, which she opened and flicked through the pages.

'What is it?'

'It's absolute proof, that's what this is. It's a journal in which he's recorded details relating to the women that he's attacked. We've got him.' Whitney handed it to George, and she peered at the different entries.

'Yes. I think this is his planning journal. From what he's written, he's used it when he's following his potential victims to try and get some picture of what they do. It's small enough to be concealed on his person. Here's an entry relating to Lorna Knight, which was written two days before her attack. Listen to this: "LK met with friend. Overheard them arranging to go to cinema on Sunday." This entry has two asterisks next to it. That might signify the date of his attack,' George said.

'How was he managing to get close enough to hear a conversation?'

'If he was following her and they met in a café. But he'd have to make sure not to be caught.'

'Or he might have placed a listening device on her phone,' Whitney said.

'Is that even possible?' George asked.

'I'm not sure. But Ellie would know. See if he's used the asterisks before.'

George flicked through the pages. 'He's done the same for "CH" which is Cheryl Hughes. He comments about her going to church every Sunday. It's very detailed, and in keeping with the profile we have of him.'

'Yeah, well, that detail has been his undoing. Let's see Gray try to wriggle out of it now.'

25

Thursday

'Frank, take photos of this lot, and in particular, some of the latter pages in the journal. No need to photograph all of it. Then send everything to forensics,' Whitney said when they returned to the incident room.

'Will do, guv,' the officer said, pulling on some disposable gloves and taking the evidence bags from her.

She then headed over to Ellie's desk. 'Is it possible to put a listening device on someone's phone?'

'Yes, guv. If you can get hold of the target phone, then a Wi-Fi app can be installed on it to enable a third party to listen.'

'Wouldn't the person see it's there?' Whitney frowned, wishing she could get to grips with all the new technology.

'It's possible to hide an app on a phone so it's not visible on a person's home screen. Most people don't look at their actual app library and only go from the screen. So it's likely they wouldn't spot it.'

She'd certainly be in that category. Her phone might have all the bells and whistles the force wanted her to have, but she hardly used any of them.

'I see. Would you be able to locate this app, if we can get hold of the phone?'

'Of course, it's easy when you know where to look.'

'Great.' Whitney headed to the board and called them all to attention. 'Meena, please will you contact Lorna Knight and ask her to bring in her phone for Ellie to check for a listening device? We know our attacker followed and made notes of his victims' movements, but if he could listen in on conversations, that would make it much easier for him to track their exact whereabouts and plan his attacks.'

'Yes, guv. Shall I explain why we want it?'

'Be evasive. I don't want to upset her further by thinking that he'd been privy to everything she was doing in such detail. Tell her she can wait while we take a quick look. It doesn't need to be out of her possession for very long.'

'Here you are, guv,' Frank said, walking over and handing her some photocopied pages.

'Thanks.' She picked up a Manila folder from the desk and slid the pages inside, on top of a wad of blank pages. She always went into an interview situation armed with a folder that appeared full. It gave the impression that they'd collected a large amount of evidence against the person they were interviewing. It was a tactic employed by many CID officers who wanted to get their suspects to talk. Sometimes, it worked. Other times, it didn't. But using the technique certainly did no harm.

'Gray's solicitor has just arrived, guv,' Doug called out.

'Okay, thanks, we'll go back now. Brian, I want you with me again, and George will continue to observe. Is there anything else before we go? Oh yes,' she added before anyone answered. 'There's something which I believe is unrelated to the case but needs investigating. Gray has a house full of brand-new goods, still with tags on. Ellie, I'd like you to look deeper into his finances and find out if he has any income other than what he earns that would enable him to purchase these goods. Or if we can find out whether someone bought them for him. I'll forward you some photos I took of these goods. Much of what he has is designer and bloody expensive. There's got to be a reason behind him having them.'

'I'm onto it, guv.'

The three of them left the incident room and made their way downstairs. George left them to observe, and they walked in to see Gray engrossed in conversation with the man sitting beside him. They stopped talking the moment Whitney and Brian entered.

Whitney placed her folder on the table and sat down. She nodded to Brian to start the recording equipment.

'Interview resumed. Joined by … Please state your name for the recording,' Whitney said to the man beside Gray.

'Tony Walsh, solicitor for Mr Kyle Gray.'

Whitney had come across Mr Walsh before, and she disliked him immensely. He'd invariably advise his clients to make no comment and was always insistent on ending an interview within minutes of it starting, citing that there couldn't possibly be anything further to discuss.

'And before we start,' Walsh continued, 'I'd like to point out on record that my client has willingly assisted in your enquiries, yet when I met with him just now, he hadn't even been offered something to drink.'

Well, that didn't take long. She resisted the urge to roll her eyes. Walsh was already being his typical self and trying to put her on the back foot.

'Noted,' she said coolly. 'Mr Gray, we have just returned from having executed the warrant to search your property. While there, we discovered a number of *unusual* items which we would like you to account for.'

Panic crossed his face. 'Look, it's not what you think. It's —' He stopped talking when Walsh rested a hand on his arm and whispered something that Whitney was unable to hear. Gray then spoke back to him but again she couldn't make out what it was.

'What *do* we think?' Whitney demanded, leaning forward in her chair and locking eyes with him.

'They've got nothing to do with attacks on women,' Gray said.

'Whitney, he's referring to the brand-new clothes and other goods, not the items found in the shed. I know you said asking him about those wasn't a priority, but by the fact that he's brought it up, it might be worth pursuing,' George said into her ear, at the exact time she'd had the same thought.

'Designer clothes which were unworn. Kitchen utensils still in their boxes. Ornaments. All manner of new and clearly expensive items. I hope you have insurance, because the cost of replacing it all would be more than I earn in ten years. And ditto for you, I would think. Unless you earn seven figures a year in your job ...?' she exaggerated, hoping that it might persuade him to admit where they came from.

A slight digression wouldn't hurt either. She'd pick her moment and go back with a question about the attacks when he was less on guard.

'No, I don't,' Gray said.

'Then perhaps you could tell us how you obtained all these things.'

'What is this to do with your investigation?' Walsh asked.

'Mr Gray?' Whitney said, ignoring the remark from the solicitor.

'I'm looking after them for someone,' Gray said.

'He's lying,' George said in her ear.

Whitney had already realised, by the heavy breathing and how he tilted his head to the side.

'Try again, Mr Gray. I want to know what you're doing with those goods. And if you wish to hurry this interview along, which you indicated previously that you did, then I suggest you give me an answer, because I can stay here all day – and night – if necessary.'

Gray glanced quickly at Walsh and then back at Whitney. 'Okay. I stole them. I've been doing it for years. I can't help it. It's a compulsion.'

Ah-ha. It was what she'd suspected. Though how he managed to steal some of the larger items beat her.

'I'm curious. Ask him how long he's been doing it and if he's ever been caught,' George said in her ear.

Whitney wasn't sure how relevant that would be but decided to ask anyway.

'How long have you had this compulsion?' she asked.

'All my life, but recently it's been getting out of control.' He bowed his head.

'Have you ever been caught?'

'Only as a teenager, nicking sweets from a shop with a gang of friends from school. Am I going to be charged?'

'We will make a decision on that later. In the meantime, I want you to take a look at a photograph of other things we found at your property.' She pulled out the photo of the balaclava and gloves and slid it over to him.

'I've never seen them before.' He pushed the sheet of paper back towards her.

'Look again, because they were found hidden in your garden shed.'

Gray audibly sighed, his face relaxing. 'Well, they're definitely not mine. I haven't been in the shed for ages, and a lot of the stuff in there belongs to the previous tenant. I just haven't got around to sorting it all out.'

'How long have you lived at Hilton Road?' Whitney asked.

'A little over three years.'

'And you expect us to believe that you still have items belonging to the previous tenant?' Whitney glanced at the solicitor, expecting him to interrupt, but he remained silent.

'Yes. It's only the shed, and I hardly ever go in there. But I'm quite certain that I've never seen the balaclava and gloves.'

'I suggest you move on, DCI Walker, because my client has nothing further to say regarding the items in the photo,' the solicitor said.

'With pleasure,' Whitney said, looking directly at Walsh and allowing herself a tiny smirk. 'Mr Gray, even if we were to believe you, there's also the matter of a journal that was found in one of the drawers in your bedroom. A journal detailing the movements of every woman you attacked.'

'B-b-but ...'

Whitney pulled out a photo of the journal entries and slid the paper over towards him. He picked it up and stared at it.

'Perhaps you'd like to read out the first entry,' Whitney suggested.

'I've never seen this before in my life. You've made it up. No way was it in my drawers.'

'I can assure you it was. "LK met with a friend. Overheard them arranging to go to the cinema on Sunday",' Whitney said, remembering the entry. 'Do you recall writing that?'

'I'm telling you, I didn't.'

'Look at the entry. Is that your handwriting?'

He stared, a look of disbelief on his face. 'It could be, I suppose. But I didn't write it.'

'Well, if it wasn't you, then who could it be?'

'How the hell do I know?'

'Do you know someone who writes like you and also has access to the chest of drawers in your bedroom?'

'Of course I don't. You're making me out to be stupid. All I know is that I didn't write it.'

'How did you overhear LK's conversation? Did you manage to plant an app on her phone?'

'What? No. I wouldn't even know how to do that. I'm telling you, it's not me. That writing might look like mine, but it's not. You have to believe me. I'm being set up.' He turned to his solicitor. 'I'm telling the truth,' he mumbled.

Whitney rubbed her hands together. It was all slotting into place nicely.

'I'd like to return to the date of birth of your former girlfriend, Deirdre Jones. The twenty-ninth of February. When we mentioned it before, you acted like it wasn't important. But the attacks we're investigating have one thing in common. The victims were all born on that day. The same as your ex-girlfriend. What do you have to say about that?' Whitney asked.

'Nothing. It's a coincidence.' He leant forward, rested his head in his hands and emitted a groan.

'All the items we found at your house are currently with our forensic team, and we expect to find DNA evidence on them that will link you to the murder victim and, quite possibly, to the attacks as well. It will help your case if you admit to what you did. The Crown Prosecution Service will take that into consideration and may be more lenient.'

He glanced up; his brows furrowed. 'Why would I admit to something I didn't do?'

He was certainly putting on a good performance, but they had the evidence in front of them. Irrefutable evidence. However much he protested that it wasn't him. Surely, his solicitor would advise him.

'Mr Gray, you haven't been able to provide us with alibis for the times of any of the attacks that we have asked you about. We also have CCTV footage showing your car in the vicinity of both the murder and attempted murder from earlier this week, *and* we've found these items at your house. What would you think in our place?'

She couldn't put it any plainer.

The solicitor leant in and said something to Gray.

'No comment,' Gray said.

'Mr Gray, do you have a laptop or computer? We didn't find either at your house,' Whitney said.

'I have a laptop, but it's missing.'

'How convenient.'

'It's true. It disappeared a few days ago. I've been using my phone to process orders for work. Why don't you believe me?'

'Mr Gray, if you think you are innocent of these crimes, then—'

'Of course, I'm innocent,' he interrupted. 'I haven't killed or attacked anyone. You're just trying to frame me so that you can solve the case. I'm not stupid. I know what goes on. And I refuse to let you use the DNA sample I gave you, because I know you'll fix it to find me guilty.' The words tumbled out of his mouth at breakneck speed.

'I'm afraid that won't be possible, Mr Gray,' Whitney said calmly. 'You consented to giving the sample and it's already with our forensics department being analysed and used to compare with DNA we found on the items in your garden shed.'

'Can they do this?' Gray asked his solicitor, running a hand through his hair.

'Unfortunately, once you've consented to giving a DNA sample, you can't later retract permission to use it. Now, Detective Chief Inspector, have you finished with your questioning? My client is not prepared to cooperate further, so either let him go, or charge him. Preferably the former.'

The solicitor had pre-empted her, because she fully intended to charge him.

'Yes, our questioning is over for the time being. Kyle Gray, we are arresting you on suspicion of the murder of Paula Moore, the attempted murder of Lorna Knight, and of the sexual assaults on Jessie Wood, Cheryl Hughes, and Tina Bennett. You do not have to say anything, but it may harm your defence if you do not mention something which you later rely on in court. Anything you do say may be given in evidence. Do you understand?'

He stared at her, open-mouthed. 'But … But … it's not true. I haven't done anything. I don't know these women.' He turned to his solicitor; panic etched across his face. 'You have to get me out of here. I know what they do to sex offenders in prison, and I'm not one of them. I'm innocent. You have to believe me.'

'Leave it with me,' the solicitor replied as if he was responding to a routine matter.

'Mr Gray, we will arrange for someone to take you into custody, where you will be officially charged.'

'What about bail?' Gray said to his solicitor.

'All in due course. We will, of course, apply for bail.'

'Good luck with that,' Brian said, turning his nose up.

'Won't I get it?' Gray asked.

'We'll apply and see,' the solicitor said, picking up his papers. 'I'll be in touch.'

'Okay, you come with me,' Brian said to Gray.

Whitney waited for everyone to leave the room and then went to see George.

'We've done it,' she said, grinning. 'In record time, too. That's got to be cause for a celebration.'

26

Friday

Whitney strolled into her office the next day with a spring in her step. She could hardly believe they'd managed to solve the murder and other assaults in less than a week. Before she'd gone home last night, she'd informed the super of the charges, and they'd agreed to wait until everything was official before contacting all the women Gray had sexually assaulted and letting them know they had someone in custody. Although Whitney wanted them to know before the press conference. Especially Lorna Knight. Whitney didn't want her finding out via the media.

Knowing they'd made an arrest wasn't going to erase the memories of what had happened for any of them, but at least it might give them some closure, knowing that the person responsible was going to be put inside for many years.

Whitney's mobile rang, and she glanced at the screen. She didn't recognise the number.

'DCI Walker,' she answered.

'Is that DCI *Whitney* Walker?' A male voice asked. His voice sounded familiar, but she couldn't place it exactly.

'Yes, it is. How may I help?'

'My name is Ted Price. My son Matt used to work with you.'

That's why he seemed familiar; they had similar-sounding voices. But what concerned Whitney was the seriousness of his tone serious. Please don't let anything have happened to Matt.

'Yes, that's right,' she said tentatively.

'I'm sorry to phone during the day – I know how busy you are – but Matt has asked me to give you a call because he's not up to speaking to anyone at the moment.'

Whitney's heart began thumping. Something bad must have occurred if Matt wanted her to know about it.

'What's happened, Mr Price?'

There was silence for a few seconds and Whitney could hear Mr Price suck in a breath. 'There was a bad car accident, and his wife, my daughter-in-law, Leigh, didn't survive. She died at the scene.'

Whitney's hand flew to her mouth. Leigh, dead? No. It can't be possible. What about Matt? Dani?

'Oh no. I'm so sorry. Matt, is he—'

'He was driving but only suffered minor injuries. The accident wasn't his fault. A lorry drove at speed straight onto the motorway instead of giving way. It hit the side of the car.'

Having known Matt for many years, she suspected that he would be plagued with guilt, even though he wasn't to blame.

'I'd like to visit Matt. Would that be possible?'

'I'm sorry, DCI Walker, but he doesn't want to see anyone

at the moment. But I can certainly tell him that you'd like to see him. He might say yes in a little while.'

'What about Dani? Was she hurt?'

'Dani wasn't with them. We'd been looking after her at the time of the accident, to give them a night out. Matt and Dani are both staying with us until we move down south in a couple of months. We've sold our house and have bought a cottage in Cornwall.'

'Are Leigh's family helping out as well?'

Whitney knew nothing about them. Matt had always kept work and home life separate. It was a testament to how much they got on that he'd confided in her about the couple undergoing the IVF treatment. Other than that, he'd told her very little about him, Leigh, and their respective families.

'Her parents live in Canada. They emigrated twenty years ago. I've spoken to them, and obviously, they're devastated at Leigh's death. They didn't mention Dani. Matt certainly doesn't want to move over there, so it's going to be left to us and Matt to bring her up.'

'He's very lucky to have your support.'

'We're his parents. It's what we do, although ...' His voice cracked. 'Sorry. It's very hard.'

'I understand. It's a difficult time for everyone. I won't keep you any longer. Please send Matt our love and condolences. I'd like to go to the funeral, if you could please let me know when it is. I'm sure others in the team would also like to attend, if that's okay with you?'

'Yes, please do come. And any of Matt's co-workers are welcome, too. I should say ex-co-workers, but I think he still feels more attached to Lenchester than the rural force he's with at the moment. He enjoys working there, but it's not challenging. Still, that was the decision Matt and Leigh made. Only one of them could have a career, and they chose her. It didn't seem right to me ... but I'm from a different generation. The one where men were expected to be the main breadwinner.' He gave a loud sigh.

'When is the funeral?' Whitney prompted.

'Sorry. It's being held at ten-thirty next Monday. It will be at the Heatherton Crematorium. Do you know where it is?'

'Yes, I do. Thank you very much for letting me know. Please tell him we're here for him at any time. And if he wants to chat, to give me a call.'

'He'll appreciate it. We'll see you on Monday,' Ted said.

Whitney replaced her phone on the desk and stared into space. A tear rolled down her cheek, and she brushed it away with the back of her hand. Why did that have to happen to Matt? He was a good man. One of the best. He didn't deserve such tragedy.

Matt and Leigh had tried so hard for a baby and eventually turned to IVF. They'd been successful at their first attempt, and he'd been so excited when she became pregnant, although he'd only shared this with Whitney. They'd decided that Leigh would pursue her career as a head nurse, and he'd be the one to take responsibility for the child and remain as a sergeant. He'd been an amazingly good officer, and she'd wanted him to take his inspector's exam. She'd missed him greatly when he left. She still did. He was so level-headed and although quiet, he could be stubborn and dig his heels in. He was the perfect person for her to work with. They dovetailed perfectly, and he wasn't afraid to pull her back if he felt she was letting her emotions get in the way.

Sighing, she forced herself to go into the incident room to break the news. She pushed open the door. The room was a hive of activity, with lots of the usual chat after a case had been solved, even though they hadn't had their ritual celebration yet. They wouldn't do that until everything had gone through and they'd heard back from the CPS.

'Can I have your attention, please?' she called out once she was standing in front of the board and could see them all.

'Hey, guv. What's wrong? Surely it can't be that bad. Not after our success this week,' Frank shouted out.

She held up her hand to silence him. 'I'm sorry to say I have just received some bad news, which I wanted to pass on to you all straight away.'

'I'm sorry, guv. I didn't realise.' Frank sat back down in his seat and focused his eyes on her.

'You weren't to know. I've just come off the phone with Matt Price's father. There was a car accident, and his wife Leigh died at the scene.'

There were several gasps and intakes of breath.

'Fuck. What about Matt and Dani?' Frank asked.

'Matt sustained some minor injuries, but he's going to be fine. It wasn't his fault. A lorry collided with them. Dani was with Matt's parents for the night and so wasn't in the car. I've passed on our love and condolences.'

She glanced across at Ellie, whose face was ashen. She'd been very close to Matt when he worked there. He'd mentored her when she first started. Whitney walked over to her desk and rested her arm around the officer's shoulders.

'I can't believe it, guv.' She gulped and reached for a tissue from the box on her desk. 'We only saw Matt a few days ago, and everything was going so well. And now this has happened. I don't know how he's going to cope.'

'It's going to be hard, but he's got his parents to help at the moment.'

'I thought they'd sold their house and are moving to Cornwall?'

Whitney frowned. 'How do you know that?'

'Matt told me. He said he'd miss them when they went. They're the only grandparents in the country. Leigh's parents live in Canada and they don't see them much, maybe only once a year, if that.'

'Yes, that's what Mr Price told me.'

'Did you speak to Matt? How is he coping?'

'No. He doesn't want to talk to anyone at the moment, but he did ask his dad to call and let us all know. The funeral is going to be next Monday at Heatherton Crematorium, and everyone is welcome to go. You can come with me if you'd like to.'

'Thank you, guv. I'll see what the others are doing. Perhaps we can all go together.' Ellie blushed and averted her eyes.

'That's a very good idea,' Whitney said, realising that the younger officer might feel uncomfortable being with a DCI, even though they had a good relationship. 'We can all support each other.'

'Guv, I've got Dr Dexter on the phone,' Doug said.

Whitney sighed. 'Can you either take a message or say I'll call her back in a little while?'

She glanced over to where Doug was standing. She could tell by the expression on his face that her comments weren't going down well. So typical of Claire.

Doug looked across at her. 'Dr Dexter said you will want to hear this, and she wants to speak to you *now*.'

Whitney sucked in a breath. She could really do without Claire's sarcastic attitude this morning. This better be worth it. 'Okay, I'm coming over.' She hurried over and took the phone from Doug. 'Yes, Claire,' she said, sounding harsher than she'd intended.

'So sorry to bother you with something related to work,' Claire said in a facetious tone.

She winced. It wasn't Claire's fault. She didn't know what they were dealing with.

'Sorry, Claire. We've just had some bad news regarding Matt, who used to work here.'

'I remember him. He couldn't stand the sight of dead bodies. Would go out of his way not to look at them any time he came across one.'

Whitney gave a dry laugh. 'Yes, that's him. His wife's died in a car accident.'

'I'm very sorry to hear that,' Claire said, her tone softer. 'I'd offer to call back later, except there's important information that you need to hear. I've had the results back from forensics, and the blood that was found in Paula Moore's mouth alongside the glove fragments wasn't hers, as I'd previously believed. She must have bitten through the gloves and actually broken the skin. This means we have the DNA of the murderer. Not only that, his blood group is very rare. It's AB negative. I'll email the results over to you.'

'Excellent. Thanks. We've found the gloves and balaclava used in the attacks, and also taken a DNA sample from the man we've charged to see if it matches up with any DNA found on them. Now we have your results, that should tie it all up nicely, and we can send everything to the CPS.'

'You've charged someone already? That's excellent news. Well done.'

Whitney frowned. Rarely, if ever, did the pathologist offer praise. Then she remembered the lecture that the woman was giving.

'Thanks, Claire. I appreciate you rushing this through for us.' She ended the call. 'Right, team. Dr Dexter also has the DNA of the attacker from blood in Paula Moore's mouth. So there will be no wriggling out of it for Gray. She also told us that the murderer has a rare blood group. I'm assuming that, too, will tie back to Gray. Doug, can you get in touch with forensics and find out when they'll have the results?'

Whitney left the incident room and went to her office. She had admin to do, but she really couldn't face it. Then again, if she did do some, it would take her mind off poor Matt and what he must be going through. She couldn't begin to imagine how awful it was for him. 'Crap. George,' she said out loud. She'd have to let her know about Matt and Leigh. She might want to attend the funeral with them. Should she call? Or maybe wait until she comes into the station. George had said she'd be in today.

She opened the document and was about to begin working on some monthly projections when the phone on her desk rang.

'Walker.'

'Guv, can you come back into the incident room? It's important,' Brian said.

She replaced the handset, skirted around her desk and opened the door to the incident room. Huddled around the desk at the front was every member of her team. Frank, Brian, Doug, Meena, and Ellie. They turned in unison as she headed towards them.

What the hell was going on?

'You're not going to like this, guv,' Brian said, taking a step towards her. 'We've just had the DNA results back from forensics, and Gray's blood type is O. He isn't a match for the blood in the victim's mouth. It looks like we have the wrong man.'

27

Friday

George pushed open the door to the incident room, expecting to hear the usual chatter and high spirits from everyone now the case had been solved.

'You've got to be kidding me,' Whitney said from where she was standing by the board. Dismay was plastered all over her face.

George stared at her friend. What had happened to elicit such a response? She glanced at the rest of the team, who were by Whitney's side, all of them subdued, and most definitely not acting in the manner she'd have expected. Whitney had been convinced that the case was solid. They had plenty of evidence, even if the motive had yet to be discovered.

She walked over to the board.

'Whitney?' she said, wanting to attract the officer's attention.

'You've arrived at just the right time. You're never going

to believe what's happened. It looks like Kyle Gray isn't our murderer. Forensics have come back, and the blood in Paula's mouth belonged to someone else. Assuming that the blood came from biting through the gloves, which Claire thinks it did. Whoever murdered her has a rare blood group, type AB negative, and that doesn't match the DNA we took from Gray. His type is O.'

'But it doesn't explain why the IP address for the person posing on social media came from his location. Unless ...'

Why hadn't she thought of it before? Because her thoughts had been stuck on Ross, instead of thinking about all possibilities in relation to the case. She'd been happy to go along with everything Whitney had deduced, instead of making sure everything was perfectly aligned.

'He's working with someone else, or he's being set up. Two scenarios to consider,' Whitney said. 'But how likely is it that there's two of them? From what we know of the attacks, they're carried out by a man on his own.'

'I believe you're correct. That he was framed. I'm sorry I didn't think about it sooner.'

Whitney frowned. 'Don't be daft. How were you expected to realise? We all got sucked in good and proper.'

It was generous of Whitney to excuse her, but the fact was, she should have given the issue more thought. Or what was the point in her being there to assist on cases?

'Are you going to release Gray from custody now you have the evidence to put him in the clear?' she asked.

'Not yet. We need to investigate this further, just in case he does turn out to be involved.' Whitney turned away from George. 'Ellie, I'd like you to investigate Gray further. See if we can discover why he's being framed or if there's any chance that he's working with someone. The rest of you, keep researching and see what comes up. For now, it's back to the drawing board.' Whitney turned back to face George, running her fingers through her mass of curls, which had worked their way loose from the tie holding them back.

'I'm very sorry to hear about the case. But you've had setbacks in the past which you've overcome.' George couldn't put her finger on it, but Whitney's reaction was more intense than she would have expected. There was something else going on, George was sure of it.

'You're right. But that's not the only thing that's happened this morning. Let's go into my office and I'll explain. Better still, we'll go to the cafeteria and grab a coffee. Is that okay with you?'

'Of course.'

They spoke very little on their way, and it wasn't until they were seated at one of the tables with their drinks that Whitney began to speak.

'We've had some bad news, I'm afraid. It's ...' Her voice cracked, and her eyes filled with tears. 'I'm sorry. It's been so hard trying to hold it together.' She picked up her mug and took a sip.

'What's happened?' George asked. Was it Tiffany? Or Ava? Or could it be something to do with Whitney's mum or brother? But surely if it was any of them, then Whitney wouldn't be at work. It had to be something else.

'Do you remember my ex-sergeant, Matt?'

'Yes, I saw him the other day when he came into the office. We worked together on a number of cases. I was always impressed by his contribution to the team.'

'Of course you did. I forgot. It's so awful. His wife, Leigh, has died, leaving him alone to take care of his daughter.'

Matt had been an integral part of Whitney's team. In fact, it was down to his insistence that she consider George's offer to help on their first case together, that she ended up in her being an official part of the department. Matt was able to see what Whitney couldn't at the time. That academic research and real-world policing could coexist.

'I'm very sorry to hear that. Please pass on my condolences when you see him.'

'At the moment he doesn't want any visitors, but the whole team will be welcome at the funeral. After that, he may be up to receiving some visitors.'

'I'd like to attend with you, if you think that's appropriate, considering I'm not a proper member of the team.'

'Yes, most definitely you can come with me. And as for you not being a proper member of the team, you are in my eyes, and—'

'Guv,' Meena called out as she reached their table. 'I'm sorry for interrupting you, but I've had an idea which I want to run by you, away from the rest of them, in case you think it's no good.'

Whitney exchanged a glance with George and raised an eyebrow.

'Sit down and explain. I trust you don't mind Dr Cavendish being here.' Whitney nodded towards the empty chair at their table.

Meena blushed, while pulling out the chair and sitting next to George. 'I'm happy to tell both of you. I was thinking that if Gray isn't our man, which it looks to be the case, we could try to draw the real killer out.'

'I take it you have a plan in mind to do this?' Whitney said, resting her arms on the table and looking directly at the officer, giving her full attention.

'We already know that the leap-year-birthday social media group is the one place that links everyone. We know, too, that the killer used this group to lead us to Gray. My idea is that we make use of the group, too.'

'In what way?'

'Why don't I post on the group and ask if anyone fancies meeting up for a night out in Lenchester?'

'Have you ever done that before?' George asked.

Did the idea have merit? That would be down to Whitney to decide.

'No, because when others have met up, it's been in other areas of the country. As far as I know, no one has suggested a local one. But the fact that it's been done in the past shouldn't arouse suspicions. I can say I want to get out and meet people. If the killer knows I'm alone, he might see me as an easy target. If we meet in a public place, then members of the team can be stationed in various places. I'll be perfectly safe. It might not work, but it's got to be worth a try. We know he's been upping his game from sexual assault to murder. We need to stop him before another woman dies.'

George kept her eyes focused on Whitney to see her reaction. Engaging in an activity like this, involving placing an officer in danger, wasn't something that was embarked on lightly.

'Won't members of the group think it strange that you haven't asked your friends to go out?' George asked.

'I can say that I have no friends in the area because I haven't lived here long,' Meena said.

'Don't they already know where you live? And what about your job? Do they know you're in the force? It seems somewhat risky,' Whitney said, drumming her fingers on the table.

'It's not risky because I haven't mentioned where I live or what I do. Although I'm a member, I've always kept a low profile. Mainly reading posts and rarely contributing. Most of them won't even know I exist.'

'George, what do you think?' Whitney said, turning to her.

George hadn't expected to be consulted because Whitney was usually well able to make up her mind when it came to operational matters.

'On the face of it, I believe it to be an idea worthy of consideration. But you must remember that just because you haven't been an active participant in the social media group, it doesn't mean that the killer hasn't researched you. He's very thorough in the way he pursues his victims.'

'George has a point, Meena.'

'I accept that there is an element of risk, but all the victims that we are aware of were active in the group. I've spent time researching the group, and they would have been known by the other members. They also spoke about the areas in which they lived, which I have never done.'

George was quiet for several seconds while considering the officer's response. 'We must never underestimate the ability of the murderer, but in this instance, I believe that Meena is correct. It's unlikely that she's known by any of the group members.'

'Okay, in that case, I'll run your idea past the super, Meena. She'll need to give her permission because we are putting you in a potentially dangerous position.'

'Um ... May I make a further suggestion, guv?' Meena said, biting down on her bottom lip.

'What is it?' Whitney asked.

'Perhaps we should wait to ask for permission until I have received some positive replies. It's not worth jumping through all the hoops if no one wants to meet me and my plan fails before it's even got off the ground.'

George nodded in agreement. Not that it was her decision, but Meena made perfect sense.

'Yes, I agree that's the way to go. Especially as the super may have to contact Chief Superintendent Douglas to get a final sign off. If he says yes and then it doesn't take place, it could backfire on me. And we all know how much delight he'd take in that,' Whitney said, rolling her eyes. She looked at her watch. 'We don't have enough time to get everything in place for you to meet with the group this evening, but tomorrow night, Saturday, would be an ideal time. When are you going to post it on the group?' Whitney asked, smiling at Meena.

Whitney had gone from being dejected to buoyant in a very short time. It was fascinating to watch.

'I can do it now, if you like, and see if anyone replies. Fingers crossed, someone will.'

'That's a great idea. As soon as one person agrees to meet up with you, I'll go to see the super. Preferably, we need a response today, or it might be too late to organise, and she'll say no. You go back to the office now and post your request, and we'll follow shortly,' Whitney said, nodding towards the entrance to the cafeteria.

'Yes, guv.'

'Don't you wish to check the post before Meena puts it up?' George asked once they were alone.

'It's not necessary. She's already told us what she'll be putting in it. Having said that, I suppose we better go back and see what, if anything, the team has turned up. We'll take our coffee with us.'

As soon as they were back in the incident room, Whitney headed over to Meena and had a quick chat with her before returning to the board where George was standing.

'Did you approve?' she asked.

'Yes. It was fine, as I knew it would be. She's going to post it now. I'll tell the rest of the team what we're planning.' Whitney cleared her throat. 'Eyes this way, everyone. I want to bring you up to speed with what we're doing. You all know that Meena was born on the twenty-ninth of February and is a member of the social media group the murderer is targeting. I've approved, in principle, an idea from Meena regarding drawing out the killer. I say "in principle" because we still have to seek permission from the super and, most likely, Douglas. But I won't be going to them until everything's in place. Meena, you can take over from here and explain to the team.'

'Yes, guv. I've put up a request in the group for someone to meet me on Saturday night at the Rose & Shamrock, which is west of the city centre. It's lively and popular with all age groups, so I thought it would be a perfect spot. I'm hoping that the killer will take the hint.'

'If he's daft enough to,' Frank said. 'He'll know straight away that it's a set-up.'

'No, he won't. I hardly ever engage on the group and certainly have never told anyone where I live or what I do for a living. Remember, Frank, there are over a thousand members. He's not going to pick me out,' Meena said.

Frank sighed loudly. 'Okay, I get that. But surely it will seem strange to the killer that suddenly a person from Lenchester, where he's recently murdered a woman and attempted to murder another, will ask to meet.'

'Umm ...' Meena faltered, looking helplessly at Whitney.

'Have you a better idea, Frank?' Whitney asked.

'No, guv,' he said, looking sheepish.

'Then we'll try this one.'

'As long as Meena isn't in any danger. That's all I'm concerned about.'

Frank's response impressed George. Along with Brian,

Meena was a fairly recent addition to the team, but she'd clearly been assimilated. It was a credit to Whitney's management style and the people she surrounded herself with.

'Meena won't be alone. We'll all be close by,' Whitney said.

'You better tell the missus that you won't be home on Saturday night then, Frank,' Doug said, grinning. 'That's if she believes you. Knowing how much you shy away from actual work, she might think you're planning to go out with another woman.'

'Shut up, Doug. But now he's brought it up ... will I be needed, guv? The wife and I do have something on tomorrow night. It's been arranged for months now.'

'Ha. I was right. I knew it,' Doug said, punching the air.

'Work on the assumption that all personal plans for tomorrow are cancelled. That's unless no one takes Meena up on her offer to meet.'

'Go and check,' Frank said.

'There's no point. It was only posted ten minutes ago,' Meena said.

'Please?' Frank begged.

'Go on, Meena, or we'll never hear the end of it,' Whitney said.

The officer went over to her desk and her fingers flew across the keyboard. She stared intently at her screen.

'Well?' Frank said.

'I've actually had a reply, guv. From a woman called Ginny. She lives on the outskirts of Lenchester, and she said she'd love to meet up tomorrow. We've arranged to meet at seven forty-five.'

An excited cheer went up from everyone in the team. Apart from Frank, who scowled. It wouldn't affect George, because she doubted she'd be allowed to go with the team because she hadn't had the necessary training required for undercover work.

'Right. In that case, the operation is now on. Subject to the super's agreement, of course. And that's where I'm heading now.'

_____

28

Friday

Whitney tapped gently on Superintendent Clyde's slightly open door and popped her head around it. 'Do you have a moment, ma'am?'

Rather a moot point because, whatever her boss was doing, Whitney would have disturbed her. This was top priority.

The super looked up and smiled. 'Come in, Whitney. How may I help you?'

Whitney sat on one of the chairs opposite the super's desk. 'Two things I need to speak to you about, ma'am. First, we've discovered that the man we charged yesterday for Paula Moore's murder and the other sexual assaults isn't who we're looking for. The blood type doesn't match that of our killer.'

'That's a shame. I thought we'd got him. I'd been discussing it with Chief Superintendent Douglas. I'll have to let him know.'

Whitney gave a frustrated sigh. Typical that Douglas now had something to moan about. 'We couldn't believe it, either. Especially after the IP address for the person posting on the social media group led back to him.'

'Social media group? You'll have to catch me up.'

'There's a group that was set up specifically for people with birthdays on the twenty-ninth of February. We've discovered that someone using an alias had links with all the women who had been attacked. We believe that Gray is either working with another person, which we doubt, or he's being framed. I've got Ellie looking deeper into him to see if we can find someone with a grudge against Gray.'

'Have you released Gray from custody?'

'No. I'm not intending to do that yet because we're planning an operation to draw out the killer. Just in case Gray is actually involved with another person, we don't want him to have the opportunity to warn him.'

'Tell me about this operation?'

'One of my officers, DC Meena Singh, has a birthday on the twenty-ninth of February and she was the one who alerted us to the existence of a social media group that they all belonged to. It's a countrywide group of over a thousand people. She suggested that she should arrange a get-together in Lenchester tomorrow night to see if we can draw out the attacker. I'll have officers stationed in various places, so she should be perfectly safe. Obviously, we need your permission to go ahead, although she has already put out feelers, and so far, one person has responded.'

Clyde stared ahead for several seconds, tapping her fingers on the desk.

Was she going to say no?

'You realise that however many precautions are put in

place, there will still be an element of risk for your officer, and that isn't something to be taken lightly.'

'Of course, ma'am. We've discussed this in detail, and if there was any other way, then that would take precedence. But this seems to be our best way forward. Now that Gray is in the clear, the investigation has taken a backwards step. We've got to be mindful of the fact that the killer is shortening his timeline. Also, he's gone from sexual assault to murder. I doubt he'll revert back. If we don't catch him soon, we could be faced with a serial killer.'

'Okay, Whitney. As far as I'm concerned, yes, you can go ahead with the operation, but I will have to get approval from Chief Superintendent Douglas.'

'Yes, ma'am. How soon can you ask him?'

'I'll do it now, while you're here.'

Whitney's eyes widened. Her previous super would never have been so relaxed about it. She should be used to Clyde, but she still managed to surprise her sometimes.

'Thanks, ma'am. But I expect Doug ... I mean the chief super will make it difficult, as it's me. You know what he's like.'

'I'm sure he'll be receptive to your idea, knowing that it has my support.'

The super picked up the handset from the phone on the desk and pressed one of the numbers. Whitney sat back in her chair and waited for the inevitable.

'Good afternoon, sir. I need to speak to you regarding an operation DCI Walker wants to undertake with her team. I —' The super paused. 'Yes, I do understand, but this really is important.' Another silence. 'Okay. I'll call back in five.' She ended the call and replaced the handset. 'I'm sure you must have got the gist of that.'

'Yes, ma'am. He's too busy to speak to you.' Whitney arched an eyebrow.

'I'll speak to him again shortly. Go ahead with planning the operation, and I'll contact you once we have permission. By the way, you won't be involving Dr Cavendish in the operation, will you?'

'No, ma'am. She'll be back here, ready to help with the interviewing if we do manage to arrest anyone.'

'Good. Because I'm sure that will be one of the chief super's questions.'

Whitney left Clyde's office and headed straight back down to the incident room.

'Listen up, everyone. The super said yes, and she's going to be speaking to Douglas shortly. She's already asked about you, George.' Whitney grinned at her friend.

'Me? Why?'

'She wanted to make sure that you were nowhere near the operation. Of course, I reassured her.' Her mobile rang, and she pulled it out of her pocket. 'It's the super. Hello, ma'am.'

'We have permission to go ahead with the operation. But there are some provisos, Whitney.'

'What are they, guv? Actually, let me guess. The buck stops with me if anything goes wrong, and I'll end up in charge of traffic?'

The super laughed. 'Not quite expressed in those words, but close enough, Whitney. I assured him that everything will be done by the book.'

'Thanks, ma'am. I'll keep you informed of progress.' She ended the call and turned back to the team. 'We have permission to proceed. Any more takers so far, Meena?'

'Still just the one, guv. But it's early days. Also, people might turn up and not bother to reply.'

'If we do draw out the killer, then he might be one of those to not let Meena know in advance that he's attending. Or he could be in the pub and station himself so he can watch without being part of the get-together. That would make more sense, otherwise, the other participants would be able to identify him,' George said.

'Yes, you're right. He's more likely to be observing than taking part. Okay, folks,' Whitney said, rubbing her hands together. 'Now the meeting's definitely on, we need to decide how we're going to proceed. I want everybody back in the office first thing tomorrow morning and we'll plan it to the nth degree. Nothing can go wrong with this operation, and not just because of Meena. My neck's on the line, too.'

29

Saturday

Whitney was seated at her desk with a mug of coffee in front of her. She'd been there since seven because she'd been unable to sleep, which was usual when something big was happening the following day. She'd spent most of the night going through all the different scenarios in her head and what they needed to be mindful of. She was confident that they would have Meena's back at all times, but that didn't mean they should be any less vigilant.

She glanced up when there was a knock at the door. Who wanted to see her this early? She wasn't expecting the team until at least eight to eight-thirty, which was their usual starting time.

'Come in,' she called out.

'Good morning,' George said as she opened the door.

'What are you doing here?' They hadn't arranged for her to attend the meeting this morning.

'I'm aware that you don't wish me to take part in the

actual operation, but I thought you could use my input during the planning stages. We need to consider the offender's profile and his likely actions, which I can help with. I'm early because I knew that you'd be here and thought you might wish to run your plans past me before explaining them to the team.'

Whitney smiled to herself. They'd come a long way since first meeting when she'd been reluctant to take George's help. And George, in turn, had been very difficult to understand, in particular her inability to pick up many social cues. They were both different now, having learnt much from each other.

'You were correct. I've been here for a while, pondering over the logistics of the operation. Is there anything that we should be mindful of? Actually ...' Her voice fell away.

'What is it?'

'I've just had a thought ... You're absolutely not allowed to be part of the operation. Both the super and Douglas agree on that front. Me, too, for that matter. I don't want Ross coming after me if we put you in danger. You're not trained like the rest of us. But, considering that the meeting is taking place in a pub, where there are members of the public, how about you going there for a drink?'

'For what purpose?' George asked, pulling out the chair in front of Whitney's desk and sitting down.

'You can observe everyone with Meena and see if there are any red flags. Note if anyone is acting suspiciously. Also, you can check out anyone in the pub who's paying particular attention to the group, in case they are the murderer and watching, like you thought might happen.'

Why hadn't she thought of that before? George was far better than the rest of them to assess the behaviour of other people there.

'Won't me sitting there on my own appear suspicious?' George asked, frowning.

'Probably, so you'll have to bring someone with you. What about Ross?' Whitney knew that George didn't have other friends to ask.

'He's visiting his family today, and I'm not sure what time he will be returning. Would Tiffany come with me?'

Whitney's insides clenched. Even though it would be perfectly safe, the thought of Tiffany being anywhere near a murderer ...

'No. Ava's a bit sniffly, and she wouldn't want to leave her. Oh ... I know ... But ...' She paused, unable to stop her lips from turning up into a smile.

'Stop being so mysterious, Whitney. Who do you have in mind?'

'We'll ask Claire.'

Whitney forced back a giggle. George and Claire out together on a Saturday night would be very interesting.

'Claire?'

'Yes, why not? You've known her for years. Longer than you've known me, in fact.'

'That is true, although only in a professional capacity through the university.'

'Think of this evening out as that. A time for you to discuss forensics, or something equally highbrow. I'll give her a call.' Whitney reached for her phone.

'What makes you think she'll agree?'

'She's invested in this case. Remember, she wants it solved quickly so she can use it in her workshop.' She glanced at her watch. 'I won't phone her mobile in case she's not on duty and is still in bed. You know how she hates mornings. I'll call the morgue.' Whitney pressed the shortcut key.

'Dr Dexter speaking.'

Whitney mouthed, 'She's answered,' to George. 'Good morning, Claire. It's Whitney.'

'Why are you phoning at this time? I've only just got into work.'

Had she chosen the wrong time to call? Maybe she should have left it until later, except she needed to get all the plans in place.

'Sorry to disturb you, but I want to ask you a favour.'

'I don't do favours,' Claire snapped.

'Hear me out, Claire. We need help with the case.'

'I thought it was all solved. What do you need from me?'

'It turns out that our suspect didn't have the rare blood group you found. We haven't yet released him, in case he's working with someone else, but we doubt that's the case because of the nature of the attacks and—'

'Come on, get to the point. I don't have all day.' Whitney glanced at George and rolled her eyes.

'I'd like you to go with George to the Rose & Shamrock pub tonight for a drink, to keep an eye on the patrons and, in particular, people at a get-together where one of my officers will be undercover. They're meeting at seven forty-five, so if you can be there by seven-thirty, that would be good.'

'I still don't understand why you need me.'

'Because George can't go on her own and Ross isn't available. Do you have plans this evening?'

'I have now, by the sounds of things.'

'Is that a yes?'

'I suppose it is. Tell George to pick me up at seven from my house. I'll message her the address.'

Should Whitney mention dress code? No, it wouldn't make any difference – Claire was out on a limb when it came to fashion.

'Thanks, Claire, we really appreciate your cooperation.'

'Well, you owe me one. And I won't forget.' Claire ended the call without even saying goodbye. But that didn't surprise Whitney. Nothing about Claire surprised her.

'That's sorted,' Whitney said, smiling at George. 'She will go with you, and you're to pick her up at seven. She'll text her address. Is that okay?'

'Yes, that will be fine.'

'I'm sure you'll have an enjoyable evening. And you can report back on the conversation.'

George frowned. 'We're not there to enjoy ourselves.'

'I was joking, George.'

'I realised that.'

Whitney was about to make a retort when there was a knock on the door that linked her office to the incident room, and Brian came in.

'Everyone's here, guv, if you want to come out to plan the operation.'

'Thanks, Brian. We're right behind you.' She gathered up her phone and went through with George. 'Good morning, team. It's good to see you all. This is likely to be a long day and night, and so my suggestion is that we plan the operation and then take a few hours off this afternoon to get some rest – providing someone remains in the office to take calls – and then we'll all meet up tonight. Dr Cavendish is joining us for the planning to provide insight into who we're looking for. She will also be at the pub, strictly as an observer and not taking part in any way. I've arranged for Dr Dexter to be with her.'

'This I have to see,' Frank said, laughing. 'Dr Dexter out on the town on a Saturday night.'

'That's enough, Frank. She's kindly agreed to accompany George, and that's all that matters.'

'Good luck, Dr C, that's all I can say,' Frank said, looking either side of him for support from the others in the team. Doug and Ellie were laughing. Brian and Meena, less so, probably because they weren't so familiar with Claire and her eccentricities.

'Dr Dexter and I have been acquaintances for many years, Frank. An evening out will not be an issue for either of us. We're not there for pleasure,' George said.

'Sorry.' Frank bowed his head, but Whitney suspected it was more to hide his laughter than to appear contrite.

'Right, that's enough time wasted on the merits, or otherwise of the evening George and Dr Dexter will be having. Meena, have you had any more people from the group agreeing to meet up with you?'

'Yes, guv. Two more women and one man have indicated they might join us but haven't messaged me privately about it. All the arrangements regarding where we're going to meet, the time, and the exact location we'll be in the pub, I've done in public rather than away from the group, to ensure that if anybody else wants to come along, they can.'

'The killer, you mean,' Frank said.

'Good work, Meena. I'm going to pass over to Dr Cavendish to give us some pointers about the killer and how we're going to identify him.'

Whitney stepped to the side, making space for George to move in front so everyone could see her.

'What we must remember is that our killer is extremely clever. He's prepared to play the long game. To our knowledge, he began assaulting women at least eighteen months ago and only now has he framed Kyle Gray for it. If it wasn't for Paula Moore actually breaking his skin when biting through the gloves, his plan would have succeeded. We also know that the killer likes to have things neat and tidy, hence him murdering Paula Moore immediately after failing in his attempt to kill Lorna Knight. If he now believes that he's failed in framing Gray, he will want to put that right as soon as he can.'

'If the motive of the killer is to frame Gray, then surely he won't try anything stupid now, not while Gray's in custody? We should assume that he's aware of that. So, shouldn't we release him? We can put a tail on him,' Brian said.

'Yes, Brian, I think that might be the way forward,' Whitney said. 'Ellie, have you had any luck in discovering who might want to frame Gray?'

'No, guv.'

'Could it be linked to all the goods he's stolen?' Doug asked.

'They come from a variety of places, and there's nothing I can find linking them,' Ellie said. 'Sorry, guv.'

'Don't apologise. You can't find what isn't there,' Whitney said.

'We should ask the super to hold a press conference and say that we had someone in custody but have released them. That way, the killer might try to frame him again. Possibly get him to go along to the pub or be close by. What do you think, guv?' Brian said.

'I like it. George, are you in agreement?'

'Yes, I am. The idea does have merit.'

'Is there anything else we should be considering?' Whitney asked George.

'If he is in the pub and watching, it will be unobtrusively. We already know that he can fly under the radar and not be seen. Take, for example, in the café where Paula Moore met him. No one remembered seeing him. That tells me he's capable of blending in with the scenery. But remember, he will be fully cognisant of what's going on at Meena's meeting, so I suspect he'll place himself far enough away not to be noticed but close enough to follow the proceedings. I'll be keeping an eye on the patrons and will be able to identify anyone who appears suspicious and will let the DCI know via text message.'

'And then we can meet up in the bathroom to discuss, if necessary. Any more questions for Dr Cavendish?' No one had. 'Right, this is how we'll operate. Brian and I will be inside the pub observing Meena's meeting. Frank and Doug, I want you outside in an unmarked car, keeping an eye on what's going on. Make a note of everyone who enters and leaves the premises. Ellie, we'll need you here at the station, available to do any searches we need on people who have turned up.'

The officer wouldn't mind not being at the sharp end of an investigation. She was much better placed at the station, researching anything they needed. She was fast and resourceful.

'Yes, guv,' Ellie said.

'I'll also have several uniformed officers in cars on standby. Any questions?'

'Yes. Meena, are you totally sure that no one knows your occupation?' Doug asked, his brows furrowed and the lines around his eyes tight.

'I can't see how anyone could know because I've never mentioned it. You know what these groups are like. Some people share absolutely everything, and others, like me, don't give anything away. Obviously, if I'm already in the killer's sight, he might have followed me and discovered where I work, but that's not very likely. Even more so, because I use my maiden name on all social media platforms.'

'Okay, that's good enough for me,' Whitney said. 'Brian, phone down to the custody suite and inform them that they can release Gray. Make sure they do it straight away, and I'll contact the super and ask her to make an announcement to the press. I'll be back in a minute.'

Whitney went into her office and called the super. Luckily, she was free and able to do as asked. She didn't need Whitney with her, which was another plus.

'It's all sorted,' Brian said when Whitney returned to the incident room.

'Good. So is the press announcement.'

They were as prepared as they could be. Now that George was on board in a more unobtrusive way, Whitney was happy. Between them, they'd make sure that Meena was safe. Whitney was convinced that they were going to be successful this evening. Her gut was telling her. Not that George would believe her. She'd love to have a wire on George so she could listen to her and Claire's conversation. And as for what Claire was going to wear, that she couldn't wait to see.

'Right. We're ready to lure out this bastard and catch him once and for all.'

30

Saturday

Whitney stared at herself in the mirror of the bathroom at the station. She'd taken her hair out of the tie and run a brush through it, although it was still wild, and had smeared on some lip gloss and added some eye shadow and mascara. It was a Saturday night, so she needed to look like she was ready to go out. Earlier in the day, she had gone home and changed into something more suitable – a summer dress with a denim jacket over her shoulders. She swapped her black work shoes for a pair of white trainers and, after giving herself one last look, she returned to the incident room for last-minute preparations.

'Hey, look at the guv, all ready for her Saturday night out on the town,' Frank said.

Whitney shook her head. Frank had certainly become cheekier than usual, and she'd put it down to retirement being only around the corner.

'Thank you, Frank,' she said, rolling her eyes. 'Is

everyone ready to go? I've been in contact with Dr Cavendish, and she's collected Dr Dexter, and they're on their way to the pub. Remember, don't acknowledge them if you see them. We don't know who'll be watching or how long they've been there. Meena, have you been contacted by anyone else?'

'Yes, guv. An older guy who's part of the group. He said he'll definitely be there.'

'That could be him,' Frank said.

'Not unless his photo isn't him, because this guy has got to be in his sixties, which is way outside the age of who we're looking for,' Meena said.

'Our profile isn't set in stone, so we shouldn't exclude anyone,' Whitney said.

'Is your old man going to be there, Meena? Keeping an eye on you,' Frank asked.

Whitney hoped not. Meena's husband now worked in security but used to be in the force. Having someone there who wasn't under her control could only lead to difficulties.

'No. He's staying in tonight. He knows I'm out on an operation but doesn't know what it's about or that I'm going to be undercover. I thought it best not to tell him.'

'Good move. It could only complicate matters. Now, good luck, everyone. Brian, we'll take your car, and I'll leave mine here,' Whitney said.

'Yes, guv, I imagined we would,' Brian said with a wry grin.

'You're not going out like that, are you?' she said to him. He was still wearing his work suit and looked very different from her. He was always the best dressed member of the team. Whitney put it down to his time at the Met. They all wore expensive clothes there.

'I was going to take off my tie and dispense with the

jacket, so I'm wearing trousers and an open-necked shirt. Is that okay?'

'I'm sure it will be fine, although considering we're meant to be out on a date, we don't want to appear too different.'

She was winding Brian up to bring some levity into the proceedings. She'd found in the past that it helped with morale to lighten the mood a little before embarking on a serious operation.

'A d-d-date?' Brian spluttered.

'What's wrong, Brian? Am I too old for you?' Whitney said, smirking.

'He'd be lucky to have you, guv,' Frank said.

'You wouldn't say no, would you, Frank?' Doug said, giving a loud laugh.

'I'm married. You know that. If I wasn't … then …'

'Okay, I think we've gone far enough. I appreciate your compliment, Frank. But you know I'm only joking, Brian. We don't have to pretend to be on a date. There'll be no holding hands or anything else. We'll just be out together as friends having a drink.'

'I knew you didn't mean it,' Brian said, the sense of relief in his voice echoed by the more relaxed expression on his face.

'Right, we all know what we're doing. Meena, we'll have eyes and ears on you the whole time. Act normally. If you want to talk to me, then go to the ladies' bathroom, and I'll follow you in there.'

'What if she just wants to go to the loo?' Frank said.

'That's fine, too. We don't have to speak while we're in there.'

'Okay, guv,' Meena said.

They all left together. Whitney with Brian, Meena on

her own, and Frank with Doug in his car.

When they reached the pub, Brian parked on the main road rather than the car park. They waited five minutes and then walked in. Meena was seated at a round table towards the back on her own with a drink in front of her.

Brian and Whitney found a table that gave them a view of the entrance and also one of Meena's table.

It was seven-twenty, and Meena had told the group to meet at seven forty-five, so now they had to wait.

'I was very sorry to hear about your ex-sergeant,' Brian said, sipping the lemonade he'd ordered.

'Yes, it was such a tragedy. Matt always kept his private life private. But the odd time that I met Leigh, I really liked her. It's going to be very hard for him. They were a devoted couple. I'll be going to the funeral on Monday to show my support for him and the family.'

'Did he continue working as a police officer after leaving here?'

'Yes. They'd decided that Leigh should pursue her career as a nurse, so after the restructure, he took a job in a much smaller force that gave him time to be with Dani after she was born. To be honest, I wasn't sure of the decision, because he'd have made such a great inspector, but it was what he wanted, and so I supported his decision.'

'And if he hadn't made that decision, then I probably wouldn't be here on your team. I remember when I first arrived how much he was missed by everyone. He was a much tougher act to follow than I'd anticipated.'

Whitney stared at Brian, observing the uncertainty in his eyes. It was the first time she'd ever heard him sound remotely lacking in confidence. He'd been the opposite to Matt when he'd arrived – brash and full of himself. He'd made it known that he was a career officer, and working at

Lenchester was simply a stepping stone to something bigger and better. Had it all been bluff?

'He was – is – greatly missed, and it perhaps was a bit hard for you. You're a very different officer from Matt. But that doesn't matter. It would be no good if we were all the same. You've been a valuable asset to the team since arriving, especially now you've settled in and become one of us, so to speak, although I'm assuming that you'll be wanting to take your inspector exams any time now, so you can move onwards and upwards.'

'Yes, I would like to take them soon. I feel that the time is right. But moving on maybe isn't such an issue for me now. Lenchester has a lot more to offer than I first thought. I'm happy being a member of your team, and also I like living here.' He averted his eyes, his cheeks a little pink.

It wasn't hard to guess what had brought on this change of heart.

'If I'm not mistaken, I think you've met someone. Or is that colour in your cheeks from the heat?' She laughed.

'I'm saying nothing,' Brian said. 'Personal life is personal and—'

'Look, someone's just joined Meena,' Whitney interrupted when a woman in her thirties, holding a glass of wine, sat at the table. 'I wonder if that's Ginny. I'll take a photo on my phone.' She pretended to be looking at something on her screen and snapped.

'And here's Dr Cavendish and Dr Dexter,' Brian said, nodding at the bar, where the pair of them were standing. 'They make an odd couple.'

Whitney had to agree. George, at over five foot ten, was elegant and understated, in a pair of dark trousers and a pale blue shirt with her cardigan draped over her shoulders. Claire, on the other hand, was even shorter than Whitney's five foot four, and looked like she'd closed her eyes before pulling out the first things she could lay her hands on to wear. True to form, nothing was matching, and her red hair sticking out at all angles. They bought their drinks and sat at a table on the opposite side of the room.

Already, it was filling up, and Whitney was careful to take photos of any males who entered. There was a mix of ages, and most people were with someone. There was one man seated alone at the bar, but he didn't look like their man. He was short and round. Nothing like the description they had from Lorna Knight and the other women who'd been assaulted.

Meena was joined by an older man in his sixties, who Whitney assumed was the man she'd mentioned. He appeared frail and not likely to be the murderer. There was another woman who looked to be in her early fifties. After an hour, Meena got up and headed to the bathroom. Whitney followed.

After checking there was no one else in there, Meena turned to her. 'It doesn't look like he's coming to my meetup.'

'I agree, but that doesn't mean he isn't here watching. Where possible, I've checked out all the males in the pub, but because it's so busy, I might have missed someone. I'll text George and ask her to come in.' She took out her phone, sent a text and within a minute, the door opened, and George came in.

'You wished to speak to me,' George said.

'Yes, have you spotted anyone suspicious? So far, I haven't.'

'Certainly no one with Meena was acting in a suspicious manner. I've scrutinised all the males in here, both those on their own and with other people, and as far as I could tell, no one was paying particular attention to you and the group.'

Meena's face fell. 'So, it looks like my plan wasn't so good after all.'

'We don't know that. Go back to your group, and we'll stay for another hour. I'll then text you, and you can use it as an excuse to leave. Where are you parked?'

'In the car park. I've got a white Honda, and it's in the back row.'

'We're out the front along the street. Once you leave, drive to where we've parked, and we'll be waiting for you. I'll instruct Frank and Doug to keep an eye on you when you exit the pub and walk to your car.'

'Okay, guv.'

'We can't all be seen coming out of the ladies together. You go first, and George and I will follow in a minute.' Her phone pinged, and she glanced at the message on the screen. 'Wait a minute. I've just heard that Gray is in the vicinity. He was heading in the direction of the pub, and uniform have stopped him. I'd given instructions for him to be apprehended if he got too close. Supposedly, he's meant to be meeting someone for a drink at a nearby bar.'

'If he's being framed, then I'd say that the killer is somewhere close. You should let Gray go for his drink because we don't want to alert the killer that we're aware of what he's doing,' George said.

'Good point. The trouble is we still don't know where he is. If he's not inside, then perhaps he's watching from somewhere. Or he might turn up later. Meena, we'll keep going as planned, so wait for my text and leave.'

'Will do, guv.'

Once Meena had left, Whitney grinned at George. 'Well,

tell me, how's it going with Claire? To quote Brian, you certainly look like an "odd couple".'

George frowned. 'Why?'

'Because you're so different.' Whitney sighed. George wouldn't get it. 'Anyway, nothing to report, I take it?'

'Unless the killer is heavily disguised, he's not in here. But that doesn't mean he won't show up.'

31

Saturday

'Okay, everyone, it looks like our guy hasn't taken the bait because he's nowhere to be seen,' Whitney said into her mic once they'd left the pub an hour later and were standing in the foyer. 'Meena's going to leave shortly and will meet Brian and me at our car. Frank and Doug, watch and make sure she gets to her car. She's in the pub car park and is driving a white Honda, which she's parked at the back. We don't want anything to happen to her outside. Our man could still be here watching out of sight somewhere.'

Disappointment coursed through Whitney. She'd been convinced that they'd catch the guy, but it now seemed unlikely. She walked to the door and scanned the area. There was nobody around, apart from a young couple who had left the pub a few seconds before Whitney and Brian and were heading hand in hand up the street towards the city centre.

'We have a full view of outside the pub, guv. I assume

Meena will go to the car park from the side entrance,' Frank said.

'I don't know, but we'll watch and see.'

Whitney texted George to let her know that they were leaving and said if they wanted to leave now, they could and that she'd phone her in the morning. George texted back almost immediately to say that they would be leaving shortly.

After a few minutes, George and Claire walked past in silence, not acknowledging Whitney or Brian. Whitney hoped the evening hadn't proved too difficult for George. If the expression on both of their faces was anything to go by, it hadn't been a riot. And the fact they'd left the moment they'd been told they could was probably an indicator of how it had gone. Not that it mattered; they were there for work, not to socialise.

Five minutes later, Meena exited the main pub area and walked past them. She cast a quick glance in their direction and gave a slight nod before turning left and heading out of the side entrance. Frank had been correct.

Once she had left, Whitney and Brian left through the front door. They walked up the road to the car and waited for Meena to arrive.

'Where is she?' Whitney muttered, glancing at her watch for the tenth time. 'It doesn't take this long to get in your car and drive a hundred yards up the road. She's been five minutes already.' She pressed her mic. 'Doug, has Meena driven out of the car park yet?'

'No, guv. Maybe she's on the phone. I watched her leave the pub, walk down the path and get into her car as you requested. No one else has walked or driven down there since Meena, nor has anyone come out of the pub from either entrance. We've been watching the whole time. She's perfectly safe.'

Was she?

Something wasn't sitting right.

Why would Meena be chatting on the phone when Whitney and Brian, both of whom were her superior officers, were waiting for her to meet them? That wasn't like Meena at all. She was one of the most reliable members of the team. Unless there had been news about her father. But would Meena even have taken a call from anyone during the operation?

The hairs rose on the back of her neck. Nothing about this was okay.

'Can you still see her car, Doug?' she asked with urgency.

'Hang on, guv. I'll look.'

What?

'I thought you watched her get into it. Have you moved?' she snapped, instantly regretting it because it wasn't his fault.

'We did watch, guv. Well, I did. Her car wasn't visible from where we'd parked, so I got out of mine and kept an eye on Meena until she'd unlocked and climbed into the front seat of her car. It was all clear, and no one tried to stop her. I made sure of it.'

Then where the hell was she? The officer couldn't just disappear into thin air.

'Are you *now* in a position where you can see her car?' she demanded after a few seconds.

'Yes, guv. And Meena's car is exactly where she'd parked it. Nothing has changed. She's got to be on the phone or doing something. It's only been a few minutes,' Doug said.

Was she overreacting? If she was, she didn't care. Meena's safety came first.

'Can you see whether she's sitting in the front seat?'

Doug let out a sigh. 'I can't, guv. I'm sorry, but it's too dark to tell. There are no lights near where she's parked.'

'Something's not right. Run down and check whether she's okay, Doug. I'm on my way and will meet you there.' She ended the call, grabbed her bag from the floor of the car and turned to Brian. 'Quick, follow me. I'm concerned about Meena. Her car's still there, but we don't know if she is.'

She leapt out of the car and ran down the street in the direction of the pub. Her feet pounded the pavement. Soon she was gasping for breath, but she didn't stop. She couldn't believe how unfit she was. Brian sprinted past her, and she ended up following him down the path that led to the car park. When they reached the white Honda, she dragged in some much-needed breaths. Doug was already there and had opened the driver's door. He was peering inside.

That told her everything.

'Meena's gone. Her handbag's on the passenger seat.' Doug went to grab it, when Whitney pulled him back.

'Stop. It's evidence. If he's got Meena, he must be on foot because no cars came out of the car park.'

'If anything happens to Meena, it will be all my fault,' Doug said, running a hand through his hair. 'I swear we thought she was safe. I watched with my own eyes when she got into the car. There was no one around. No one. And now—'

'Doug, stop. Our priority now is to find her. Anything else will be discussed later. She pressed her mic. 'Frank, get backup here straight away. Meena's missing. I want the whole area cut off. At the moment, they're on foot, but we don't know if he's got a car somewhere close. We ...' Her voice cracked, but she covered it with a cough. She had to remain strong. For Meena and the rest of the team. 'We can't let him get away.'

'I'm on it, guv,' Frank said.

Whitney scanned the area. If he had got Meena, then where would he go, and how could he disappear without being spotted? There was only one way in and one way out of the car park. Was he hiding in one of the parked cars?

'Check all the cars,' she said to Doug and Brian. 'I'll take the ones closest, and you split up and take the others.'

There were at least twenty cars dotted around the car park, and she took the two adjacent to Meena's Honda, a blue Mini, and a maroon Golf. She peered in all the windows, and both were empty. She tried the boots, but they were locked. She then went over to a red Toyota and peered into the window.

'Guv, over here,' Brian shouted from where he was standing beside a brick wall that stood about two feet in height.

She ran over, with Doug following.

'What is it?' she asked.

'Look at how scuffed the grass is beneath the wall.' He shone his torch on to the grassed area. 'Someone has jumped over there. It could be him with Meena.'

Whitney stared at the ground that Brian had lit up. Someone had definitely been there. Whether it was the killer with Meena, it wasn't possible to tell, but it was the only lead they had.

'Where does this wasteland lead to?' she asked, turning to face the officers.

'I don't know, guv,' Brian said.

'Me neither,' Doug added.

That made three of them. Despite living in Lenchester her entire life, she wasn't familiar with this part of the city.

'Shall we split up and each take a different direction?' Brian asked.

'No. It's too dangerous. Look at the way the grass is scuffed more on that side. I'd say that if he's dragging Meena and she's resisting, then it makes sense that they're heading west. We'll go that way. But keep quiet. We don't want to alert him.' Whitney turned on the torch app on her phone, climbed over the wall and headed in that direction, praying that she'd got it right.

They ran a few steps when Brian sidled over to her. 'Guv, I can hear a noise. It sounds like voices,' he whispered.

She held up her hand to indicate they should stop moving. They stood perfectly still and listened. Echoing from north of where they were heading was the muffled sound of someone shouting.

'Quick, this way,' she said, racing in the direction of the sound.

She ran through the undergrowth and over a clump over thistles. A thorn stabbed her leg, and she forced back a groan. They didn't want to alert the killer.

They continued running until they reached a small clearing. She stopped and shone her torch. The beam landed on a man struggling with a woman.

It was Meena. Her arms flailing.

Brian barged past Whitney, sprinted towards them, and grabbed the man around the neck. 'Get off her,' he yelled, yanking him off Meena and throwing him to the ground.

The man rolled to the side, jumped up, and took off, stumbling slightly.

Doug and Brian took off after him.

He'd only got five metres when Brian did a flying tackle,

grabbed hold of the assailant's body and forced him to the ground, landing on top of him.

Whitney ran to Meena and pulled her into her arms. 'It's okay. You're okay. It's safe, now,' she whispered. Just because Meena was an officer, it didn't mean that she wouldn't be affected by what had happened. She needed to be reassured.

'Guv, am I glad to see you,' Meena said, giving a shaky smile and pulling out of Whitney's hold. 'He was in my car. I don't know how he got in there because it was locked. I'm sure of it. I remember double-checking before going into the pub.'

'We'll find out what happened later. Wait here for a moment. I won't be long.'

She ran over to Brian, who was straddled across the killer's face-down body, pinning him to the ground. 'Cuff him,' she said to Doug.

He pulled out his handcuffs, crouched down, and grabbed both of the assailant's arms, and slipped on the cuffs. Brian got off the man and pulled him by the arm until he was standing.

'Who the hell are you?' Brian said, pulling off the black balaclava.

Whitney's jaw dropped. What the ...?

It was Wilson Neash. The disabled man who lived opposite Gray and came to see them with Josie Merton.

'You?' she spluttered. 'But you're—'

'Not the pathetic disabled busybody you thought I was,' Neash snarled, his top lip curling. 'You're bloody lucky this lot arrived when they did,' he said to Meena, who had walked over to where they were all standing, smoothing down her crumpled top.

'My officer can take care of herself,' Whitney said, not allowing him to believe he could have succeeded.

'What?' Neash said, his eyes darting from Meena to Whitney.

'Yes, that's right. Meena's a police officer and was working undercover. So you're not as clever as you think. Wilson Neash, I'm arresting you on suspicion of the murder of Paula Moore, the attempted murder of Lorna Knight, and for sexual assaults on Jessie Wood, Cheryl Hughes, and Tina Bennett. You do not have to say anything, but it may harm your defence if you do not mention something which you later rely on in court. Anything you do say may be given in evidence. Do you understand?'

'Whatever,' he grunted.

She turned her back on him and headed over to the uniformed officers who'd joined them. 'Take him away,' she said.

32

Sunday

'Are you up?' Whitney said when George answered her phone.

George glanced at the clock. It was seven-thirty in the morning. She'd been in her study since six, wanting to get some reading done in preparation for the research project she was about to start. Ross had suggested they go out for the day if the weather was good, to get away from all the unpacking and sorting. She could hear him stirring upstairs.

'Yes.'

'How quickly can you get here? We've caught the murderer. He went after Meena when she left the pub.'

'Why didn't you phone last night?'

'Because by the time he'd been processed, it was late, and I didn't want to disturb you. We're interviewing him when his solicitor arrives later this morning, which is why I've called now, hoping that you'll be able to observe. And …

you'll never guess in a million years who the murderer turned out to be.'

George hated these games. Was she meant to name everyone they'd come across during the investigation before being told who he was?

'Whitney, I don't intend to guess. Tell me who it is.'

'It's Wilson Neash. You remember him, the—'

'Disabled man who came to see us with Josie Merton. They live opposite Kyle Gray. Goodness me. So the disability was an act. There was nothing about the way he behaved which caused me to suspect him.'

That was the second time she'd slipped up. Was she so preoccupied with her personal life that vital evidence had eluded her? She couldn't let that happen again.

'I know, right? He had both of us well and truly fooled when he came here. He seemed so gentle and submissive and let Josie Merton do all the talking. Now we know for certain that he was framing Gray. But we don't know why.'

'Was Josie involved?'

'I don't believe so, but we'll have to look into it. I think he just used her. What time can you get here?'

'In an hour.' She stood up from her desk and headed towards the door. She'd need to explain to Ross that their day out together would have to be postponed.

'We're not expecting his solicitor until ten, so that gives us plenty of time to prepare.'

'How's Meena, after the ordeal?' George had almost forgotten to ask.

'She was okay last night, but I suspect the shock might hit her today. I've told her not to come in and to spend time at home with her family. I'll give her a call later.'

'She may need some counselling.'

'Yes, I know. We have procedures in place for times like these, so no need to worry about her.'

After ending the call with Whitney, George informed Ross that their plans were changing and then headed into Lenchester. When she arrived, at a few minutes before eight-thirty, she went straight to the incident room, where Whitney was standing near the board with the others.

'Ah, George, you're here. Good. We have a search warrant for Wilson Neash's house. His solicitor's been in touch and put back the interview until eleven-thirty, so that gives us time to make a thorough search of his place and see what evidence we can turn up.'

'I've been pondering how we could have been so taken in by him when he came to the station. Then again, because he left most of the talking to Josie, it took the focus off of him. He ...' Her voice fell away as she caught sight of the names that had been written on the board.

It had been staring her in the face the whole time, and she hadn't seen it.

'What is it?' Whitney asked.

George pointed at the board. 'The man Paula Moore met with at the café. He was called Shanon Lewis.'

'What about it?'

'Can't you see? How did I not notice sooner?' She hit her forehead with the palm of her hand. If only she'd been concentrating properly during the investigation and not had her head full of Ross's proposal, then they could have discovered who the murderer was sooner. Not that she could have prevented it from happening, but certainly, they wouldn't have had to put Meena in danger.

'Sorry, you'll have to tell me. I'm totally lost here,' Whitney said, shaking her head.

'*Shanon Lewis* is an anagram of *Wilson Neash*.'

'You mean all this time, the name of the murderer was staring us in the face?' Whitney said, open-mouthed, gawping at the board.

'Yes,' George said.

'Listen up, everyone. George has just pointed out that the name *Shanon Lewis* is an anagram of *Wilson Neash*.'

'So he was playing with us the whole time. Coming in to see us. Leading us to Gray.' Doug said.

'What a wanker,' Frank said. 'Why the hell would he do that? I suppose he thought he was too clever for us to work it out. The arrogant bastard. Well, he didn't get away with it. Good call, Dr C.'

Except George didn't see it that way. Discovering it straight away would have made it a good call, not seeing it after the event.

'It's more evidence for us to present to the CPS. We'll meet you at Neash's house, and we'll conduct the search.'

George drove Whitney out to Hilton Road in Cotton Fields, and they waited for Frank and Doug to arrive before going into the house.

'Frank, go out into the garden and check what's out there, see if there's a shed and what's in it. Doug, you take the living room and kitchen, and we'll go upstairs.'

'Why do you always take the upstairs, guv?' Frank asked.

'You know what, Frank. That's a very good question, and one I don't have an answer for. Maybe I like rummaging through people's clothes.' Whitney glanced at George and grinned.

'Or maybe it's because that's where we find most of the evidence,' Frank said, arching an eyebrow.

'That could be the case, but right now, it doesn't matter because we don't have all day to complete this search. So, off you go. Come on, George.'

Whitney marched up the narrow stairs with George behind.

Frank had been right about them always searching upstairs, at least when George was with her that's what they did. But George had put it down to habit rather than anything else, and over the years that they'd known each other, despite her outward appearance, Whitney was a creature of habit.

'Where do you want to look first?' George asked.

'I'll take the front room, and you take the back. The bathroom will most likely be in between the two.'

George glanced at her friend. 'Is everything okay? You don't seem your normal self.'

'You're right. I'm cross with myself for allowing Meena to be attacked. I thought everything had been covered, but it hadn't. Neash somehow managed to get into the back of Meena's car, without being seen, and wait for her. I couldn't sleep last night going over and over what could have happened if we hadn't rescued her in time. I was so concerned with catching the bastard that I went along with an ill-thought-out plan.'

'It wasn't "ill thought out". And you did everything by the book. All undercover operations come with an element of risk. Focus on the fact that Meena is fine and Neash is in custody. Replaying everything won't change it. If anything, it will stop you from focusing on what's important at the moment, and that's ensuring that Neash is successfully prosecuted for what he's done.'

'You're right, of course. You're fast becoming the person who knows me best. And who'd have thought it when you consider you're not exactly top of the class in respect of social cues.'

'Is that a compliment?' George wasn't sure what Whitney meant by that.

'I'll leave you to work that out. In a way I suppose we're lucky it was Meena he went for because we had her covered. What if he'd decided to attack another woman at the meeting?'

'He wouldn't have. We know how he planned everything in detail. Even with short notice, he'd have made sure to prepare. It wouldn't fit his profile for him to randomly select someone else.'

Whitney nodded'. You're right, of course. Okay, let's start. Here are your gloves.'

George slipped on the gloves and went to the back room, which was set up as an office. There was a desk along the far wall, and on there were two laptops, both open. She pressed keys on both of them but they were locked.

'George, come and look in the bedroom,' Whitney said, poking her head into the room. 'We'll need to take these with us and send them down to forensics. Anything of use that you could see in his computers?'

'Nothing. I couldn't get in. Shall we call Ellie and see if she can help?'

'Not yet. Come and see what I've found.'

George followed Whitney into the bedroom. On the bed was a box with the lid lying beside it. Whitney picked up a Polaroid photo of Lorna Knight and held it out for her to look at, followed by a hair slide.

'His trophies,' George said.

'Why didn't he leave them in Gray's house rather than keeping them for himself?'

'There could be several reasons, including him deriving pleasure from the assaults in their own right and not simply because of his intent to frame Gray. But this should help you frame your interview questions.'

'Definitely.'

'Guv.' Doug walked into the room, holding what looked like a photograph album in his hand. 'Look at this. I found it in the sideboard.'

He handed it to Whitney and stood beside her and George while each page was turned over.

'It's like a shrine to this one woman,' Whitney said.

George agreed. All the photos featured the same woman, and in some of them she was with Neash. There were also theatre tickets, train tickets, and dried flowers. 'Some of these photos look as if they were taken without her knowledge. I suspect he was following her. In this one, she's sitting in a café with another woman, and this is snapped from outside. You can see the reflection of the glass.'

'Well, we know that he's an expert in stalking, so that could be how he learnt to be so discreet. Maybe this woman ended the relationship with him, and he was so devastated that he decided to stalk her. But who is she?' Whitney turned to George. 'Do you think this could be related to his motivation for the assaults and murder?'

'Until we interview him, we won't know. But it's highly likely, considering that this has been so lovingly created, and it's dedicated to only one person.'

'Right. We've seen enough. Bag up the evidence. We've plenty to discuss with Neash.'

33

Sunday

'Ellie, we need to get into these laptops, can you help?' Whitney said when they arrived back at the station.

'Leave it with me, guv,' Ellie said, taking them from her.

'I'd like to know if there's anything we can use in the interview.' Whitney said, glancing at her watch. 'We've still got some time before the solicitor is here, let's grab a coffee and bring it back here,' she said, turning to George.

When they returned, ten minutes later, Ellie beckoned them over. 'I've got into this one, guv.' She handed a laptop to Whitney, who took it over to an empty desk and stood to the side while George started going through it.

'Interesting,' George muttered.

'What is it?'

'I've found several spreadsheets, and from all of the detailed entries, I'd say that once he decided who from the social media group he was going to target, he'd locate them from their IP address so he could start tracking them and their movements and decide a time when he could attack them,' George said.

'Does he use a separate spreadsheet for each victim?'

'There are a number of different workbooks. Jessie Wood is the first name, so it looks like he started his attacks with her, assuming that everything is in chronological order, which I believe it is.'

'Are there any victims we don't know about?' Whitney asked.

'There's a Belinda Frampton and also someone between Cheryl and Tina.'

'So that's two more. I'll ask Ellie to find out more. We want to charge him for all of the attacks, not just the ones we're aware of. Is there anything on the computer that explains why he started with Jessie Wood?'

'Not that I've discovered, but this really has been a cursory look,' George said.

'Forensics might come up with something.'

'Guv. Neash's solicitor has arrived,' Frank called out.

'We're on our way.'

When Whitney and Brian entered the interview room, the solicitor was flicking through some papers, and Wilson Neash was sitting upright in the green plastic chair, a belligerent expression plastered across his face. The clothes he had been wearing during Meena's assault had been sent to forensics, and now he had on a blue T-shirt and a pair of grey jogging bottoms. Whitney sat opposite him, and he rolled his eyes in contempt.

If that was the way the man wanted to play it, Whitney was happy to oblige. He wouldn't get the better of her.

She placed her folder on the table and indicated to Brian to start the recording equipment.

'Interview on Sunday, September 18. Those present: DCI

Walker, DS Chapman and ...' She nodded at the man sitting opposite Brian.

'Roy Evans, solicitor.'

'And ...' She stared at Neash.

'Wilson. Leonard. Neash,' the man said in a patronising manner.

'Mr Neash, we're here to discuss with you the recent murder of Paula Moore, the attempted murder of Lorna Knight, sexual assaults on a number of women, and the attempted rape of a police officer.' Whitney opened the folder in front of her.

'No comment.'

Whitney could cheerfully slap every suspect who said 'no comment'. It wouldn't make any difference. She'd continue and wait for him to start talking. They invariably did, once she'd pushed the right buttons.

'When we searched your house, we found some very interesting items.' She opened the folder and slid over a photocopy of the album cover. 'Let's start with this, shall we?'

Neash glanced down at the photo and clenched his fists. 'No comment,' he said through clenched teeth.

'Really? From all the photos and keepsakes in the album, I'd say the woman is very important to you. Why don't you tell me about her?' Whitney leant back in the chair and stared directly at Neash, the hint of a smile on her face.

'No.'

Well, that was better than the "no comment" Maybe she'd crack him sooner rather than later.

'Okay, we'll come back to that later. While we were searching your house, in your office, we found two laptops, and on one of them there were spreadsheets containing details of women you have stalked, raped and, in the case of Paula Moore, murdered. We have more than enough evidence to charge you, whether you cooperate or not. But what we're really interested in, is why you framed Kyle Gray for them all?'

Neash stiffened.

'You've hit a nerve there, Whitney,' George said in her ear. 'His anger towards Kyle Gray was blatantly obvious when you mentioned his name. His nostrils flared, and he made a jerky movement with his head. And now he's closing his eyes in an attempt to distance himself from his memories. It's classic stuff. Push him hard.'

'Mr Neash,' Whitney snapped, causing him to open his eyes and scowl in her direction. 'Your body language when I mentioned Kyle Gray was very interesting. Clearly, you feel considerable anger towards him. Perhaps you'd like to tell me about it.'

He scowled. 'No comment.'

'Come on, Mr Neash. You can tell me. Kyle Gray rubs you up the wrong way, big time. What did he do? It must have been really bad if you were prepared to commit rape and murder simply to frame him.' The man's eyebrow twitched. 'Especially as you would have known that if caught, you'd be spending the rest of your life in prison. What on earth could be worth you doing that?'

She locked eyes with him, and he stared right back, almost as if he couldn't break the link between them.

'I'll tell you what that bastard did,' Neash finally said, his eyes blazing. 'He destroyed my life.' He paused, and his eyes glazed over a little.

Good. Now she was getting somewhere.

'How did he do that?' Whitney asked.

'He took away, Deirdre, the one woman I ever loved.

We'd been together since school, but when he came along with all his fancy clothes and typical salesman patter she changed. He showered her with gifts, things that I could never have afforded in a month of Sundays, and suddenly, I was out on my ear, and instead, she wanted him. It was like the twenty years of us being together meant nothing. And you know what? It didn't even last.'

'Did you try to get her back when they had finished?' Whitney asked.

'I didn't know they'd split up until it was too late. It wasn't until I saw her death announced in the paper two years ago that I found out she'd had cancer and died. I would have taken her back if she'd asked. But she didn't.'

So that was the motivation. A broken heart. Bloody hell, talk about going to the extreme. But it wasn't for her to judge. She wanted a full confession from him. One that would stand up in court should he decide to plead not guilty and opt for a trial.

'We know Deirdre had a twenty-ninth of February birthday, and you only targeted women with the same. Why? It couldn't have been easy finding targets.'

'That was the whole point. To make it all mean something.'

'It all seems a very complicated way of getting your revenge. Why didn't you arrange for him to be beaten up instead? Or even murder him? Then it would all have been over. But this?' Whitney said, fixing him with an incredulous stare.

'That's why you and me are different. You're a copper. You can only think inside the box. To me, it was perfectly straightforward. I wanted to put him in hell, just like I've been since he walked into my life and wrecked it. Death or being beaten up wouldn't come anywhere close to what he deserved. I wanted him in prison and labelled a sex offender for the rest of his life.' He thrust out his chin and looked down his nose at Whitney and Brian.

'Whitney, if you want to get more from him, then pander to his arrogance. Tell him how clever he is,' George said.

'Okay, I get it now. Smart move on your part, and you're right, I wouldn't have twigged. Why don't you tell us exactly how you managed to frame Gray?' Whitney relaxed her shoulders and sat back in the chair.

She'd let him feel superior for now. Because it wouldn't be for long.

Neash turned and looked at his solicitor. 'Fuck it, why shouldn't I tell you? It's not like I'm denying anything.'

The solicitor shook his head and let out a sigh.

Whitney stole a glance at Brian, who was, like her, leaning back, waiting to hear the rest of the story, already conscious that Neash had admitted everything.

'The floor's yours,' Whitney said, gesturing with her hand.

'I kept an eye on Gray after I knew that Deirdre was dead and saw that he was on his own. I couldn't believe my luck when the house opposite where he lived came up to rent. I'd never met him in person, so I was confident he wouldn't know who I was. And even if he had seen a photo of me from the past, I made sure to look very different.'

'Why did you pretend to be disabled? Surely simply changing your outward appearance would've done the job,' Whitney asked, curious why he'd gone to such lengths.

'I wanted to make sure that no one connected me to Gray. My mother was disabled, and the thing about being in a wheelchair is that people don't pay you any attention. If they're used to seeing a disabled man, they won't recognise me when I'm able-bodied. People often only see the disability and not the person. I work from home anyway, so it made no difference to my working life. No one saw me behind closed doors. And outside, I was invisible. It was inspired, if I say so myself.'

She couldn't disagree. Not that she'd tell him that.

'And Josie, was she part of this?'

Neash rolled his eyes. 'Do me a favour. I've got more intelligence in my little finger than she has in her whole head. I just used her, so you didn't start suspecting me. Pathetic woman. I let her think that coming to you was all her idea.'

'But what if she hadn't seen the press conference on the television?' Whitney asked.

'She keeps her telly on all day and always watches the news. I knew she'd see it.'

'And your plan to infiltrate the social media group. How did you come up with it?' Whitney asked.

'I'd decided to target women born on the twenty-ninth of February and knew about this group because Deirdre had been a member of it. I used a fake name and sent the IP address to Gray's house. It was so easy. Once in the group, I friended women who lived within a forty-mile radius of Lenchester. I methodically discovered all about them. I had a selection of women in my sights, and from there, chose the easiest targets.'

'Had you targeted my officer before last night?'

'No. I didn't realise she was an officer, and she hadn't been on my radar at all. But I couldn't resist going to the meeting. Well, I didn't actually attend, or I'd have noticed police in there. Once Meena was inside, I let myself into her car. I had wondered if it was a set-up, but I made sure to have Gray in the frame anyway, in case it wasn't. What caught me out was Meena being one of you lot. A stupid error on my part. If I'd have figured that out, I wouldn't be here.' He stared at Whitney, drumming the fingers from both hands on the table.

'What I don't understand is how you managed to get into my officer's car, which was locked?'

'Easy. I've got a device that can capture a fob's signal from a distance.'

Whitney could seriously slap the smug expression from his face. But of course, she wouldn't. No way would she jeopardise the case.

'I see. How did you manage to frame Kyle Gray and have him in the vicinity of all the attacks?' Whitney asked,

'That was easy. I hacked into his computer, found out where his appointments were going to be, and made fake appointments for him when it was during the day. Discovered he was on a dating app, so made fake dates with him to make sure his car would be seen in the vicinity. It's such elementary stuff, a kid could do it.'

'And the anagram of your name when arranging to meet Paula Moore? What was that all about?'

Neash sat back in his chair, his hands behind his head. 'You worked that out, did you? I didn't think you would. But you can't have sussed it until recently, or you would've brought me in for questioning. It was a game I played with myself. I wanted to see how clever you were. It turns out, not very.' He leant back in the chair and steepled his fingers behind his head.

'Except you're here under arrest. So I'd say we did well.' Whitney paused for a moment. 'Why did you move from rape to murder?'

Neash lowered his arms until his hands were in his lap. Whitney couldn't fathom the expression on his face.

'This became more to him than simple revenge,' George said in her ear.

'I suggest that you got off on it, didn't you?'

'No comment.'

'You started off by raping these women with a clear motive of framing Kyle Gray. But you enjoyed it more than you thought you would. You derived a feeling of power from it. And then it got to the stage where you had to strangle your victims because it gave you sexual satisfaction. Am I right?' Whitney demanded, leaning forward and locking eyes with him.

'So what if I did?' He glared angrily at Whitney.

'And when you told them if they screamed that you'd cut out their tongue, what was that all about?'

'It was a threat. It meant nothing. And even if it did, so what? Are you now trying to psychoanalyse me? Because you're not smart enough.'

The solicitor tapped him on the arm, leant in, and said something quietly.

'That's it. My client won't be answering any more questions. He's given you as much as you're going to get today,' the solicitor said.

Whitney didn't care. She had enough to present to the Crown Prosecution Service. Neash had admitted everything, which meant if he pleaded guilty, then he'd go straight for sentencing. She hoped so. Otherwise, all the girls who'd been attacked would have to relive their experience in court.

'Fine. I'll arrange for someone to take you back to the cell.' Whitney gathered up her folder and left the interview room with Brian.

George was in the corridor waiting for them.

'Nicely done,' George said. 'He opened up far more than I thought he would.'

'Thanks. Brian, go to the custody suite and arrange for Neash to be escorted back. We'll see you back upstairs.'

'Yes, guv.'

He walked on ahead, and Whitney and George took the lift upstairs. When they stepped out, the super was walking along the corridor.

'Whitney, I was on the way to speak to you, to thank you and the team for a job well done,' she said.

'Thank you, ma'am.'

'How's DC Singh?'

'She was a little shaken, obviously, and I'll be making a full report regarding what happened. I've given her a couple of days off, and once she's back, we will sit down together and talk it through.'

'Be sure to advise her that there is counselling available for her, should she need it.'

Whitney was hardly going to forget that. There were protocols in place, and she would follow them.

'Yes, ma'am. I'll make sure to do that.'

'We need to arrange a press conference to announce that the murder has been solved and to inform the public about the historic sexual assault cases. There may have been others, and it will encourage women to come forward.'

'On Neash's laptops we did find evidence of other attacks, ma'am. I've asked DC Naylor to look into them and we'll follow up as soon as she has anything.'

'Good. With a bit of luck, you will have found them all.'

'Yes, ma'am. I'd like to inform the victims that we have charged someone, before you announce it to the press. We'll get onto that straight away.'

'Of course. Once you have, let me know and also make sure I have all the necessary information for the press conference? There's no need for you to attend, unless you specifically wish to.'

'Thank you, ma'am, but no. I'll leave it to you. I have work that requires my attention. I'll ensure all the case details are with you shortly. I'm assuming that we won't yet be releasing names.'

'Not until the CPS has decided whether or not to press charges, which is a formality, as you know.'

'Dr Dexter, the pathologist, will be delighted at the result,' Whitney said.

The super frowned. 'For any specific reason?'

'She's using the case for a workshop to illustrate how pathology works with the police.'

'Oh, I see. Well, as long as confidentiality isn't breached, I see no harm in it.'

'It definitely won't be, ma'am.'

The super turned and headed back the way she'd come.

'It was very considerate of Superintendent Clyde to say thank you,' George said once they were out of earshot.

'You're telling me. Can you imagine Jamieson being like that?' Whitney said, referring to her previous boss who so rarely set foot in their old incident room that anyone would have been forgiven for thinking that he didn't know it existed. 'Right, now Frank can have the celebration he'd been asking for. Will you be coming to the pub with us? I wanted to find out how your evening with Claire went.'

'No, I've got to get home. Thanks for asking, though,' George said.

'And Claire?' Whitney sighed. Getting information from George was like pushing treacle uphill.

'We discussed the workshop that she's going to be giving and also some of the current research findings in both of our fields.'

'And that's it? Nothing personal, just boring work?' Whitney shook her head.

'It's not boring to us.'

'Sorry, I know that. I just thought that being out together you might have ... I don't know ... told a few jokes, talked about Ross and Ralph ...'

'Whitney, why would I discuss personal matters with Claire when I have you?'

'True. In which case, please tell me if the reason you're going home now and not coming to the pub is because you're going to give Ross your answer?'

'It means I'll be talking to him about it. I'll see you tomorrow at the funeral.'

George turned and left Whitney staring at her retreating back. Would there be a wedding or not?

34

Monday

The chapel at the crematorium was full, and George, Whitney, Ellie, Frank, and Doug had only been able to get seats at the back. The service had been both poignant and funny as a celebration of Leigh's life took place. Once the service was over, they filed outside into the bright, sunny day.

'For such a private couple, they certainly have a lot of friends and were well liked,' Whitney said.

'A lot of them were from the amateur dramatic society that they both belonged to,' Ellie said with a dismissive wave of her hand.

'What? Matt was into am-dram?' Whitney said.

She could no more imagine him on stage spouting Shakespeare than she could see Dickhead Douglas inviting her out for a meal. Never going to happen.

'Leigh was the one who acted, and Matt helped out behind the scenes, painting scenery and stuff like that.'

'After all the years of working with him, he never once mentioned it to me. But you were very close with him, weren't you?'

'We were at work, and we did occasionally socialise with them. Dean and I went to watch the play *Abigail's Party*. Leigh was amazing in the lead role,' Ellie said.

'I'd loved to have seen it. Do you know what his plans are for the future? Have you been in touch with him?' Whitney asked Ellie.

'I did phone and spoke to him briefly. He's thinking of relocating to Cornwall when his parents move there so they can help with the baby.'

'What about work?'

'He said he'll apply for a job at one of the local forces.'

'What about Leigh's family, are they happy with his decision?'

'He didn't say. I'm not sure whether they're in a position to help or not, being in Canada. They're here for the funeral, but I don't know when they're planning to go back. It must be so awful for them,' Ellie said.

'I'll be in touch with him before he goes.'

'Yes, I know he'll be glad to hear from you. He's always asking how you're doing.'

'Were you invited back to the house after the funeral?' Whitney asked.

'No. It's just very close family.'

'Okay, I'll see you all back at the office.'

Whitney headed over to George's car with her.

'Were you upset because Ellie knew more about Matt's plans than you did?' George asked.

'Typical of you to get straight to the point,' Whitney said, giving a hollow laugh. 'Not really, because that was Matt.

Well ... maybe a little. But I'm glad he confided in someone else, other than me. Remember, I was his boss, and even though I did know certain things going on in his life, there was still distance between us. I will try to see him, though, before he leaves. Cornwall is hours away. Not sure I could live there with all those winding roads.'

'It's a beautiful place, and there's some stunning scenery and historic sites to look at. Ross and I have discussed going there for a holiday at some time.'

'Speaking of Ross, did you have your discussion yesterday, and if so, what was the upshot?' Whitney asked, looking at her friend.

'I'm going to say yes,' George said.

Whitney took a step back in shock. George had taken far less time to decide than she would have expected.

'George, that's fantastic.' She gave the woman a big hug. 'What about bridesmaids? Do you know, in my whole life I've never been one? Or maybe you think I'm too old? Or maybe you have others lined up?'

'I haven't actually given it any thought. I'll let you know when the time comes.'

'I can't wait. I hope you let me help choose your dress.'

'Whitney, slow down. I'm not having a full white wedding. I have no desire to parade myself in front of hundreds of people. It will be a quiet affair, with only a few, very select, people attending.'

'Oh, I see.' Whitney couldn't hide the dejected tone in her voice. If it was going to be very small, then she probably won't even be invited.

'But you will be one of them.'

∾

GET ANOTHER BOOK FOR FREE!

TO INSTANTLY RECEIVE the free novella, **The Night Shift**, featuring Whitney when she was a Detective Sergeant, ten years ago, sign up for Sally Rigby's free author newsletter at www.sallyrigby.com

READ MORE ABOUT CAVENDISH & WALKER

DEADLY GAMES - Cavendish & Walker Book 1

A killer is playing cat and mouse....... and winning.

DCI Whitney Walker wants to save her career. Forensic psychologist, Dr Georgina Cavendish, wants to avenge the death of her student.

Sparks fly when real world policing meets academic theory, and it's not a pretty sight.

When two more bodies are discovered, Walker and Cavendish form an uneasy alliance. But are they in time to save the next victim?

Deadly Games is the first book in the Cavendish and Walker crime fiction series. If you like serial killer thrillers and psychological intrigue, then you'll love Sally Rigby's page-turning book.

Pick up *Deadly Games* today to read Cavendish & Walker's first case.

FATAL JUSTICE - Cavendish & Walker Book 2

A vigilante's on the loose, dishing out their kind of justice...

A string of mutilated bodies sees Detective Chief Inspector Whitney Walker back in action. But when she discovers the victims have all been grooming young girls, she fears a vigilante is on the loose. And while she understands the motive, no one is above the law.

Once again, she turns to forensic psychologist, Dr Georgina Cavendish, to unravel the cryptic clues. But will they be able to save the next victim from a gruesome death?

Fatal Justice is the second book in the Cavendish & Walker crime fiction series. If you like your mysteries dark, and with a twist, pick up a copy of Sally Rigby's book today.

∽

DEATH TRACK - Cavendish & Walker Book 3

Catch the train if you dare...

After a teenage boy is found dead on a Lenchester train, Detective Chief Inspector Whitney Walker believes they're being targeted by the notorious Carriage Killer, who chooses a local rail network, commits four murders, and moves on.

Against her wishes, Walker's boss brings in officers from another force to help the investigation and prevent more deaths, but she's forced to defend her team against this outside interference.

Forensic psychologist, Dr Georgina Cavendish, is by her side in an attempt to bring to an end this killing spree. But how can they get into the mind of a killer who has already killed twelve times in two years without leaving a single clue behind?

For fans of Rachel Abbott, L J Ross and Angela Marsons, *Death Track* is the third in the Cavendish & Walker series. A gripping serial killer thriller that will have you hooked.

~

LETHAL SECRET - Cavendish & Walker Book 4

Someone has a secret. A secret worth killing for....

When a series of suicides, linked to the Wellness Spirit Centre, turn out to be murder, it brings together DCI Whitney Walker and forensic psychologist Dr Georgina Cavendish for another investigation. But as they delve deeper, they come across a tangle of secrets and the very real risk that the killer will strike again.

As the clock ticks down, the only way forward is to infiltrate the centre. But the outcome is disastrous, in more ways than one.

For fans of Angela Marsons, Rachel Abbott and M A Comley, *Lethal Secret* is the fourth book in the Cavendish & Walker crime fiction series.

~

LAST BREATH - Cavendish & Walker Book 5

Has the Lenchester Strangler returned?

When a murderer leaves a familiar pink scarf as his calling card, Detective Chief Inspector Whitney Walker is forced to dig into a cold case, not sure if she's looking for a killer or a copycat.

With a growing pile of bodies, and no clues, she turns to forensic psychologist, Dr Georgina Cavendish, despite their relationship being at an all-time low.

Can they overcome the bad blood between them to solve the

unsolvable?

For fans of Rachel Abbott, Angela Marsons and M A Comley, *Last Breath* is the fifth book in the Cavendish & Walker crime fiction series.

~

FINAL VERDICT - Cavendish & Walker Book 6

The judge has spoken......everyone must die.

When a killer starts murdering lawyers in a prestigious law firm, and every lead takes them to a dead end, DCI Whitney Walker finds herself grappling for a motive.

What links these deaths, and why use a lethal injection?

Alongside forensic psychologist, Dr Georgina Cavendish, they close in on the killer, while all the time trying to not let their personal lives get in the way of the investigation.

For fans of Rachel Abbott, Mark Dawson and M A Comley, Final Verdict is the sixth in the Cavendish & Walker series. A fast paced murder mystery which will keep you guessing.

~

RITUAL DEMISE - Cavendish & Walker Book 7

Someone is watching.... No one is safe

The once tranquil woods in a picturesque part of Lenchester have become the bloody stage to a series of ritualistic murders. With no suspects, Detective Chief Inspector Whitney Walker is once again forced to call on the services of forensic psychologist Dr Georgina Cavendish.

But this murderer isn't like any they've faced before. The murders are highly elaborate, but different in their own way and, with the clock ticking, they need to get inside the killer's head before it's too late.

For fans of Angela Marsons, Rachel Abbott and L J Ross. Ritual Demise is the seventh book in the Cavendish & Walker crime fiction series.

MORTAL REMAINS - Cavendish & Walker Book 8

Someone's playing with fire.... There's no escape.

A serial arsonist is on the loose and as the death toll continues to mount DCI Whitney Walker calls on forensic psychologist Dr Georgina Cavendish for help.

But Lenchester isn't the only thing burning. There are monumental changes taking place within the police force and there's a chance Whitney might lose the job she loves. She has to find the killer before that happens. Before any more lives are lost.

Mortal Remains is the eighth book in the acclaimed Cavendish & Walker series. Perfect for fans of Angela Marsons, Rachel Abbott and L J Ross.

SILENT GRAVES - Cavendish & Walker Book 9

Nothing remains buried forever...

When the bodies of two teenage girls are discovered on a building site, DCI Whitney Walker knows she's on the hunt for a killer. The problem is the murders happened in 1980 and this is her first case with the new team. What makes it even tougher is that with budgetary restrictions in place, she only has two weeks to solve it.

Once again, she enlists the help of forensic psychologist Dr Georgina Cavendish, but as she digs deeper into the past, she uncovers hidden truths that reverberate through the decades and into the present.

Silent Graves is the ninth book in the acclaimed Cavendish & Walker series. Perfect for fans of L J Ross, J M Dalgleish and Rachel Abbott.

∼

KILL SHOT - Cavendish & Walker Book 10

The game is over.....there's nowhere to hide.

When Lenchester's most famous sportsman is shot dead, DCI Whitney Walker and her team are thrown into the world of snooker.

She calls on forensic psychologist Dr Georgina Cavendish to assist, but the investigation takes them in a direction which has far-reaching, international ramifications.

Much to Whitney's annoyance, an officer from one of the Met's special squads is sent to assist.

But as everyone knows...three's a crowd.

Kill Shot is the tenth book in the acclaimed Cavendish & Walker series. Perfect for fans of Simon McCleave, J M Dalgleish, J R Ellis and Faith Martin.

DARK SECRETS - Cavendish & Walker Book 11

An uninvited guest...a deadly secret....and a terrible crime.

When a well-loved family of five are found dead sitting around their dining table with an untouched meal in front of them, it sends shockwaves throughout the community.

Was it a murder suicide, or was someone else involved?

It's one of DCI Whitney Walker's most baffling cases, and even with the help of forensic psychologist Dr Georgina Cavendish, they struggle to find any clues or motives to help them catch the killer.

But with a community in mourning and growing pressure to get answers, Cavendish and Walker are forced to go deeper into a murderer's mind than they've ever gone before.

Dark Secrets is the eleventh book in the Cavendish & Walker series. Perfect for fans of Angela Marsons, Joy Ellis and Rachel McLean.

BROKEN SCREAMS - Cavendish & Walker Book 12

Scream all you want, no one can hear you....

When an attempted murder is linked to a string of unsolved sexual attacks, Detective Chief Inspector Whitney Walker is incensed. All those women who still have sleepless nights because the man who terrorises their dreams is still on the loose.

Calling on forensic psychologist Dr Georgina Cavendish to help, they follow the clues and are alarmed to discover the victims all had one thing in common. Their birthdays were on the 29th February. The same date as a female officer on Whitney's team.

As the clock ticks down and they're no nearer to finding the truth, can they stop the villain before he makes sure his next victim will never scream again.

Broken Screams is the twelfth book in the acclaimed Cavendish & Walker series and is perfect for fans of Angela Marsons, Helen H Durrant and Rachel McClean.

OTHER BOOKS BY SALLY RIGBY

WEB OF LIES: A Midlands Crime Thriller (Detective Sebastian Clifford - Book 1)

A trail of secrets. A dangerous discovery. A deadly turn.

Police officer Sebastian Clifford never planned on becoming a private investigator. But when a scandal leads to the disbandment of his London based special squad, he finds himself out of a job. That is, until his cousin calls on him to investigate her husband's high-profile death, and prove that it wasn't a suicide.

Clifford's reluctant to get involved, but the more he digs, the more evidence he finds. With his ability to remember everything he's ever seen, he's the perfect person to untangle the layers of deceit.

He meets Detective Constable Bird, an underutilised detective at Market Harborough's police force, who refuses to give him access to the records he's requested unless he allows her to help with the investigation. Clifford isn't thrilled. The last time he worked as part of a team it ended his career.

But with time running out, Clifford is out of options. Together they must wade through the web of lies in the hope that they'll find the truth before it kills them.

Web of Lies is the first in the new Detective Sebastian Clifford series. Perfect for readers of Joy Ellis, Robert Galbraith and Mark Dawson.

∾

SPEAK NO EVIL: A Midlands Crime Thriller (Detective Sebastian Clifford - Book 2)

What happens when someone's too scared to speak?

Ex-police officer Sebastian Clifford had decided to limit his work as a private investigator, until Detective Constable Bird, aka Birdie, asks for his help.

Twelve months ago a young girl was abandoned on the streets of Market Harborough in shocking circumstances. Since then the child has barely spoken and with the police unable to trace her identity, they've given up.

The social services team in charge of the case worry that the child has an intellectual disability but Birdie and her aunt, who's fostering the little girl, disagree and believe she's gifted and intelligent, but something bad happened and she's living in constant fear.

Clifford trusts Birdie's instinct and together they work to find out who the girl is, so she can be freed from the past. But as secrets are uncovered, the pair realise it's not just the child who's in danger.

Speak No Evil is the second in the Detective Sebastian Clifford series. Perfect for readers of Faith Martin, Matt Brolly and Joy Ellis.

∾

NEVER TOO LATE: A Midlands Crime Thriller (Detective Sebastian Clifford - Book 3)

A vicious attack. A dirty secret. And a chance for justice

Ex-police officer Sebastian Clifford is quickly finding that life as a private investigator is never quiet. His doors have only been open a few weeks when DCI Whitney Walker approaches him to investigate the brutal attack that left her older brother, Rob, with irreversible brain damage.

For twenty years Rob had no memory of that night, but lately things are coming back to him, and Whitney's worried that her brother might, once again, be in danger.

Clifford knows only too well what it's like be haunted by the past, and so he agrees to help. But the deeper he digs, the more secrets he uncovers, and soon he discovers that Rob's not the only one in danger.

Never Too Late is the third in the Detective Sebastian Clifford series, perfect for readers who love gripping crime fiction.

∾

HIDDEN FROM SIGHT: A Midlands Crime Thriller (Detective Sebastian Clifford - Book 4)

A million pound heist. A man on the run. And a gang hellbent on seeking revenge.

When private investigator Detective Sebastian Clifford is asked by his former society girlfriend to locate her fiance, who's disappeared along with some valuable pieces of art, he's reluctant to help. He'd left the aristocratic world behind, for good reason. But when his ex starts receiving threatening letters Clifford is left with no choice.

With the help of his partner Lucinda Bird, aka Birdie, they start digging and find themselves drawn into London's underworld. But it's hard to see the truth between the shadows and lies. Until a clue leads them in the direction of Clifford's nemesis and he realises they're all in more danger than he thought. The race is on to find the missing man and the art before lives are lost.

A perfect mix of mystery, intrigue and danger that will delight fans of detective stories. '*Hidden from Sight*' is the fourth in the bestselling, fast-paced, Midland Crime Thriller series, featuring Clifford and Birdie, and the most gripping yet. Tap the link, grab your copy, and see if you can solve the crime.

WRITING AS AMANDA RIGBY

Sally also writes psychological thrillers as **Amanda Rigby**, in collaboration with another author.

REMEMBER ME?: A brand new addictive psychological thriller that you won't be able to put down in 2021

A perfect life...

Paul Henderson leads a normal life. A deputy headteacher at a good school, a loving relationship with girlfriend Jenna, and a baby on the way. Everything *seems* perfect.

A shocking message...

Until Paul receives a message from his ex-fiance Nicole. Beautiful, ambitious and fierce, Nicole is everything Jenna is not. And now it seems Nicole is back, and she has a score to settle with Paul...

A deadly secret.

But Paul can't understand how Nicole is back. Because he's pretty sure he killed her with his own bare hands....

Which means, someone else knows the truth about what happened that night. And they'll stop at nothing to make Paul pay...

A brand new psychological thriller that will keep you guessing till the end! Perfect for fans of Sue Watson, Nina Manning, Shalini Boland

I WILL FIND YOU: An addictive psychological crime thriller to keep you gripped in 2022

Three sisters...One terrible secret

Ashleigh: A creative, free spirit and loyal. But Ash is tormented by her demons and a past that refuses to be laid to rest.

Jessica: Perfect wife and loving mother. But although Jessica might seem to have it all, she lives a secret life built on lies.

Grace: An outsider, always looking in, Grace has never known the love of her sisters and her resentment can make her do bad things.

When Ashleigh goes missing, Jessica and Grace do all they can to find their eldest sister. But the longer Ashleigh is missing, the more secrets and lies these women are hiding threaten to tear this family apart.

Can they find Ashleigh before it's too late or is it sometimes safer to stay hidden?

ACKNOWLEDGMENTS

This book wouldn't be here without the input of many people.

First, I'd like to thank Rebecca, my editor, for picking up the reins on this series and making so many insightful suggestions. Also, thanks to Kate who does such an excellent job with the final edit.

To my Advanced Reader Team, thanks so much. Once again, you've been amazing and together we've made the book the best it can be.

To Stuart, thanks for another fabulous and perfect cover.

I'd also like to thank Pete for your input. Finally, thanks, as always, to my family for your support.

ABOUT THE AUTHOR

Sally Rigby was born in Northampton, UK. After leaving university she worked in magazines and radio, before finally embarking on a career lecturing in both further and higher education. Sally has always had the travel bug and after living in Manchester and London moved overseas. From 2001 she has lived with her family in New Zealand (apart from five years in Australia), which she considers to be the most beautiful place in the world.

Sally is the author of the acclaimed Cavendish and Walker series, and the more recent Detective Sebastian Clifford series. In collaboration with another author, she also writes psychological thrillers for Boldwood Books under the pen-name Amanda Rigby,

Sally has always loved crime fiction books, films and TV programmes. She has a particular fascination with the psychology of serial killers.

Check out her website for a FREE prequel story.....
www.sallyrigby.com

Made in United States
Orlando, FL
24 July 2022

20135568R00167